# The Caravan at the Edge of Doom

## FOUL PROPHECY

First published in Great Britain 2022 by Farshore

An imprint of HarperCollins*Publishers*
1 London Bridge Street, London SE1 9GF

farshore.co.uk

HarperCollins*Publishers*
1st Floor, Watermarque Building,
Ringsend Road, Dublin 4, Ireland



ISBN 978 1 4052 9829 2
Printed and Bound in the UK using 100% renewable electricity
at CPI Group (UK) Ltd
1

A CIP catalogue record for this title is available from the British Library.

MIX
Paper from responsible sources
FSC™ C007454

This book is produced from independently certified FSC™ paper to ensure responsible forest management.

For more information visit: www.harpercollins.co.uk/green

JIM BECKETT

ILLUSTRATED BY OLIA MUZA

*For Tuuli and Lyra – J.B.*

For Mamba and Orysia,
my Legendary cats! – O.M.

# PART ONE

## RESTLESS SOULS

# 1

## 2:30 p.m. MONDAY

### 19 hours and 30 minutes until Eternal Damnation

For a moment, I wondered why no one else seemed bothered about the man trying to climb in through our classroom window. Then I realised he was probably dead, and it all made sense.

Actually, it didn't *all* make sense. Him being a Restless Soul awaiting his passage *Beyond* only explained why I could see him and my non-Visionary classmates couldn't. It didn't explain why he wanted to break in to our maths lesson.

I glanced across at Bess, sitting beside me. My new best friend was doodling a hamster on a skateboard. I was pretty sure she hadn't noticed our ghostly intruder.

'For the third time, Harley,' said Mr Canoe. 'Where's your maths book?'

I looked up at my stressed-out teacher. Unfortunately, Mr Canoe had one of those voices that was hard to listen to. It wasn't his fault, but I often found myself zoning out even when I wasn't being distracted by a Restless Soul attempting to climb through the window.

'Sorry, sir,' I said. 'It's erm –' The dead man was banging on the glass and shouting now, so by this point it was clear that no one else in the room could see or hear him. For me, though, all this noise was making it really hard to come up with a quality excuse for my missing maths book (which in truth I'd ripped to shreds during my recent visit to the Land of the Dead – and I didn't think it would be a good idea to mention that).

I was still struggling for an excuse when the Restless Soul successfully scrambled through the window's narrow opening like a slippery spider. Sliding into the room, he landed head first on Steven's desk, knocking his pencil case to the floor. Naturally, Steven assumed it was Kenny who'd knocked his pencil case to the floor (because that was the main thing Kenny did). So, Steven knocked Kenny's pencil case to the floor in revenge. Kenny's pencil case landed right where the sneaky Restless Soul was tiptoeing towards me, causing him to trip and crash into Taylor's desk. Naturally,

Taylor blamed Kenny and thumped him.

Meanwhile, Mr Canoe hadn't noticed any of this because he was still looking at me, waiting for an explanation about my missing book.

'Well?' he said sternly.

'Sorry, I left it at home,' I said.

Then Mr Canoe launched into a lecture about equipment and organisation while the Restless Soul stood in the middle of the classroom shouting, 'Harley Lenton? Which one of you is Harley? I've got an important message for Harley Lenton, the Gatekeeper of Kesmitherly.'

I looked down at my desk so that the shouty dead window-sneaker wouldn't catch my eye.

'Are you listening to me, Harley?' snapped Mr Canoe.

'Yeah, I'm trying to, sir,' I said, peering up at my teacher.

'So *you're* Harley!' said the Restless Soul, stepping towards me.

'*Trying* to?' said Mr Canoe. 'And what's that supposed to mean? Is there something more interesting *blah blah blah* –'

I attempted to look apologetic, but I couldn't really listen to his lecture about packing my bag while this Restless Soul was *also* getting impatient with me. They both went on and on, while Taylor and Kenny walloped each other behind them. I was *trying* to concentrate, but there was just too much happening.

'You need to come *now*, Harley!' yelled the Restless Soul. 'We're all trapped! BK bust up the tea machine so we can't get through. You need to come and fix it *blah blah blah* –'

'. . . it is a statistical fact,' continued Mr Canoe, 'that students who forget their protractors *blah blah blah* –'

'. . . come on, Harley, it's your Visionary Duty!' said the Restless Soul. 'You're the Gatekeeper *blah blah blah* . . .'

'. . . now I'm sure none of us can forget Miss Prudenza's assembly about the boy who lost his pencil *blah blah blah* . . .'

'. . . there are fifteen more Restless Souls waiting in that coach, Harley. We all wanna get going ***now***! We've had enough of this life *blah blah blah* . . .'

'. . . without all the work from today's lesson, how will you revise –'

'Just STOP!' I yelled. 'Please *stop* . . .'

And everyone stopped. Taylor stopped thumping Kenny. The Restless Soul stopped begging me to fulfil my Visionary Duty. Mr Canoe stared at me like I'd cut off his tie and dunked it in his coffee.

'Not you, sir,' I mumbled. 'I didn't mean you. Sorry.'

But as far as every living person in the room was concerned, I definitely *had* meant Mr Canoe – because no one else had been talking when I shouted *stop*. I felt terrible. I liked Mr Canoe, and it wasn't his fault he had a boring voice and could never live up to the memory of Miss Delaporte, the best teacher ever.

'Stay behind at the end,' he growled, striding furiously back to his trigonometry.

I stared down at my desk, but I could feel the judging eyes of my classmates burning into me from every direction. This was the trouble with being a Visionary whose late grandparents' caravan toilet was a Portal of Doom. Stuff kept *happening*.

It had been like this ever since primary school with Olly, my friend who turned out to be dead rather than imaginary. But I'd only known about my family's Visionary Duty since half-term, when I had to rescue my little brother from the Land of the Dead after he accidentally passed *Beyond* in Nana's wheelie bag. (Officially, this made me a Legendary Hero *down there* – which really wasn't as good as it sounded.) After my grandparents passed through themselves, I became the new Gatekeeper of Kesmitherly, responsible for guiding Restless Souls through the Portal of Doom. Again, this sounded grander than it was – all I had to do was make a cup of *Special Tea* for the Souls who got dropped off at the caravan each morning, then wait for them to pop into the loo. And thanks to my grandparents' parting gift of a Self-Service Tea Machine, I hadn't even needed to do that. But being the Gatekeeper of a Portal of Doom was still a massive hassle for a twelve-year-old who didn't want the attention.

'Pssst, Harley!'

The lesson-intruding Restless Soul quietly slipped a note on to the desk I shared with Bess. Then he tiptoed away and scrambled swiftly out of the window, apparently as embarrassed about my outburst as I was.

'How did you do that?' gasped Bess in wonder, picking up the note – which from her point of view had literally *appeared* on our desk.

Mr Canoe swung round, his owl eyes staring unblinkingly. 'Whatever information is contained within this note you're passing, Harley,' he said, too exasperated to raise his voice in anger, 'I doubt it conveys anything of such great consequence that it cannot wait until the end of the lesson. Bess – you stay behind too.'

'No!' I yelped. 'Please, sir. It wasn't Bess's fault. It was just me. Don't make Bess stay behind. Please, Mr Canoe –'

But he just snarled softly and returned to his algebra.

This was turning into the worst day ever. Not only had I looked like a total weirdo and got Bess into trouble, I now had *this* to deal with:

KEY SNAPPED OFF TEA MACHINE.
PLEASE CAN YOU FIX IT AFTER SCHOOL?
P.S. THERE'S BEEN ANOTHER PROPHECY IN
THE LAND OF THE DEAD!
BK ☺

Mr Canoe had been wrong about this note being of no great consequence. BK was the driver who brought the Restless Souls to our caravan every morning. His message confirmed that today's Souls had been unable to pass *Beyond* – and that was a *massive* deal, of *enormous* consequence. I couldn't help feeling Miss Delaporte would've been more understanding.

As soon as I got out of detention, I ran round the corner to find BK and his coach full of dead people.

# 2

## 3:53 p.m. MONDAY

### 18 hours and 7 minutes until Eternal Damnation

The ghostly coach wound its way through Kesmitherly towards the patch of wild lonely moorland where the caravan had sat for more years than anyone could remember.

I was sitting at the front, directly behind the driver. BK was enormous and sweaty and sang too much, but he was friendly, and he was a Visionary. Also, he was alive – unlike his passengers. There were sixteen of them today, sitting in pairs behind us, staring out of the coach's grimy windows at the disturbingly tidy streets.

'I'm sorry, pet,' said BK, as we sat in a queue of traffic

to get past the roadworks. 'I don't know me own strength! I just gave it the gentlest of little twiddles, and it came off in me hand!' He held up the little silver key that was meant to be attached to the back of the Self-Service Tea Machine.

'Don't worry,' I said. 'I can brew up some *Special Tea* the old-fashioned way today, then get Mum and Dad to come out and fix it later.'

'Cheers, pet. Thanks for being so understanding.' With one giant hand on the steering wheel, he reached round and held out a bag of sweets. 'Mint Imperial? Grandest mint you can get, that is. Posh mint. How was your afternoon anyways, pet?'

'Okay,' I mumbled, popping the manky mint into my mouth.

'You don't sound sure, pet.' Somehow, BK always knew when I wasn't as okay as I said. He was as kind as he was sweaty. And he was very sweaty.

So, for a moment, I thought about giving him an honest answer about how my afternoon had been. Mr Canoe had only kept Bess back for a few minutes after the lesson – which was good – but he'd spent those minutes warning her about the hazards of falling in with a bad crowd (me) and the importance of avoiding fidgety rude children (also me). Then he'd said that from tomorrow she should sit across the other side of the room, at a desk next to Ambary and Orlando (*not* me).

He said it would be better if I sat on my own. And he was probably right.

So now Bess would be friends with Ambary and Orlando and that lot, instead of me. Ever since she'd moved to Kesmitherly just before half-term, I'd known this would happen eventually – and now that annoying ghost had sealed the deal. The trouble was, during our short and happy friendship, I'd told Bess EVERYTHING. About the Portal of Doom in my late grandparents' caravan toilet, about being a Legendary Hero in the Land of the Dead – all that crazy stuff. I hoped she wouldn't mention any of it to Ambary and Orlando and that lot because they'd definitely think I'd made it up to impress the new girl, and then I'd look even more sad and desperate. Bess had just believed it all for some reason. She wasn't even that bothered. Bess was so great.

I decided not to tell BK any of this, though, because the thought of saying it out loud was just too depressing. So, I just sucked on my weirdly stale mint and stared at the red traffic light.

'Sorry about sending Bert in with that note,' said BK. 'Only I couldn't risk coming myself because teachers get suspicious when they see a big feller like me hanging around. That's why I sent Bert in. I hope he didn't cause any bother, you know, coming through the window like that. I remember from my own childhood how hard it can be when a ghost comes in your classroom and none of your pals can even *see* it. I do understand, pet.'

BK understood! BK *always* understood! That set me right off and I burst into tears.

'It was a nightmare, BK!' I sobbed. 'I couldn't listen to Bert and Mr Canoe at the same time and I ended up looking like a weirdo *and* getting Bess into trouble – just like in primary school when Olly was always getting *me* into trouble! But this was worse because Bess isn't even dead! And now Ambary and Orlando and that lot will easily steal Bess away from me. They already think I'm odd because Zoe's uncle saw me floating around the ceiling of the Ragged Goose – you know, when I'd gained Inlightenment after my quest in the Land of the Dead . . .'

BK nodded sympathetically.

'Being a Visionary is embarrassing!' I continued. 'Maybe if I'd had a chance to explain to Bess what had happened back there – about Bert climbing through the window and shouting at me – maybe she'd have understood. But I couldn't talk to her because Mr Canoe let her out before me. And I can't talk to her now because she's probably with Ambary and Orlando and that lot – and anyway, we've got these Restless Souls to deal with – even though the whole *point* of having a Self-Service Tea Machine was for me to be able to concentrate on school and friends and having a life *instead* of helping the Dead pass *Beyond* . . .'

And my tears had set BK off because it didn't take much, and now we were both sobbing away, and he kept steering the coach up the kerb and on to the pavement and nearly driving into lamp posts and prams and dogs.

'You'll be all right, pet!' he bawled. 'I bet you're wrong about Bess. I bet she still thinks you're great – you're a Legendary Hero, for crying out loud!'

'Only in the Land of the Dead!' I wailed.

'But that's the biggest land!' BK sniffled. 'You're brave and strong and noble, just like them Legendary Heroes of old, pet! You know, Bilbamýn the Bold, Vileeda the Valiant, Craemog the Intrepid – and all those other Heroes who slayed the Mythical Monsters with their swords and spears –'

'That's just *stories*, BK!' I howled. 'They didn't really slay all those monsters. I *know* because I've *met* those monsters! They're all down there, working as Beast Guardians of the Twelve Tasks on the Path of Heroes. They just sit there, bored out of their minds . . .'

'I can relate to that,' BK blubbed. 'I should've been on telly, you know. In the movies! Not motoring about at all hours, picking up Restless Souls . . .'

'I know, you mention it a lot,' I sobbed.

Then we sat quietly for a moment, sniffling and dabbing our eyes while an elderly man shuffled over the zebra crossing to Meg's Mini Mart. After that, BK let out a contented sigh, and the coach pulled away towards the edge of Kesmitherly.

'Ooh, that's better,' he said. 'It's good to get it all out, eh, pet?'

I sniffed in agreement. Having a good cry while our ghostly coach kept mounting the kerb and narrowly missing a load of living pedestrians who couldn't even see us really had helped. I turned my thoughts towards the challenge ahead.

Sixteen mugs of *Special Tea*, then sixteen explosions as the Restless Souls popped into the Portal of Doom and passed *Beyond*. But brewing up sixteen mugs of *Special Tea* on the caravan's tiny hob would take ages. To be honest, although the Self-Service Tea Machine had been a thoughtful gift, it could've been *more* thoughtful. My grandparents could have given me one of those Digital Soul Adjusters that were being installed in Portals of Doom all over the world. But Pops and Grandpa had insisted I'd be better off with a 'classic' machine from 1976 because it was 'sturdy' and 'reliable' . . . Now the snapped-off key was lying on the coach's dashboard, glinting at me in the afternoon sun. 'PLEASE CAN YOU FIX IT AFTER SCHOOL?' the note had said, just before the P.S. about a prophecy –

Hold on a minute! In all the maths drama and boring tea stuff, I'd totally forgotten to ask BK about the *interesting* part of his note!

'The prophecy!' I said. 'Your note said *P.S. there's been another prophecy in the Land of the Dead*. Do you know what it is?'

'Something about a *foul surge*,' said BK. 'Hold on, I jotted it down on one of these napkins.' Keeping one giant hand on the wheel, BK riffled through a pile of burger cartons and sandwich wrappers until he found a napkin with some words scribbled on it. He passed it behind without taking his eyes off the road, and I read aloud:

'Your smile lights up my heart like the new street lighting on the Risborough bypass –'

'No, not that,' he said, hurriedly reaching out and turning the napkin over. 'That was something, erm, else. Other side.'

I smiled at the thought of BK getting romantic on a napkin from Chicken Town. Then I read the prophecy from the Land of the Dead on the other side.

**WHEN AN EXCESS OF FOULNESS DESCENDS,**
**ONLY AN ALMIGHTY SURGE**
**SHALL CLEANSE THIS PLACE.**

'What does it mean?' I asked.

'Not sure, pet. The other drivers were coming up with all sorts of ideas at breakfast. Apparently, it's caused a big stir *Beyond*.'

I got my phone out and texted Olly.

(After thirty years of lingering in the Land of the Living as a mischievous Restless Soul, Olly had eventually passed through. Now he loved it down there, hanging out with the other kids who'd been electrocuted while climbing pylons to fetch Frisbees. He'd been even happier since I'd reunited him with his police-officer dad, who, it turned out, *hadn't* been trying to arrest him since they'd died together – he'd only been chasing Olly for a hug.)

Hi Olly. You heard about this new prophecy?

It was worth asking, even though he'd probably take ages to reply because he hardly ever checked his phone. Olly died in 1989, before texting and the internet, but someone had loaned him an old handset, so he did keep in touch a bit. The only other people I could ask about the prophecy were my grandparents, and there was no point messaging them. I'd be more likely to get a reply from Mr Purry Paws, our old cat.

After hitting SEND, I scrolled through past messages between me and Bess. It was mostly stuff about school, and my experiences in the Land of the Dead, and her experiences of living above a pub. Since my chat with BK, I felt a bit better about it all. Some of the messages even made me smile.

BK steered the coach off the road and we bumped across the heathery moor. As we approached the spot where the rusty old caravan had sat for longer than anyone could remember, I looked out of the window. The caravan had been my grandparents' home for most of my life, and although I'd become self-conscious about its spooky reputation, it was a place full of happy, cosy memories. Usually, it could be seen from the roadside, covered in weeds as if it were part of the natural landscape . . .

But not today. For the first time in forever, the caravan was gone.

# 3

## 4:21 p.m. MONDAY

### 17 hours and 39 minutes until Eternal Damnation

BK rushed me back home and I burst through the front door.

'Mum! Dad!'

I found them in the lounge, trying to get Malcolm to walk by coaxing him across the room with snacks as if they were training a dog. Ever since they'd missed my little brother taking his first steps in the Land of the Dead, they'd been desperate to get him walking again. But he just sat on his bum and waggled his Diddy Dino at them, giggling.

'He's a late walker because he was an early talker,' Mum reassured herself, eating the broccoli that Malcolm couldn't

be bothered to fetch.

'Perhaps he needs to be hungrier?' pondered Dad.

'The caravan's been stolen!' I announced.

'You what, love?' said Dad.

'The caravan!' I yelled. 'It's gone – stolen, with the Portal of Doom in it! Now the Restless Souls of the Hesitant Dead can't pass *Beyond* and they're all hanging around Kesmitherly. We need to call the police.'

Mum and Dad looked at each other. For some reason they weren't leaping into action, so I figured I should keep talking until they got over the shock and took control of the situation.

'BK was there until one o'clock,' I said, 'trying to fix the wind-up key back into the tea machine because he'd snapped it off. The caravan can't have been missing for more than four hours.'

'Four hours?' said Mum. 'The thieves could have towed it more than two hundred miles by now, Harley.'

Mum was right, and the thought knocked me back on to the sofa in despair. I'd been running on adrenaline since we arrived at the empty patch of moor and now I was empty. It was time for my parents to step up.

'Okay,' I said. 'So that is far. But the caravan should be easy to spot, shouldn't it? And the police have helicopters and stuff, so can you call them, please?'

Dad inhaled deeply. 'Can't do that, love,' he said, shaking his head. 'See, the thing about that caravan is it's not actually *ours*.'

I sat up, reenergised by the catastrophe of this latest revelation. 'Why isn't it ours?' I asked. 'Did you sell it?'

'No, no. Course not,' said Dad defensively. 'That was your grandparents' home – we would never sell it. It's just . . . we didn't *buy* it. Thing is, no one really owns it. It's the shell of a Portal of Doom. It's meant to be hidden away, so the ordinary living don't find it and start prying about. But of course the old caravan's never been *hidden* in a traditional sense. See, your classic Portal of Doom would be squirreled away at the back of a cave on top of a mountain, or behind a mysterious tapestry in the locked room of an ancient castle, or in a booby-trapped shrine in the depths of the jungle –'

'Yeah, yeah,' I said, getting impatient. 'But my grandparents spent their last few years protecting a Portal of Doom in a caravan toilet.'

'Yes. And the Gatekeeper before them was there for decades,' said Mum. 'That caravan's been parked on the same spot, looking creepy and abandoned, for longer than anyone can remember. People stay away because they think it's haunted, and no one would ever want to steal it because it's so grimy and overgrown –'

'But someone *has* stolen it!'

'Yeah,' said Dad. 'It's a bit of a problem.'

'It's a *massive* problem!' I said, hitting a cushion in exasperation. 'What'll happen to all those Restless Souls? We've ***got*** to find the caravan . . . It's our Visionary Duty!'

My parents looked unconvinced. The trouble was, as far as they were concerned, it *wasn't* their duty. They'd rejected the Gatekeeper job years ago; that was why the responsibility for guiding Restless Souls through my grandparents' caravan toilet had skipped a generation and landed on my shoulders. I couldn't blame them. For Mum and Dad, normal life was just too precious. Mind you, I hadn't exactly *wanted* to protect and serve a Portal of Doom either.

But right now, someone had to do something. Restless Souls, unlike most Dead, couldn't transfer directly *Beyond*. Without their allocated Portal, they'd be stuck here, wandering in aimless misery for eternity. So, getting the caravan back was bigger than Life or Death – for no Soul should be denied their eternal rest. Besides, the last thing I needed was a bunch of annoying dead people hanging around Kesmitherly, climbing into maths lessons and embarrassing me whenever they felt like it.

'I tell you what,' said Mum, 'there might be a way. That patch of moor where the caravan's parked is private land . . .'

We followed Mum through to the kitchen, where she went down on her hands and knees and rummaged about at the back of a cupboard full of carrier bags and empty ice-cream tubs. Then she brought out an old shoebox and blew the dust off it dramatically, like a wizard with an ancient book of spells.

Malcolm went 'Oooh!', Mum sneezed, and Dad fetched the dustpan and brush. Then Mum opened the box and sifted through a pile of crinkly yellowed papers.

'I've got a feeling we may have something here from Sue the Landowner, in amongst Nana's old things . . . Aha!'

Mum selected an ancient document from the pile and carefully laid it out on the floor as we gathered round.

'Good thinking, love,' said Dad. 'Is this Sue the Landowner's decree from back in the seventeen hundreds or whatnot?'

'Yes,' said Mum. 'This is legal written proof from the eighteenth century that no one's allowed to move that caravan!'

'Eighteenth century?' I said, confused. 'But the caravan's got tyres and plastic bits and a gas hob. This decree must be about a different caravan.'

'You're right, Harley love,' said Dad. 'A bunch of helpful Visionaries upgraded the caravan in the 1960s so it didn't look out of place. But this decree is still valid, since it refers to any old caravan left on that patch of land. Look.'

*Be it herein known that upon this day in the Year of Our Lord 1742, it is hereby decreed that Mrs Suzanna Lempington, landowner, doth bequeath this patch of land – namely that betwixt the hawthorn tree and the clump of occasionally pink-flowering heather, at a point one mile to the east of the parish church at Kesmitherly and one mile to the north of Fingle's Pond – as a safe haven for one knackered old caravan. Yea, one completely unsuspicious knackered old caravan that shalt be forever ignored by commoners and noblemen alike, for 'tis just an old caravan, honest, nothing to see here, walk on by, just like ye always have.*

*Be it known to the reader hereof, that none shall ever remove said caravan, under pain of death, within a leasehold of one thousand years.*

*As witnessed upon this, the twelfth day of November 1742 by the right upstanding Hieronymus Ticklethwaite, Beadle, Mayor, Justice of the Peace etc. etc.*

*Signed (Witness) – Hieronymus Ticklethwaite*

*Signed (Landowner) – Su*

'Oh dear,' said Mum. 'The ink on Sue's signature has faded away.'

'What a shame,' Dad sighed. 'Otherwise, this ancient legal document would've proved that no living person has the right to move the caravan. Oh well.'

Mum put the decree back in its shoebox and Dad went and peeled some potatoes.

'Well, what do we do now?' I said, watching my stupidly relaxed parents in disbelief. 'We can't just leave it!'

'What *can* we do?' said Dad.

'We could forge the signature?' I suggested. 'No one would know. And the caravan is ours anyway, so it wouldn't even be a proper lie. You know, we'd be doing it for the good of the Restless Souls –' I trailed off as Mum and Dad stared at me disapprovingly. Unsurprisingly, they weren't up for something as dishonest and illegal as that; my parents hated rule-breaking even more than I did.

'I'm sure there's some other way,' said Dad.

'Well, I could go *down there* and find Sue the Landowner,' I said. 'Get her to re-sign the decree?'

'Oh no!' said Mum. 'That'd be far too risky. A journey into the Land of the Dead, just to get a signature on an ancient document? No, I wouldn't want you going *Beyond*, Harley, not again.'

'Anyway, you can't get down there without the caravan,' said Dad. 'And it's better not to disturb the Dead with admin. Although I'm sure Sue wouldn't mind. She's always been a great supporter of us Visionaries, from what I've heard . . . But don't you worry about it, Harley. You go on up and do your homework, and your mum and I can take care of this caravan problem. We'll sort something out just as soon as I'm done with these potatoes.'

Dad went back to his peeling and Mum looked at a leaflet about gutter clearance. I stomped off to my room in despair.

As soon as I got there, Bess called, which totally freaked me out. I stared at my phone. Why was she calling? Was it just to tell me what a loser I was? Ambary and Orlando and that lot must've put her up to it.

The phone buzzed and buzzed, then it stopped buzzing and went to voicemail.

I should just ignore it. Delete the voicemail. Pretend none of this had ever happened. That'd be the safest option.

But what if Bess *hadn't* phoned to call me a loser?

Curiosity got the better of me. I listened to the message.

'Hey, Harley, are you okay? Bet you can't guess where I am.' She paused for about half a second, which really wasn't long enough for me to guess where she was, then whispered, 'I'm at the wrecker's yard in Risborough. Did you know your caravan's here? I followed it on my bike! When I got home, there were all these people – and outside the pub was your grandparents' caravan, sitting on the back of this big truck –'

I stuck the phone closer to my ear and closed my bedroom door to soften the noise of the washing machine. I didn't want to miss any of this momentous and strange news.

'It was these people doing a Tidy the Village campaign. Their leader's like a politician or something and she was moaning at my mum about the gravel in the hanging baskets. So obviously I didn't say anything because I put that gravel there, but anyway my mum seemed more cross with these moany people than with me –'

I knew all about the Tidy Village People. They were a bunch of nosy busybodies obsessed with – well, tidying the village, obviously. Their leader was Ambary Meadow's mum, and she was kind of famous in Kesmitherly. Janet the Lollipop Lady reckoned Councillor Meadows could be the next prime minister, though I'm not sure she meant that as a compliment. Still, most people seemed to think that tidying up was a good cause, especially if someone else was going to do it for them. So they let Ambary's mum and her cronies take charge and boss everyone around. Flowers were planted, the library memorial was scrubbed, and a brand-new 'Welcome to Kesmitherly' sign was built on the roundabout out of bits of old tractors.

Then the campaign stepped up a notch and become more aggressive. People were intimidated into hiding their bins and washing their windows. They tried to force

Chicken Town and the betting shop to close by having a team of volunteers tut and sigh every time a customer thought about going in. They pressured Meg's Mini Mart into having a permanent display of fresh avocados and soda bread even though they couldn't sell it. Teenagers were banned from sitting on the memorial. Pensioners were only allowed to queue at the post office if they'd polished their walking sticks. Now it seemed they'd been harassing Bess's mums to tidy up the Ragged Goose.

'– they were on about how the Red Lion pub at Osselton has lovely hanging baskets burgeoning with crimfunanfimums,' Bess continued. 'I mean, what even *is* burgeoning? And what even *is* a crimfunanfimum? Am I saying it right? Anyway, you need to come down here, Harley, 'cos I don't reckon they should've taken your caravan like that, and I heard one of those moany people mumbling to another one that it's going to be CRUSHED IN THE MORNING! Come down now, Harley. I haven't got a plan for how we're gonna save it yet, but if you come, we can think of one together. I'll be waiting for you by the gate.'

I put the phone down and allowed myself a great big grin to go with the warm feeling inside. Bess didn't think I was a loser at all! She *hadn't* been badmouthing me with Ambary and Orlando and that lot. We were still friends! Bess was looking out for me – and she wanted us to meet up and form a plan *together*! This was wonderful news!

On the other hand, my grandparents' caravan had been towed to a wrecker's yard and was going to be crushed in the morning. This was *terrible* news! If the caravan was crushed, the Portal of Doom would be destroyed. There'd be no way down for the Restless Souls who'd been allocated to our Portal – and no way back *up* for any Living Souls who passed through by mistake.

I ran downstairs to tell my parents we needed to drive round there with Sue's decree straight away. Maybe now that the caravan was under imminent threat of extinction, I could persuade them to forge the signature so we could prove it had been towed illegally and rescue it from being crushed. And maybe if we promised the Tidy Village People that we'd clean it up, paint it, plant flowers round it – maybe they'd let us have it back.

When I got to the kitchen, Mum and Dad were on a call together. They had the phone on speaker, and they looked serious.

'Okay, well, thank you, Mr Canoe,' said Dad. 'Yes, we'll speak to Harley. I'm sure this won't happen again. Goodbye.'

'Goodbye,' said the voice of my professionally concerned maths teacher.

Mum ended the call. They turned and looked at me.

'That was Mr Canoe,' said Mum. 'He said you had a bad afternoon, Harley. Poor behaviour, no homework. And back to your old pranks, like in primary school with Olly.'

'It wasn't me,' I said. 'It was a Restless Soul –'

'We understand that, love,' said Dad. 'But you mustn't let your Visionary Duty get in the way of your schoolwork. Some things are more important.'

I stared at them in disbelief. How could one little detention with Mr Canoe be *more important* than condemning a bunch of Restless Souls to an eternity of misery in Kesmitherly? And then I realised, as I looked at my parents' serious, worried faces, that I couldn't tell them Bess's news about the caravan after all. If I did, they'd only come up with some boring excuse for why we shouldn't go to the wrecker's yard and rescue it.

For Mum and Dad, a lost maths book would always be a bigger deal than a lost Soul.

But for me it was different. Nana had made *me* the new Gatekeeper of Kesmitherly, and she'd sealed the deal with a chocolate biscuit. I'd taken that biscuit. I must rescue the caravan.

'Sorry about my poor behaviour in maths,' I said, hanging my head in shame. 'I promise I won't do anything like this again.' I traipsed off guiltily to my room. Then a few minutes later, I tiptoed down the hallway, snuck out the front door and ran round the corner to meet BK and his ghostly coach.

# 4

## 4:57 p.m. MONDAY

### 17 hours and 3 minutes until Eternal Damnation

As we sat in a queue of traffic at the roadworks, I stared at the red light. Without Sue the Landowner's signature to prove that the caravan belonged on the moor, I was struggling to come up with a rescue plan that didn't involve sneaking into the wrecker's yard and stealing it back. My brain felt tired, and I found my gaze wandering from the red traffic light to the driver's mirror. Behind me, the Restless Souls were chatting excitably, sharing theories of what to expect *Beyond*.

'Well, I've heard the afterlife is run by a very wise, but very judgmental goose,' said a Soul in a hospital gown with a bunch of droopy flowers. 'If you've been good, you're rewarded with nearly everything you ever wanted! Not everything, just *nearly* everything. But if you've been bad, they *show you* everything you ever wanted, then feed it all to a crocodile who laughs at you while he eats it. Afterwards, a goblin with a face the same as yours but backwards –'

'No, it's not like that,' interrupted another Restless Soul who was dressed as a clown. 'It's not like being alive at all. It's like you become air. Just float around.'

'No, no, no!' said a younger Restless Soul in a suit. 'My auntie told me what it's really like – and she should know because she's already down there. She told us all about it during a seance. Trouble is, our Ouija board is very sticky from juice spillages, so the glass doesn't move as smoothly as it used to. So, Auntie *might* have said that existence *Beyond* is *blissful,* or she might've said it's *ticklish.* Then again, my sister thought she might've been forecasting a *light drizzle*, so . . .'

It was interesting hearing all these stories about what it *might* be like down there. Obviously, none of them was right. Though, in a way, they were all a little bit right. I thought back to the first time I'd looked out over the Back of Beyond and seen the infinitely swarming crowds, and I wondered how I'd describe it. I guess it felt bigger than Life, but also smaller. Like being stretched and squashed at the same time.

That was only one part of it anyway. Before these Souls

reached the Back of Beyond, they'd have to whoosh down the Flume of Infinite Terror and meet their Guide, who'd lead them through the Nothing. After that, if they were lucky, they might get to hang out and have picnics with their dead relatives or whoever was waiting for them. Hopefully, they'd never end up *Beneath*, where all the Resentful Beasts were waiting – to bite and claw and sting and slash, in an eternity of slow-motion vengeance against humanity . . .

Behind me, the Restless Souls continued their discussion, but I didn't join in. They'd find out what *Beyond* was really like soon enough. Besides, if I told them I'd been to the Land of the Dead and come back out again, I'd basically be advertising the fact that I was a Legendary Hero. I'd look like a right big-head.

Leaving Kesmitherly behind, we sped down the main road towards the outskirts of Risborough. We passed the sauce factory where my grandparents had spent many happy years bottling Grimston's Sweet Relish, and snaked our way through the industrial estate.

As we pulled up at the wrecker's yard, I saw Bess waiting with her bike beside the huge metal gates. She hadn't seen me yet because I was in the ghostly coach. (According to BK, it wasn't that non-Visionaries *couldn't* see it, it was just that they *didn't* see it. I hadn't fully got to grips with this idea, but it was clear that no ordinary living people ever seemed to notice us when we were in his coach.) BK parked up and I jumped out and ran over to Bess.

'Hey, Harley!' she shout-whispered. 'Where's your bike? How did you get here?'

'I got a lift,' I said. 'Hey, thanks for calling.'

'That's all right –' Bess's eyes went wide with terror as she looked up at something behind me. 'Harley,' she whispered. 'When I say *run*, run. One, two, three –'

I turned to see what had freaked her out. It was only BK – then I remembered how I'd felt the first time I'd seen him. Before I could explain, he lunged at Bess and produced a lolly from her ear.

'Aaaagghhh!' she yelped.

'Hello, pet,' said BK. 'You must be Bess. Fancy finding one of those in there!' He held out the lolly and Bess took it cautiously.

'This is BK,' I said. 'He looks scary, but he's actually not.'

'Who looks scary?' asked BK, crestfallen.

'I'm guessing the wrecker's yard is closed,' I said, avoiding BK's question as I stared up at the giant gates. They were as tall as a house and as wide as another house, and they were locked shut with a padlock the size of my head. Beyond them lay rows upon rows of crunched and bent and smashed-up vehicles piled on top of each other. I couldn't see it, but the caravan was in there somewhere – hopefully still unsquashed.

But how to get in? Could we climb over the gates? Cut

a hole in the fence? Maybe we could stack the Restless Souls into a ghostly human pyramid –

'Bert could get through those gates, no problem!' said one of the Restless Souls.

'Yeah, go on, Bert!' said another. 'Use your skills!'

'Let us in, won't you, pal?'

'We all want to pass through, Bert.'

'Go on, Bert.'

'Please, Bert.'

'*Can* you do it, Bert?' I asked, trying to spot my maths lesson intruder among the group of Restless Souls cajoling him to break in.

'Who's Bert?' said Bess. 'Who are you talking to, Harley?'

'There's a whole load of –' I began. But at that moment, the wiry ghost who'd climbed into our maths lesson this afternoon stepped sheepishly out from the huddle of Restless Souls.

'Sorry if I got you in trouble earlier,' he mumbled.

'That's okay,' I said through gritted teeth. (It really wasn't.)

'What's okay?' said Bess.

BK leaned down and whispered into my ear. 'You might have to describe things to your friend, pet. I've got a feeling she's not *one of us*.'

I turned to Bess. 'There's a load of Restless Souls here,' I explained, slightly embarrassed for some reason. 'They seem to think that this one – Bert – can get us through the gates. Bert came into our classroom earlier and brought that note. He's who I was shouting at when I got in trouble with Mr Canoe.'

I turned away from Bess because I really didn't want to see her my-friend's-a-weirdo-but-I'm-going-to-smile-politely-because-I'm-nice face. Also, I really *did* want Bert to see my I'm-still-cross-that-you-made-me-look-like-a-weirdo-this-afternoon face.

The Restless Souls gathered round him.

'Bert's an expert lock picker,' said one of them.

'He was a professional burglar when he was alive,' said another. 'He broke into all kinds of places. Cracked safes, got past alarms and CCTV. Picking a padlock will be a doddle for Bert. He's a champion criminal!'

'Can you get us in, Bert?' I asked.

'I can,' said Bert hesitantly. 'But I'd rather not.'

A great clamour of disappointed moans arose from the Restless Souls.

'Why not?' I asked.

'I don't want to do any more of that,' said Bert. 'Since I died, I've been feeling terrible about my life of thieving. I was so good at it – never got caught, not once. Then I died peacefully in my sleep, happily surrounded by massive piles of cash and stolen goods. And now I regret it. You see, I'd always planned to one day quit my thieving and give my stolen cash away to good causes like pandas and that. Then I died before I got the chance to mend my wicked ways. That's why my Soul is so restless. But at least now that I'm dead I can renounce my life of crime completely, and never break in anywhere ever again.'

'But you broke in to a classroom full of children earlier,' I pointed out.

'That wasn't breaking in,' said Bert. 'The window was open.'

I wasn't sure the law would be in complete agreement with Bert's defence, but I let it go. Somehow, I needed to persuade this reformed offender to break the law just one more time. I wasn't happy about it, but this was a crisis – who knew how many Restless Souls would be trapped in an eternity of misery if I didn't get through this gate and prevent that Portal of Doom from being crushed?

'What's happening?' whispered Bess.

'Bert *can* break in, but he doesn't want to,' I said, not bothering to hide my annoyance at Bert's attitude. 'He reckons it'd be immoral or something.'

'But they stole your caravan!' said Bess. 'Those Tidy Village People have done all the immorality here. Bert would just be helping to put things right. In fact, if Bert does this, he'd be making up for all those years of crime. He'd be a Hero!'

Bert looked up. I was about to suggest that picking a padlock to get into a wrecker's yard would ***not*** make up for years of crime, and was *definitely not* like being a Hero. But then I saw that Bess's rousing speech had had a powerful effect on the reluctant robber – so I joined in.

'Your brave deed would be celebrated for generations to come,' I said. 'You'd be an *inspiration* to remorseful wrongdoers everywhere!'

'Would it make up for all those ice creams I stole from small children when their parents weren't looking?' asked Bert hopefully. 'All those handbags I stole from frail old ladies? All those shoes I stole at the bowling alley? All the jewellery I stole from my aunt? All the gifts I stole from under Christmas trees? All the flowers I stole from graves? All the buffets I helped myself to at the funerals of complete strangers?'

*NO!* I thought. *No, no, no, no, no. Not even a tiny bit close, you old meanie.*

'Yes,' I said. 'If you pick this padlock now, it'll make up for all of that.'

Five minutes later, Bess and I were inside the caravan. It hadn't been crushed, but it was hemmed in between rows of piled-up scrap vehicles, and the end of the aisle was blocked off by a truck. There was no hope of towing the caravan to freedom. Meanwhile, some of the Souls were becoming *too* restless – clambering over bonnets, fiddling with gear sticks, playing Frisbee with hubcaps – and BK would be picking up a new coachload at dawn.

So, until we could come up with a plan for breaking the caravan out, I got on with brewing a round of *Special Tea*. I'd already tried poking the silver key in the back of the Self-Service Tea Machine to wind it up, but it was well and truly broken. So I grabbed the tin marked *Special Teabags*, lit the gas hob, and boiled the kettle.

'Is this it?' said Bess, opening the bathroom door. 'Wow! The legendary Portal of Doom. It really does look like a toilet.'

Outside, I could hear BK singing to the Restless Souls, trying to keep them entertained while they waited. I stuck my head out the door and called him over. 'There's no milk, no sugar and no biscuits,' I whispered. 'Do you reckon you could persuade them to drink it straight?'

BK shook his head gravely. Then a smile crept on to his face. 'Posh mints!' he said, patting his pocket.

Inside, Bess was putting a *Special Teabag* in each mug. There were only six mugs, so we were doing them in batches and washing up in between. I passed the first batch round. Soon, Restless Souls were queuing for the Portal of Doom, sucking BK's manky mints as they waited. The first one popped into the caravan to use the loo –

*BOOM!*

'Whoa!' said Bess, as the caravan shook with what sounded like an explosion but was actually the Portal of

Doom slamming shut after the Soul had passed through. Every few minutes, there was another *BOOM!* as one by one, the Restless Souls tinkled their way *Beyond*. And although Bess couldn't see or hear the Dead, no one could miss the thick clouds of hot green smoke that seeped out from under the bathroom door after each passing.

'That is some epic sorcery!' said Bess.

I was just brewing up the second batch when I noticed an eerie hush. The Restless Souls had stopped chatting. BK had stopped singing. I peeped through a gap in the curtain. The remaining Dead were nowhere to be seen.

But now I could hear new voices.

Someone was coming. And they sounded alive.

# 5

## 5:28 p.m. MONDAY

### 16 hours and 32 minutes until Eternal Damnation

'Someone's coming,' I mouthed to Bess. 'Stay down and don't make a sound.'

Squatting on the floor, I held the caravan door shut from the inside, motioning Bess to do the same. I didn't know where BK had gone, but it made sense for him to hide. I reckoned he'd get into a lot more trouble than a couple of kids if he got caught on private property.

As the voices came nearer, I could make out what they were saying.

'. . . so I'm sure you will appreciate the importance of removing the riff-raff and their rubbish, of *cleaning up* those elements of society who bring shame upon our community . . .'

'It's *her*!' whispered Bess. 'It's that councillor who came to the pub earlier! The one from the Tidy Village People – the one who took the caravan!'

'You know she's Ambary's mum?' I whispered.

'No!' gasped Bess in disbelief.

I nodded.

'. . . this dirty old caravan has been abandoned on the picturesque moor beside our village for as long as anyone can remember,' Councillor Meadows continued. 'An absolute eyesore for so many years – I can't imagine anyone will miss it!' She laughed snootily. 'So, you say it will be crushed tomorrow morning at ten o'clock?'

'Yeah, we'll crush it about ten,' said a man's voice. He sounded tired and annoyed. 'But it's gonna cost extra, remember? Because of the short notice and because I've opened up special for you tonight, after hours –'

'Yes, yes,' said Councillor Meadows. 'My committee will be quite happy to pay the extra, thank you. I really can't think of a better use of campaign funds. Getting rid of things like this is what we exist for.'

'All right,' said the man. 'Come on then, let's step into the office to sort out the paperwork, and you can pay the deposit.'

'Mum?' said a familiar voice.

'Yes, Ambary?'

Ambary! *She* was here too?!

'Can me and Rocky-Nathaniel stay here and look round the scrapyard?'

'Of course you can,' replied her mum indulgently.

'Cool!' said a younger voice – Ambary's little brother, presumably.

'It's not safe for unsupervised children,' said the scrap dealer gruffly.

'As I say,' asserted the councillor, 'we have the funds to cover *any* extra costs that may arise. Now come along. To your office!'

The scrap dealer sighed loudly, as their footsteps receded into the distance.

'Is this old caravan getting crushed in the morning?' asked Rocky-Nathaniel gleefully. He sounded like a right brat.

'Yeah,' said Ambary. 'So we may as well help ourselves to whatever's inside. There might be some cash stuffed down the back of a chair. Or a priceless antique clock or something.'

'Are we looting?' asked Rocky-Nathaniel.

'Yeah, I suppose,' Ambary replied.

'Cool.'

'Go on then, in you go.'

'Why don't you go in first?' said Rocky-Nathaniel.

'You're older than me. Unless you're scared? You don't believe those rumours about it being haunted, do you?'

'No!' Ambary laughed in a fake, exaggerated way. 'It's just . . . I *dare you* to go in.'

'Double dare you!' said Rocky-Nathaniel.

'Triple dare you!' said Ambary.

'Aw, that's the biggest!' whined Rocky-Nathaniel. 'Okay, here goes.'

Rocky-Nathaniel tried to open the door. Bess and I held it firmly, but the outside handle was longer, giving Rocky-Nathaniel more leverage. It took all our strength to keep it shut, even though he was smaller than us and there was only one of him.

'Here, let me have a go,' said Ambary. She wrenched at it and nearly snapped my fingers off. The door flew open – and there she was. Ambary Meadows. The most popular girl in our year group. She stared at me and Bess, squatting in an old caravan in a scrapyard. Tomorrow she'd tell Orlando and all the other popular kids –

'What are *you* doing here?' gasped Ambary.

'What are *you* doing here?' said Bess.

'I'm here with my mum,' Ambary replied. 'We've got *permission* to be here. She's important.'

'Yeah, well, this is Harley's caravan,' said Bess. 'So, we've got permission to be *in here*. Anyway, no one's given you permission for *looting*!'

'What are you talking about?' said Ambary. 'This isn't Harley's. It's that smelly, haunted caravan from the edge of Kesmitherly. It's a famous ancient relic, abandoned in long-ago historical times. It doesn't belong to anyone. Mum had it towed away and now she's getting it crushed because it spoils our village.' Ambary peered at me warily. 'Is this some weird game? Are you back into that creepy "imaginary friend" stuff, like in primary school?'

I shot a panicked glance towards the caravan's miniature bathroom. I doubt Ambary even noticed.

But Bess did.

'Whatever happens, you're not coming in *here*,' she said, stepping into the tiny toilet room and pulling the door shut behind her.

'Why would we want to go in *there*?' said Ambary, wrinkling her face in disgust.

'She's in a toilet!' said Rocky-Nathaniel.

I still hadn't spoken. I felt like anything I said could be used as evidence against me. And while I understood that Bess was being amazingly loyal and kind by shutting herself in the toilet to protect the Portal of Doom, she was also drawing a lot of unwanted attention to it.

'You can't come in!' Bess shouted.

Ambary turned to me with a look of revulsion. 'What have you done to her?' she asked accusingly. 'I thought Bess was all right when she first arrived. But after a week of sitting next to you, she's turned completely weird. Have you been doing your creepy psycho spells on her or something –?'

Ambary was interrupted by an explosion which knocked her and Rocky-Nathaniel to the ground and flattened me against the wall. It was the usual, standard *BOOM!* – the seventh one that evening. And if Bess had been a Restless Soul who'd just drunk a mug of *Special Tea*, it would've been perfectly unremarkable. But she wasn't, and she hadn't. So, why –?

The toilet door swung open and green smoke billowed out.

'That is gross!' said Ambary, coughing and spluttering as the stinky fumes stung our eyes. But when the smoke cleared, she saw how much worse than "gross" it was. 'Where's Bess? What've you done with her? Where is she –?'

'You've *exploded* her!' gasped Rocky-Nathaniel. 'You really *are* a witch!'

'This is too creepy,' said Ambary. 'Come on, Rocky-Nathaniel. Let's get out of here before she does her witchcraft on us too!'

They ran off in the direction of the office, which was in a Portakabin at the end of a row of crushed vehicles.

For a moment I stood rooted to the spot. I just didn't get it. Bess hadn't drunk any *Special Tea*. She wasn't a Visionary. And presumably she hadn't even – you know – *used* the toilet. And yet she'd passed through the Portal of Doom with all the usual explosive smoky drama. But why? How? *Was* I a witch?

I reached into my pocket – but there was no point. Bess's phone was here, sitting among the dirty mugs. I couldn't even call her!

There was nothing else for it. I'd have to follow her down, find her, and get her out – just like when Malcolm accidentally passed through. At least my little brother had been with Nana. Bess was alone, and it didn't even make sense that she'd gone down. She wasn't dead. It was against all the rules!

I put three *Special Teabags* into a mug and filled it with tepid water from the kettle. I squeezed and stirred impatiently, then downed it in one. I made another, and another, slurping and guzzling *Special Tea* by the mugful. I didn't even care that it tasted awful, just like normal tea. I just needed to get it down me, then get me down there – through the Portal to Bess.

Adrenaline sped up the natural processes and I was soon ready to use the caravan's tiny bathroom. There'd been no time to psych myself up for a journey into the Land of the Dead. I had no snacks, no weapons.

I just had to get my friend back.

I sat on the Portal of Doom, stared at the fluffy pink hand towel, and released my destiny . . .

But nothing happened. No explosion. The Portal of Doom didn't open. I was just sitting. Like it was a normal toilet.

There was an urgent knocking on the caravan door.

'Harley! Bess!' It was BK. 'Hurry up – they're coming. Them kids have told their mum some nonsense about Bess exploding in the toilet. Come on, you two! The guard dogs have been released – I'll meet you back at the coach. Hurry!'

As I washed my hands, I could hear savage barking nearby. I leapt out of the caravan and ran. Behind me, the snarling hounds were closing in. I looked round and there they were – three of them – vicious, slavering creatures with hungry eyes. There was no way I could outrun them, so I clambered up the mountainous wall of scrapped vehicles, dodging their gnashing jaws. I leapt from a squashed Ford to a mangled Mercedes, squeezing between a twisted Toyota and a wrecked Renault. The dogs were snapping at my heels, but their paws were slipping – they couldn't get a grip on the crushed cars' shiny surfaces. Vaulting a Vauxhall and leapfrogging a crumpled Chrysler, I slid down a Saab's sunroof to solid ground, and ran through the open gate, pulling it shut behind me. As I glanced back into the yard, I locked eyes with a menacing figure striding behind the snarling dogs. Ambary's mum stared straight at me with a look of pure hatred and wild vengeance . . .

'Come on, pet – hop in!' yelled BK, screeching the coach to a standstill in front of me. I jumped in through the open door and we sped off into the anonymous streets of Risborough Industrial Estate.

As I slumped into the seat, my heart pounding, the remaining Restless Souls gathered round me, wide-eyed. Bert had passed through, along with five others; I'd tried to encourage the noisiest Souls to join the front of the queue, but in the end it had come down to whoever was most desperate. The final ten were a random bunch, as groups of Restless Souls awaiting their departure *Beyond* tended to be, but they were all quite worked up after my escape from the vicious hounds.

'That was amazing!' said the Soul dressed as a clown.

'Those dogs were terrifying!' said the Soul with the droopy flowers.

'Does anybody know what happened to the Portal of Doom, and when can we go back there?' asked a wrinkly Soul in a woollen jumper.

I didn't know, so I didn't answer. I just sat there, quietly panting, trying not to think about the fact that I'd just led my friend into the Land of the Dead, and for some reason I couldn't follow her.

# 6

## 5:59 p.m. MONDAY

### 16 hours and 1 minute until Eternal Damnation

'What happened to your pal?' asked BK when eventually the Restless Souls had moved back down the coach to chat among themselves. 'Did she go off on her bike?'

'She passed through,' I said.

'You what?' BK slammed on the brakes as we reached the roadworks. 'Through the Portal? How?'

'I don't know,' I said. 'She went in, then BOOM, she was gone. I don't know how or why. She hadn't even drunk any tea.'

'That doesn't make sense,' said BK.

'I know,' I said. 'And when I *did* drink the *Special Tea*

and tried to follow her, the Portal didn't work. I couldn't pass through. It's like it's broken.'

As we passed the Ragged Goose, I turned away from the pub in shame. I couldn't bear to think about Bess's mums. Did they even know she'd followed the caravan to the wrecker's yard? How long until they'd wonder where their daughter was? It was too awful.

BK parked near my house.

'So, what we gonna do next?' he whispered. 'I've still got to get this lot through somehow.' He gestured to the Restless Souls sitting behind us.

'I don't know,' I said. 'But we can't go back to the caravan. They're bound to have called the police. And there'd be no point anyway; the Portal's broken.'

I looked over at my house. Mum and Dad would already be cross with me for sneaking out. It'd get so much worse when they found out I'd broken the law *and* accidentally sent my friend to the Land of the Dead.

And it really *was* all my fault. I should never have told Bess about the caravan and the Portal of Doom. I'd put her at risk and now she was gone. And why? Why did I tell her? I guess I'd been showing off. Trying to impress my new friend. Trying to make myself look interesting. And then I'd imagined her abandoning me and going off with Ambary and Orlando and that lot – when in fact she'd been tracking down the Portal of Doom that *I* was meant to be responsible for. She'd been so loyal. And look how I'd repaid that loyalty!

Ambary's mum had probably called my parents already. She'd probably called everyone. By now, the whole of Biddumshire would think I'd murdered Bess.

And maybe I had.

'I can't go home,' I said. 'I have to get *Beyond*.' I turned to my favourite driver of the Dead. 'BK, are you *sure* I can't pass through a different Portal?'

BK exhaled deeply. 'Sorry, pet. Every Restless Soul and every Visionary is allocated a specific Portal of Doom. You can't pass through the wrong one – it just doesn't work. That's why being a driver of the Dead is more complicated than people realise.' He held out his bag of stinky mints and I took one sadly. 'But hey, don't be glum,' he said. 'There's *always* another way. As long as you don't mind something a little . . . *unconventional*.' BK stood up and turned to address the remaining Souls. 'Strap yourselves in, folks! We've got one more stop before *Beyond* – and it's your favourite!'

The coach sped along the bypass then turned off into Pickerton Service Station. BK drove past the coach park and the car park and the petrol station and the burger restaurant, then up a grass verge and through a bush.

'Here we are,' he said. 'Suppertime.'

The Drivers of the Dead Transport Cafe was hidden round the back of Pickerton Service Station. I'd never seen it before because it was on the other side of a high grass embankment, beyond the food stalls and arcade games. I guess most other people hadn't seen it either because, like the coach, it was a ghostly transport cafe, unseeable to non-Visionaries.

Inside, the cafe was teeming with Restless Souls. Every table was full, with many Souls standing. As BK squeezed through the crowd, I had a sense that something unusual was going on. Conversations were tense and urgent – this wasn't the typical vibe of people stopping for a break mid-journey. And in the excitable chatter bouncing off the greasy walls, I kept hearing the words 'Portal' and 'broken' – it couldn't be a coincidence.

'Are we the only Visionaries here?' I asked BK, feeling a little self-conscious as I raised my voice to be heard.

'Oh no, this joint's run by a Visionary,' said BK. 'Lovely lady called Morgana. Old pal of mine.' He looked misty-eyed, as if Morgana might've been more than an old pal. 'See, Morgana and me, and the other drivers and cafe staff, we're all alive. We're just not quite *as alive* as you, Harley. We're what's known as Dying Visionaries. Our days are numbered. But we've made them into a very big number by volunteering to help out with the Restless Souls. My driving, and Morgana's waitressing, earns us a few extra years *up here.* It's a nifty way of delaying the inevitable . . .'

'Like doing a gap year before university?' I asked, remembering my cousin Vinny, who'd spent eleven months working at the sauce factory to save enough money to sit on some trains for a fortnight.

'Well, I wouldn't know about *university*,' said BK. 'But Morgana might. She's a lady of high educational acumen.'

We'd finally squeezed our way through to the counter, behind which sat a tired-looking waitress, wearily sipping a Coke. She seemed strangely unbusy, considering the crowds.

'Hey, Morgana!' said BK, grinning like a loon.

'BK!' said the waitress, her face brightening as she looked up to see my companion. And as she walked over to us, I recognised her – and she recognised me.

'Harley Lenton?'

'Miss Delaporte?'

The old waitress in this hidden transport cafe for drivers of the Dead was none other than my favourite teacher of all time: Miss Delaporte! *Morgana* Delaporte. I hadn't seen her since Year 5 when the head teacher suddenly announced her early retirement one Tuesday afternoon. Some of the other kids claimed she'd been sacked because of her *unconventional methods*, but that never bothered me. Miss Delaporte had looked out for me, and listened to me, and she was the only one who took me seriously when I talked about Olly, my "imaginary" friend who turned out to be dead. And now it made sense why – like me, she'd been able to *see* him!

'You two know each other?' said BK. 'What are the chances of that, eh?'

'I used to teach Harley,' said Miss Delaporte, going all dewy-eyed. 'How's it going up at St Clotilde's?'

I shrugged. 'Okay.'

'Hey, I tell you what, it's a bit funny in here tonight, Morgana,' said BK, looking round at the hordes of Restless Souls.

'You're telling me,' said Morgana. 'I've been rushed off my feet.'

'What's going on?' said BK. 'Hold on a minute. Before we get into any deep and meaningful conversation –' He pulled out a crumpled sheet of paper from his pocket and slid it across the counter. 'Could we order supper, please?'

'Are you buying for all your passengers again?' asked Miss Delaporte, picking up the list of orders with an affectionate smile. 'He's too generous, this one,' she said, looking at me but pointing at BK. 'A big old softie.'

BK smiled shyly, and they both laughed. It was all very friendly between these two.

'And what about for you?' Miss Delaporte asked.

'Liver and onions for me, please,' said BK. 'And a cuppa. Harley? Come on, my shout. Order whatever you want.'

I looked at the menu board behind my old teacher who now ran a transport cafe for drivers of the Dead.

'Can I have a chocolate sundae and a Coke, please?' I asked.

Miss Delaporte added it to the list. Then she wandered over to the kitchen hatch and barked out the orders into the greasy steam beyond.

'How long has she worked here?' I asked.

'Morgana?' BK thought for a moment. 'Ooh, about two years, three months and fourteen days . . . I reckon maybe, approximately. I haven't really noticed.'

BK looked away. Was he blushing?

I guess I should've been glad that my favourite driver of the Dead had a crush on my favourite teacher, but to be honest it was a bit weird. I couldn't quite decide if it was weirder because we were in a hidden cafe full of dead people, or if that made it less weird. That two years and three months added up, though – I guess that would've been around the time she'd mysteriously retired.

Miss Delaporte came back to the counter with our drinks and leaned in close to give us the lowdown. 'Here's the deal, far as I can tell,' she said, conspiratorially. 'Word is, all the local Portals have been playing up this evening. In the last half hour, drivers have been dropping off Souls to wait here, while they've been driving around to see what's what. Apparently, Portals are malfunctioning right across Biddumshire – possibly further afield. And it seems like they all stopped working around the same time. Maybe at the exact same moment.'

'Would that moment be 5:40 this evening?' I asked nervously.

Miss Delaporte nodded. 'Something like that. Happened to yours too, did it?'

I looked at my shoes as BK explained to my old teacher what had happened to Bess. The whole thing felt suddenly too sad and awful to talk about.

Miss Delaporte leaned in closer. 'Harley,' she said, so gently, so kindly, just like all those times before. 'You can get her back. You can get your friend back *and* you can fix the Portals.'

I looked up.

'What did you have in mind, Morgana?' asked BK, staring admiringly at my old teacher.

Miss Delaporte leaned in even closer and whispered: 'The Dead Plumbers Society.'

BK gasped. 'Do you think it's them?'

'Maybe,' said Miss Delaporte. 'There's been a lot of talk tonight, among the drivers. But whether the Legendary Dead Plumbers Society caused the problem or not, they're sure as beans the only ones who can fix it. It was them that rigged up the Portals of Doom, way back when. Before that, Restless Souls had no easy way of getting through to *Beyond*. That's why there were so many ghosts in the old days.'

'But what about . . .' BK looked around furtively, then lowered his voice, 'their leader? You know – the notorious Quince. I've heard a few stories . . .'

*Stories.* Here we go. Always with the stories.

'Word is,' said Miss Delaporte, 'Quince *isn't* their leader any more. The Dead Plumbers Society threw her out! Too dangerous, I heard. Some say she went on the rampage with her transcendental tools, then took herself off into the wilds. Another driver reckoned the Legendary Pipe Wrench of Destiny was taken away from her because she refused to share its light of Hope. I don't know, maybe all that purgatorial gloop went to her head – that, or the power. See, apparently, Quince knows a secret. A terrible, powerful secret . . .'

My head was spinning with questions. 'Transcendental . . . Pipe Wrench . . . Quince?'

'Quince was the leader of the Dead Plumbers Society,' Miss Delaporte recapped. 'And if you ask me, she'd be the starting point for anyone who happened to be on a quest to fix the Portals of Doom. Quince is mad, bad and dangerous, but she's also the greatest transcendental plumber in the history of Death.'

'But what *is* transcendental plumbing?' I asked.

'Well,' said BK, 'from my understanding, it's like plumbing, only more transcendental. Does that sound about right to you, Morgana?'

Miss Delaporte nodded. 'That's pretty much it. An advanced, complicated, slightly magical version of plumbing . . . Ah, supper's ready!'

Miss Delaporte brought the plates of food over from the kitchen hatch, and BK and I passed them back to the Restless Souls from our coach, who were hanging around in an awkward huddle by the door.

'Hey, what about this prophecy?' asked BK, as he settled down to his liver and onions.

'**WHEN AN EXCESS OF FOULNESS DESCENDS, ONLY AN ALMIGHTY SURGE SHALL CLEANSE THIS PLACE**,' said Miss Delaporte, slowly and mysteriously.

'Yeah,' I said, tucking into my sundae. 'That prophecy.'

My old teacher leaned forward. I noticed she had a bit of egg on her glasses. 'You want to know what I think?' she asked. 'I think the prophecy has something to do with all this.' She nodded towards the crowd of Restless Souls.

'You should go down there and sort it all out,' said BK.

He was looking at me – they both were.

'You really should, Harley,' said Miss Delaporte, smiling excitably. 'You need to rescue your friend anyway. Makes perfect sense for you to pass *Beyond* and fix the Portals of Doom while you're there!'

'Go on, pet,' said BK, nudging me. 'Why not, eh? You *are* a Legendary Hero!'

I smiled feebly. I really wasn't in the mood for any more Heroism. On the other hand, I really did need to find Bess.

'Okay,' I said. 'But with the Portal of Doom out of action, I'll need another way in.'

'I think Morgana might be able to help you out with that,' said BK, winking knowingly at my old teacher.

Miss Delaporte glanced about to make sure no one was listening.

'I can get you through,' she whispered. 'But you can't tell a Soul. My way is . . . Well, it's not what you might call *officially sanctioned*.'

'Is it safe?' I asked.

'Fairly safe,' said Miss Delaporte, thoughtfully. 'But we have to keep it hush-hush. My way *is* quicker though. None of that sliding down the Flume of Infinite Terror and waiting around for your Guide to the Back of Beyond . . .'

BK was too excited to contain himself. 'Morgana can

arrange a Soul Swap that'll transport you directly into the Back of Beyond!' he announced proudly.

'A Soul Swap?' I said.

'A Soul Swap,' said Miss Delaporte. 'It's one in, one out. So, as soon as you go *down there*, we need to bring another Soul *up here* – to maintain the natural balance. You just need to choose a Soul in *Beyond* to swap with. We pass you IN and pull them OUT – then they hang around up here as collateral, until you return. Any thoughts? Maybe a pet who's passed through . . .?'

'Mr Purry Paws,' I said. 'Yeah, okay. Our old cat. But will he be all right?'

'He'll love it!' said Miss Delaporte. 'I can feed him fish and burgers and ice cream, and all those other things cats love.'

'And what happens when I'm ready to come out?' I asked. 'How do I get back up?'

'You just tap your heels together and say "There's no place like home" three times,' said Miss Delaporte.

'Really?'

'No, not really.' She giggled. 'You'll have to get out the normal way for Living Visionaries who pass through on purpose. You know, same as last time – along the Path of Heroes to the Fire Exit. Oh yes, we've heard all about your previous Heroic adventures round here, Harley! You're quite the legend in this cafe.'

Miss Delaporte pointed to a tiny photo of me pinned to a notice board on the wall beside her. At the top of the pinboard were the words 'Local Legends.' I hadn't noticed my picture at first because it was dwarfed by a double page spread from *The Risborough Gazette* celebrating the runners-up from Biddumshire's annual egg-eating contest.

'So, the Soul Swap is one way only?' I asked nervously. 'And to get Back to Life I have to cross the River Betwixt and travel along the Path of Heroes to the Fire Exit, completing the Twelve Tasks within twenty-four hours to avoid Eternal Damnation?'

'Yeah, but you've done it before, haven't you, pet?' said BK. 'It'll be a piece of cake.'

I had done it before. And it was at the top of my list of things I never wanted to do again. For starters, I'd probably have to do *all* the Tasks this time - because the Archivist (who sat in the ancient library at the end of the Path, writing down the stories of every Legendary Hero who journeyed into the Land of the Dead) was annoyingly strict. But there was something else that was troubling me about this plan.

'If I DO find Bess, and we DO make it along the Path of Heroes to the Archive, and we DO pass Back to Life through the Fire Exit . . . *where* exactly would we come out?'

'Through the Portal of Doom in the caravan, of course,' said BK. A forkful of liver and onions paused on the way to his mouth, quivering greasily. 'Oh.'

'So, if I don't get the Portals fixed, me and Bess will be

trapped *Beyond*,' I clarified. 'And if we don't make it out before 10 a.m., the caravan and the Portal will be crushed, and we'll be trapped *Beyond*. So, I haven't got twenty-four hours. I've got just over fifteen to get in, find Bess, fix the Portals, and get us Back to Life – or it's Eternal Damnation for both of us.'

BK chewed thoughtfully.

'There is one other thing,' said Miss Delaporte. 'When you come out, your cat will have to swap back in – otherwise the Portal won't open for you, even if you have got it fixed.'

'But how will you know when I'm coming back?' I asked.

'Send me a text when you're ready,' said my favourite ex-teacher. 'Honestly, don't look so *worried*, Harley! A Soul Swap only goes wrong if the substitute Soul decides to stay out.'

'How often does that happen?' I asked.

'Quite a lot, actually,' said Miss Delaporte. 'But Legendary Heroism doesn't come risk-free, eh?'

As we got our phones out to exchange numbers, I was already going off this Soul Swap idea. Mr Purry Paws had seemed quite happy in the Land of the Dead when I'd seen him there with my grandparents. But what if he changed his mind, given another taste of Life?

It was a risk I'd have to take. I needed to get Bess out, and Miss Delaporte's Soul Swap was the only way. Besides, if I stayed here, everyone would think I was a murderer and I'd go to prison – and who would look after the stupid caravan then?

I promised BK I'd be back before 10 a.m. so that we could somehow prevent the crushing. For a moment, I slightly wished I had that ancient decree with me to see if I could get Sue the Landowner to sign it while I was down there. But I'd have enough on my plate finding Bess and getting the Portals fixed – and anyway, it'd still make more sense to forge the signature than go through all that rigmarole.

'I'd best be off too, pet,' said BK. 'I've got *so many* pick-ups to catch up on. I'll be driving all night.' He put down his mug – I think it was his third coffee – and I could tell by the way he stood up that he was about to sing.

*'I'll drive all ni-igh-igh-igh-igh-igh-ight*
*To save every Reeee-stless Soul,*
*I'll drive and I'll dri-i-i-i-i-ive,*
*Then I'll stop for a sau-sage roll.'*

Some of the Restless Souls were clapping and cheering, and BK didn't need much encouragement. He climbed on to a table, playing air guitar to the tune in his head. Soon everyone was whooping and whistling. It was a happily bonkers scene, but I left it behind and followed Miss Delaporte past the counter and through the kitchen to a small door out the back.

'Behold,' she said. 'My Soul Swapping Gateway – WAIT! Harley, before I show you, you must *promise* not to tell another Soul about this – Living or Dead!'

'I promise,' I said, completely remembering why she'd always been my favourite teacher. The *unconventional methods* that Ambary and Orlando and that lot claimed she got sacked for – I reckoned those were what made her so great.

'Very well,' she said. 'And remember what I taught you in Year 5. *There are always at least two ways of looking at everything. Sometimes, many more.*'

I nodded, because I really *did* remember her saying that. She'd said it to our head teacher, Miss Stemper, many, many times.

'Good,' said Miss Delaporte. 'Now behold – this time, really behold – my Soul Swapping Gateway to *Beyond*!'

She swung open the door to reveal a small cleaning cupboard. There was a mop, a bucket, a broom, a pile of damp cloths, several large bottles of bleach, a vacuum cleaner, a blinding flash of light that set my brain on fire – then I was floating – I was no longer in the cafe – I felt Mr Purry Paws slink past me, rubbing his back against my leg, and everything went blank.

# PART TWO

# 7

## 7:02 p.m. MONDAY

### 14 hours and 58 minutes until Eternal Damnation

I awoke in darkness so dark it was bright. Or maybe it was brightness so bright it was dark? Either way, I couldn't see where I was, but I knew instantly it was the Back of Beyond. Perhaps it was the smell – a sort of mucky-clean, garlic-toothpaste smell. Or perhaps it wasn't a smell at all. Perhaps it was an understanding beyond the perception of the Living. The point is, I *knew* I was there before I could *sense* it. You know, see or feel or hear or smell or . . . what was the other one? Taste, that was it. This was a place beyond taste. No, wait – I *could* taste something. The Back of Beyond tasted like ice cream! But maybe that was because I'd just eaten ice cream.

Gradually, my ears flickered into place and the volume rose on a muffled hum, which eventually became voices.

'Look who it is!' came Nana's voice.

'Back already?' came Grandpa's voice.

'She's still tuning in,' said Gran's voice. 'Here she comes.'

Suddenly my eyes turned on with a flash and there they were – my grandparents! My lovely, weird grandparents, smiling down at me through the haze. It was like a weird, happy dream. It was so great to see them!

'Hello, Harley!' said Nana, her wispy hair glimmering in the strange under-glow of *Beyond*.

'We didn't expect to see *you* back so soon!' said Pops, his eyes blinking in amazement through his thick glasses.

'It's so lovely to have you here,' said Gran, gleefully hugging a muddy football (I must've arrived in the middle of one of her keepy-uppy marathons).

'Hello,' I said, stretching my legs along the comfy rug I seemed to be lying on.

'You're not dead, are you?' Grandpa knelt beside me, his brow furrowed with concern as his beard quivered in the breeze.

'No, it's all right, I'm not dead,' I said. 'At least, I don't think I am. I came through a Soul Swapping Gateway . . .'

'Morgana's?' said Pops. 'At the transport cafe, out the back of Pickerton Services?'

'Yeah,' I said. 'And guess what? Morgana's my old teacher from Year 5, Miss Delaporte!'

'Fancy that,' said Nana. 'What a small world.'

I sat up, slowly taking in my surroundings. Last time I'd been down here, I hadn't really had a chance to see where the Dead lived – not *lived*, but you know what I mean. I hadn't seen their homes, their everyday hanging out places, because we'd spent most of our time at a massive picnic. As I looked around, I realised we were near that same spot. The rug I'd materialised on to was in an outdoor area that overlooked the Happy Meadow. Here, a few weeks earlier, gazillions of Restless Souls had gathered to welcome a prophesied Legendary Hero (who'd turned out, unexpectedly, to be me).

My grandparents' place felt like it had been scrabbled together from bits and bobs of appealing randomness – a bit like them, I suppose. It was like a garden because there were trees and flowers dotted around, but it also had carpets and furniture. There was even a pair of curtains on a rail between two trees, separating nowhere in particular from nowhere else in particular. There were no walls or fences, so it was hard to tell where my grandparents' area ended and their neighbours' began.

HARLEY
KESMITHERLY
EMENT
PROPHECY
HARLEY
HAR

Further up the hill, past what *felt* like the edge of their place, were all kinds of homes. Some had walls and doors and windows, some had been dug out of the earth or carved out of the rock or woven together from plants and trees. There were homes made from stone, wood, bricks, grass, glass, dung, canvas, and everything else. And there were people everywhere. Sitting, chatting, cooking, snoozing, playing, singing, dancing, digging.

'Do you sleep out in the open?' I asked.

'Oh no,' said Grandpa, 'not at our age. We all bunk up in there.' He pointed towards a nearby tree with a rusty old caravan nestled in its branches.

'We were very happy with our most recent living arrangement,' said Nana, 'so we're sticking with it for now. But we can always change our minds later. That's the wonderful thing about eternity!'

'So, who did you swap with?' asked Pops.

'Mr Purry Paws,' I said hesitantly, hoping no one would mind I'd temporarily resurrected the cat.

'That'll explain why he hasn't touched his milk this evening,' said Gran.

Pops shook his head warily. 'I hope he doesn't wander off,' he said. 'He's not the most trustworthy of cats, that Mr Purry Paws. Bit of a loose cannon, if you ask me. Not sure I'd want to rely on him in a Soul Swap situation.'

Gran rolled her eyes at Pops' doom and gloom attitude

and sat down beside me. 'And what brings you here, Harley?' she asked. 'Is it to do with this new prophecy?'

I hesitated before answering. BK and Miss Delaporte were keen to believe I was here on a Noble Quest to uncover the mystery of the malfunctioning Portals of Doom and get them fixed. But to be honest, I wasn't sure if I'd have bothered coming down just for that. I mean, it wasn't exactly my job – and I didn't really know where to start. My only lead was Quince, the ex-leader of the Legendary Dead Plumbers Society, and I had no idea where to find her or even if she existed. Anyway, I just didn't have the headspace to worry about some vague prophecy while my friend was missing.

No. I had to find Bess. That's what I was down here for. Everything else could wait.

'My friend –' I began, struggling to find the words to explain about Bess without getting too emotional. But I didn't get far before we were interrupted by a clamour of excitable shouting.

'Oy! Oy! Oy! Harley-arley-arley! Vroom! Vroom! VROOM!'

'Olly!' I gasped, as a manic swirl of turquoise shell suit exploded into my eyeballs and earholes. And here he was, my old best friend who'd turned out to be dead rather than imaginary. I don't think I'd ever been so pleased to see him. He was with his Soul mates, Elektra, Sparky and Frazzle. The four of them came charging into the compound, whooping and hollering and leaping over bushes and furniture.

'Harley-arley-arley!' yelled Sparky.

'Vroom! Vroom! VROOM!' yelled Elektra.

'Neeeeeooowww!' yelled Frazzle.

They seemed pleased to see me. It was great to see them too. I took a deep breath; things would get lively now.

'Vroom! Vroom! VROOM!' said Olly again, whipping out his yo-yo and spinning a high-octane move he called the Vortexitor. Sparky and Frazzle shot up the tree beside us, and leapt off a high branch *into* the Vortexitor, spinning round with it.

'Hey, Harley, what you been up to?' said Elektra, vaulting into an armchair opposite me.

'Hi, Elektra,' I said, not even trying to match their mad energy, which Olly reckoned was a side effect of the high-voltage shocks that had brought them *Beyond* in the first place. (These four supercharged pals had only started hanging out because of their shared love of climbing electricity pylons – a pastime that was fortunately much safer down here.)

Eventually, the others stopped spinning and sat down with Elektra and my grandparents to listen to my tragic tale of Bess's disappearance. It was a bigger audience than I'd hoped for, but at least everyone was sympathetic. Taking a deep breath, I told how my new best friend – best *living* friend – had unexpectedly passed through the Portal of Doom while protecting it from the most popular girl in our year and her bratty brother. I explained that all the other Portals seemed to have mysteriously broken at the same time too. And then I explained that our caravan was scheduled to be crushed at 10 a.m., so if I didn't get me and Bess out before then, our Portal of Doom would be destroyed and we'd be trapped here forever.

'Oh, Harley,' said Nana, as she and Gran and Grandpa hugged me.

'Nightmare,' said Olly.

'That's sad,' said Elektra.

'But why did it happen?' asked Pops, frowning. 'Why would the Portal pull Bess through and then stop working?'

'I wonder if it's got anything to do with the dragons?' said Frazzle mysteriously.

'Bet it has,' said Elektra.

'Dragons?' said Nana.

'We been up Craggy Hill, watching the dragons come in,' said Olly.

'They might *not* be dragons,' said Sparky, who'd died a bit older than the other pylon kids. 'But there really is a whole load of massive flying things coming this way. Like *thousands* of them!'

'And some of the kids up there were talking about broken Portals,' said Elektra. 'There's something dodgy going on.'

'An existential crisis,' said Frazzle, looking pleased with himself. 'Caused by dragons.'

'Is it linked to the prophecy?' I asked.

Olly stared at me blankly. 'What prophecy?'

'I texted you about it,' I said.

'Yeah, sorry, Harley-arley-arley, my phone ain't been working so good since I dropped it off a pylon.'

I was so pleased to see Olly, and for some crazy reason I couldn't shake the feeling he might be helpful – somehow, with something – even though it didn't make any sense to think that. Olly just wasn't the sort of person who could ever be helpful in a helpful sort of way. I guess things were just more fun with him around. You know, depending on what kind of mood I was in.

'Those kids up Craggy Hill were talking about a prophecy too,' said Sparky.

'Yeah,' said Elektra. 'Something about *foulness descending*?'

'**WHEN AN EXCESS OF FOULNESS DESCENDS, ONLY AN ALMIGHTY SURGE SHALL CLEANSE THIS PLACE**,' said Nana.

'That's the one,' said Elektra.

'We'll come to that,' said Gran. 'But first, we need to find Bess.'

'I guess I should start by travelling to the Front of Beyond to see if she came down the Flume of Infinite Terror like a normal Restless Soul,' I said.

My grandparents exchanged troubled glances like I'd said something outrageous.

'Don't you think she'll come down the flume?' I asked, puzzled.

'Oh no, it's not that,' said Nana. 'I mean, yes – Bess will come down like usual, I expect. It's a very sensible place to begin searching for her. It's just –' She trailed off, as if struggling to share some difficult news.

'*You* mustn't go, Harley,' said Pops, who never had any trouble saying what he thought. 'Someone else should go and get her. You need to stay here.'

I was flabbergasted. What fresh nonsense was this? I'd come down here with the express purpose of finding Bess – why would I let someone else go after her?

'We'll go!' said Elektra, leaping to her feet.

'Yeah!' said Sparky, as he and Frazzle and Olly assembled beside her.

'Oy! Oy! Oy!' said Olly. 'I can guide Bess through the Nothing, Harley-arley-arley! 'Cos that'd be proper tough otherwise. Imagine trying to get through the Nothing on your own when you ain't never done it.'

I tried to smile, but I was *not* happy with this arrangement. 'It's kind of you,' I said, 'but I'd rather go myself if that's okay.'

The pylon friends deflated.

'No, it's not okay,' said Pops. Gran gave him one of her looks – but he was clearly saying what my other grandparents were thinking.

'Why?' I asked, exasperated. 'Why can't I go and find my friend?'

'Because you're a Legendary Hero,' said Nana.

'That doesn't make any sense!' I whined.

'Look,' said Gran, guiding me gently over to the curtains and pulling them open a crack. 'See? Over there?'

My heart sank. 'Harley Fans.'

Gran nodded.

One of the challenges of being an official Legendary Hero in the Land of the Dead was dealing with the obsessive fans. My official fan club had been way too excited about meeting me last time I was down – and that was before I'd even done anything.

'The stories of your epic deeds have spread far and wide, Harley,' said Nana. 'These fans have been hanging around here a lot lately, desperately hoping for the second quest of Harley the Legendary Hero. I'm afraid they're more bonkers than ever. It's really not safe for you to go out there.'

Suddenly, Pops charged at the Harley Fans, waving his arms and yelling. They scattered like pigeons, only to reconvene a few seconds later, just like pigeons.

'He does that from time to time,' said Gran. 'It doesn't get rid of them, but it helps Pops sleep if he's had a good run around.'

'They haven't seen you yet,' said Grandpa, pulling the curtains shut. 'As soon as they know you're here, there'll be so much fuss. It'll be hopeless trying to get anywhere. Better you let your friends go after Bess.'

'And you should let them go soon,' said Gran pointedly.

'Yes, you should!' declared Pops, striding back over, full of energy after his charging about. 'Because otherwise your heart will shrivel and your brains will melt and your bones will fall out and your ears will go floppy –' Gran gave Pops a stern look and he stopped sulkily. 'She knows it all anyway,' he mumbled.

He was right. The others may have been too tactful to go on about it, but Pops was only saying what we all knew. The fact was that if Bess and I didn't get Back to Life before the caravan was crushed, we'd be trapped here. And unlike my dead companions, we'd carry on ageing forever. Our hearts would shrivel and our brains would melt and our bones would fall out and our ears would go floppy – forever and ever and ever. The Land of the Dead was no place for the Living to linger. Most of this lot were too polite to mention it, but I needed to keep thoughts of Eternal Damnation at the forefront of my mind. For Bess's sake.

'Poor Bess, she must be terrified,' said Grandpa. 'Won't have a clue where she is, or what's going on.'

'We should get over there quick,' said Sparky. 'Harley's mate'll be freaking out.'

I stood up and stared purposefully in what I hoped was the right direction.

'I'm going,' I said decisively. I kept my eyes fixed on the horizon, avoiding everyone's gaze as they watched me with what I hoped were *Wow, she sure is a Hero!* expressions, but may well have been *Wow, she sure is stubborn!* expressions.

I stood, I stared defiantly, but I didn't go.

Because at that moment, Bess arrived, having made

her way from the Portal of Doom to the Back of Beyond entirely alone.

Like a true Hero.

# 8

## 7:23 p.m. MONDAY

### 14 hours and 37 minutes until Eternal Damnation

'Bess!' I said. 'Wow.'

'Hey, Harley!' Bess looked tired, but she was still smiling.

I felt so relieved I couldn't speak, could hardly think. I mean, we were still in the Land of the Dead, but she was here – safe!

'Bess?' said Olly.

'How did you do that?' said Elektra, in awe. 'All the way from the Flume of Infinite Terror, through the Nothing, along the Road to the Back of Beyond . . . that was epic!'

'Awesome!' said Sparky.

'Amazing!' said Frazzle. 'How long did it take you? Like,

less than two hours? And without a Guide – that must be some kind of record!'

'Pleased to meet you, Bess,' said Nana. 'That was certainly very impressive.'

'So brave!' said Gran.

'Oy! Oy! Oy! Bess, check this out,' said Olly, whipping out his yo-yo and doing some of his most impressive moves, including the celebration classic, Spinny Spinny Spinny Yeah Yeah Yeah.

'How did you even do it without a Guide?' asked Grandpa, his beard quivering with admiration.

'Well, it's all thanks to Harley, to be honest,' said Bess, smiling at me. 'She'd told me all about it, so . . . I knew what to expect.'

Bess was so great. No wonder everyone loved her. I immediately forgave my family and friends for giving her a better welcome than I got. She deserved it. I mean, it did seem *a little bit* over the top, all this talk of her bravery. You know, compared to when *I* arrived just now, courageously swapping my Soul with a cat – *on purpose*. You know, to ***save*** her.

'It was exactly like you described,' said Bess, turning to me. 'Except the Flume of Infinite Terror was dry. There was none of that gloopy slime going down it. Just a bit in the splash pool at the bottom.'

'No gloop, but you went down it anyway?' said Frazzle, wide-eyed.

'That must've been proper scary!' said Olly.

'No purgatorial gloop?' said Gran. 'Are you sure?'

'Yeah,' said Bess. 'It was sticky, like it had been gloopy recently, but there was nothing flowing when I was there.'

The grandparents exchanged worried glances.

'Sounds like it's been turned off,' said Nana uneasily.

Grandpa nodded. 'Which would've created a vacuum in the system, sucking the Portals open for a moment before sealing them permanently shut. Bess must have been pulled in at that precise instant.'

Pops was fuming. 'Turning off the purgatorial gloop will prevent all future Restless Souls from passing *Beyond*!' he raged. 'What kind of scoundrel would do something as terrible and unnatural and wicked as that?!'

At that moment, a throbbing growl of engines cut through our conversation. Dark shadows crawled across the land as gusts of warm air swept through the compound.

'Feels like a storm's brewing,' said Nana ominously.

'Those ain't no storm clouds,' said Olly.

Above us, an enormous fleet of airships filled the sky in every direction, casting their shadows over the land. The air was thick with the droning hum of their engines, like the buzz of a trillion swarming locusts.

'Dragons!' said Frazzle.

'Blimps,' said Pops.

'Airships,' said Gran. 'Sent by the Management, I'll bet.'

One by one, each airship unrolled a gigantic screen beneath its cabin. We looked up at the one nearest us – it must've been the size of a football pitch. Sirens wailed to attract the attention of anyone who might've somehow missed this aerial invasion. Each of the screens lit up with a message:

**ATTENTION**
**BY ORDER OF THE MANAGEMENT**

The sirens stopped, and in the silence that followed, the message grew:

**ATTENTION *PLEASE***
**BY ORDER OF THE MANAGEMENT**

An image appeared on the screen – on every screen from here to the horizon. A man with a big moustache, cycling down a street. He was trying to look normal, like a normal, down-to-earth, bike-riding man. But the more he tried to look normal, the more he wobbled along like a baked potato with legs. After a few seconds, the bike-riding scene cut to a close-up of the same man's enormous, moustachioed face –

'It's that geezer from the committee!' said Olly.

'Oh yeah,' I said. Olly was right. The giant face on the screen belonged to a member of the grumpy old Hero Welcoming Committee who'd tried to stop me from rescuing Malcolm. This was the man who Olly had humiliated in front of his colleagues. And now, here he was again, beaming out of a thousand giant screens.

'What's he doing up there?' said Olly.

'He's the leader of the new Management,' said Nana in a tone of strong disapproval.

'Busybodies from various committees who've joined together to "manage" *Beyond*,' said Gran. 'No one's asked for them or voted for them, but here they are!'

'Bunch of bossy old twits if you ask me!' said Pops.

'So, why does everyone go along with it?' I asked.

'I think most people are just relieved that someone's taking charge and organising things so they don't have to,' said Nana. 'The Dead tend to be very laidback about politics.'

'But you have to keep an eye out for these upstarts,' said Pops, growling at Big Moustache. 'They're always trouble.'

Above us, Big Moustache's throat clearance boomed out of a thousand speakers, reverberating through the sky like thunder.

'Citizens of *Beyond*,' he declared. 'The Management advises you to immediately stop what you're doing and listen to me. I bring serious news. Some of you may have heard rumours about functional difficulties affecting the passage of Restless Souls between *Before* and *Beyond*. Our chief scientists have today confirmed that the Portals have ceased to open, and the purgatorial gloop has ceased to flow. However, there is no cause for alarm. The closing of the Portals and the disruption to the gloop's flow is a natural consequence of OVERCROWDING. The Land of the Dead is FULL. We cannot accommodate any more Restless Souls of the Hesitant Dead. Our scientists are working on a solution and we will update you shortly. In the meantime, there is no need to PANIC.'

The word 'panic' was accompanied by a noise like twelve thousand pianos being dropped on to twelve thousand greenhouses. There were fireworks and klaxons and sirens and flashes of lightning and everyone jumped out of their skins. Then the words OVERCROWDING and FULL and DON'T PANIC flashed and swirled over the screens as deafening roars and squeals continued to rain down upon us. The whole thing was totally mad and unexpected. The Land of the Dead full? It just didn't sound . . . realistic. I mean, how could it even be possible? Wasn't death meant to be infinite or something? On the other hand, there were *a lot* of Souls down here . . . Maybe overcrowding did account for the Portals shutting and the gloop ceasing to flow?

The bangs and whoops and crashes were too loud for me to hear what anyone else thought about all this. But after a while, the noisy clamour crossfaded into the gentle sounds of twittering birds and giggling babies as Big Moustache's face reappeared on the screens.

'Good afternoon,' he said calmly. 'Welcome to the Management's latest update on the population crisis, as we continue our hard work for the benefit of All Souls. Taking advice from our official scientists, we have invested in a plan to ease the burden of overcrowding. From today, we shall begin rounding up and evicting all Undesirables from the Land of the Dead.'

This announcement created quite a stir.

'Eviction?' gasped Gran.

'Oh dear, this is a worry!' said Nana, shaking her head.

'What are these rascals playing at?' snarled Pops.

'The Management wishes to assure everyone that we are, as always, following the science,' continued Big Moustache calmly. 'As many of you will have heard, there has been a prophecy. **WHEN AN EXCESS OF FOULNESS DESCENDS, ONLY AN ALMIGHTY SURGE SHALL CLEANSE THIS PLACE**. Clearly, this **EXCESS OF FOULNESS** refers to the large numbers of Undesirable Souls who have recently **DESCENDED** and are currently attempting to remain *Beyond*. So, as you can see, the eviction of surplus Dead is a perfectly natural and scientific solution to our overcrowding situation as we work together to **CLEANSE THIS PLACE**. Moreover, it is perfectly natural and logical that we should target the Undesirable Dead – that is to say, those monsters and Villains who bring fear and misery to the average, hard-resting, peaceful Soul. It is for these reasons that the Management has been working tirelessly to develop an **ALMIGHTY SURGE** in order to remove these Undesirables.'

Big Moustache stared out of a thousand airborne screens at the Back of Beyond. But as I looked up at him, I couldn't help feeling his sharp eyes were burning directly into me. It was just like earlier – like Ambary's mum! *That* was who he reminded me of! Even though he looked nothing like her. It was those eyes, the way they cut through me and made me feel like I was a bin bag full of muck, spilling over their new carpet.

'Have a good day,' said Big Moustache, as the screens rolled back up and the blimps sailed ominously away.

'This all smells rather fishy to me,' said Grandpa sceptically. 'I'm not convinced there's anything natural or scientific about this at all . . .'

'Me neither,' said a familiar voice behind me.

I turned to see J-Wolf, the teenage techno-prodigy who'd fixed up the Self-Service Tea Machine for our caravan. He made all kinds of whizzy gadgets for the Dead, and my grandparents loved him, especially Grandpa. Right now, J-Wolf was sitting in some kind of hover-capsule, floating towards us on a gentle hum of hot air.

'Harley the Legend,' he said, hovering casually. 'Long time.'

'Hi, J-Wolf,' I said. 'What do *you* think's going on then?'

'Don't know yet,' he said, drifting gently to the ground and stepping out of his hover-capsule. 'But I don't trust them "official" scientists, you get me? This thing ain't "natural", I'm telling you – like G-Pax says.' J-Wolf nodded to Grandpa. 'And check this out,' he continued, looking at his phone. 'Professor Yaxis and Doctor Radar have just gone on holiday – *together*.'

'Hmm, that *is* a coincidence,' said Grandpa. 'Two highly

respected scientists who *didn't* endorse the Management. Both going on holiday today, of all days . . .'

'Better step up work on the secret project, innit.' J-Wolf and Grandpa exchanged knowing glances.

'What's the secret project?' I asked.

'It's a little something we've been working on ever since this new Management turned up,' said Grandpa. He came closer and lowered his voice. 'Basically, it's –'

'No disrespect, G-Pax,' J-Wolf interrupted, 'but it's like top top TOP secret. We can't tell *anyone*. For their own safety, you get me?'

'Yes, yes, of course,' said Grandpa. He looked sheepish, and I wasn't sure if that was because he was being told what to do by a teenager, or because he felt embarrassed about almost giving away their big secret. I was intrigued, not least by Grandpa's curious techno-bromance with J-Wolf. I guess J-Wolf was the grandson he'd never had. Apart from Malcolm.

But as mysterious as all this Management skulduggery was, Bess and I couldn't afford to get involved. This was dead people's business. And although it was tempting to hang around and see how it turned out, we'd have to leave them to it. We had a caravan to save.

I looked around the compound. Grandpa was in deep discussion with J-Wolf about their secret project. Pops was toying with a catapult, aiming it at the blimps then the Harley Fans then back at the blimps. Nana and Gran were watching Elektra, Sparky, Bess and Frazzle as they leapt in and out of Olly's yo-yo moves. It was a great atmosphere. Honestly, if it weren't for the risk of Eternal Damnation, it would've been like a holiday. But the fact was that Bess and I couldn't afford to get too comfortable. We were just way too alive for this place – and it looked like it would be down to me to point this out.

'Bess, we've got to get Back to Life,' I said. 'If we get stuck here, we'll carry on getting older and older and older *forever.* In ten years, we'll be twenty-two. In eighteen years, we'll be thirty –'

'Thirty!?' Bess went green, and Nana pulled up a chair for her to sit down. The prospect of being so ancient had made her feel sick, and I hadn't even got to the part about our muscles falling off and our brains melting. Olly and Elektra rushed to her side.

'Steady, Harley-arley-arley!' said Olly. 'No need to bring it on strong like that . . .'

'You're right, Harley,' said Bess earnestly. 'We'd better get going.' She looked sadly at her new friends and they looked sadly back.

'I wish you could stay,' said Frazzle.

'You two would have been such a help unravelling the true meaning of the prophecy and fighting back against the evil Management,' said Elektra.

'It would've been a right laugh!' said Olly.

'Maybe we could stay a *bit* longer?' said Bess pleadingly, like she was begging my permission. 'I really like it here, and there's so much I haven't seen . . .'

'Yeah, but it's not really up to me –' I began.

'Come on, Harley-arley-arley! Vroom! Vroom! VROOM!' said Olly.

This situation was ridiculous. They were acting like I was *making* us go back. It wasn't my fault we'd start shrivelling up and wasting away – it was just Nature!

'Harley and Bess must return to the Land of the Living,' said Nana. I turned to my friends with a told-you-so expression, relieved that a wise old grown-up had supported my point of view. Unfortunately, Nana hadn't finished. 'But before you go, you must fulfil your destiny,' she said, turning to me.

'Really?' I whined.

'The Land of the Dead is in crisis,' said Gran. 'You, Harley, are a Legendary Hero. We need your help.'

'Yay!' said Bess, running back over to Olly's yo-yo extravaganza.

This was so unfair.

'Okay,' I said, wandering back to Nana and Gran after a few minutes of huffing and sighing. 'So, where do I start? BK and Miss Delaporte said something about Quince and the Dead Plumbers Society.'

'Yes,' said Nana. 'That would be a good place to begin.

But don't be too hasty, Harley. Have patience. We must see what comes to pass.'

Patience?! I loved Nana but what was she on about? I took a deep breath and tried to convince myself that me and Bess would still have time to whip up the Path of Heroes to the Archive *after* I'd worked out what was really going on here with the Management and these broken Portals . . . But this slowly-slowly approach was making me anxious. Bess was too chilled out too – how quickly she seemed to forget about the horrific prospect of becoming thirty! Why was everyone down here so laidback about Eternal Damnation?

I decided to take matters into my own hands.

Ducking behind trees and furniture, I crept over to the edge of my grandparents' compound and snuck out when no one was looking. I kept a close watch on the Harley Fans, tiptoeing round them at a distance. So far, they hadn't spotted me –

'Hey! Look! It's Harley the Legendary Hero! Over there!'

I swung round to see a horde of crazy people surging towards me from the other direction – and now they were coming at me from every side. There was nowhere to hide, and within moments the Harley Fans had surrounded me, snapping selfies and holding out marker pens for me to autograph their Harley T-shirts and hats and scarves and bags and mugs. I froze, unsure what to do next. If I went along with it, I'd look like some sort of big-headed diva, as if

I deserved this attention. On the other hand, if I *didn't* start posing for snaps and signing hats, I'd look plain rude, like it was beneath me . . .

So, I went with the flow, greeting my fans and signing whatever they handed me. Out the corner of my eye, I could see Bess smiling and pointing. Olly and the others joined her, and I could see them all witnessing my moment of looking like a proper Legendary Hero. To be honest, it made me feel pretty good.

But now the crowd was getting intense. Bigger fans were elbowing smaller fans aside. There was jostling, and I was getting swept along in the crowd. Through a gap in the mob, I could just make out Nana's worried face. Then the gap closed, and I was engulfed by sweaty maniacs, barging each other aside to get closer to their Legendary Hero. Luckily, just when I thought I was going to be crushed, a squad of security guards came to my rescue. Forming a protective ring around me, they kept the fans at bay, while shuffling me away from the compound towards a waiting helicopter.

'Where am I going?' I yelled, dimly aware of my friends and grandparents calling to me from beyond the security buffer and the gaggle of fans. I couldn't hear what they were saying, and as the noise of the helicopter grew, their distant shouts were drowned completely.

'Luxury Coast,' yelled the nearest security guard in

reply, guiding me forcefully into the helicopter. 'You're a Legendary Hero, Harley. Don't need to slum it round here with the riff-raff any more. You've got an island waiting for you. An island of your very own.'

# 9

## 7:55 p.m. MONDAY

### 14 hours and 5 minutes until Eternal Damnation

As the helicopter rose rapidly into the weirdly glowing under-sky of *Beyond*, I waved sadly at the little people below. I realised now why my grandparents had been so worried about the Harley Fans spotting me. Olly had once explained to me what happened to Legendary Heroes when they – sorry, *we* – returned *Beyond*. Apparently, once we were dead, it was customary for us Legendary Heroes to get whisked off to our own private islands for an eternity of luxurious retirement. Obviously, I hadn't been expecting this *today* because I wasn't dead. Clearly someone had made a mistake. I just needed to explain that I was too alive and busy to retire, and everything could be put right.

'Excuse me!' I shouted at the serious-looking official sitting beside me. 'Hello, excuse me!' I shouted again, struggling to be heard over the deafening chop-chop-chop of the rotor blades.

'Yes, Miss Lenton?' he replied, like I was important.

'I'm not ready to retire,' I shouted.

'You'll change your mind once we get there,' he said and went back to looking at his phone.

'No, you don't understand,' I said. 'I'm not dead!' He put his headphones in and stared out of the window.

Well, that was that. What now? I needed to get back to the others, I needed to find Quince, I needed to get me and Bess along the Path of Heroes to the Archive, I needed to save the caravan . . .

I swallowed my panic and looked out of the window at the strange world below. We were flying along the route of the River Betwixt, the great waterway that separated the Back of Beyond from the eerie Badlands Beyond the Back of Beyond. Understandably, the pilot was staying firmly on this side of the river where it was sunny and cheerful. The other side was shrouded in ominous swirling mists, like a relentlessly miserable soup. That was where the Path of Heroes lay, stretching perilously above the Resentful Beasts of *Beneath*. Dotted along the miles and miles of rocky, narrow path, were the Twelve Tasks – and at the end was the Archive, where the Fire Exit would ignite for a true Legendary Hero who had successfully completed the Tasks within the time limit. This was the only route Back to Life for Visionaries and Living Souls who'd come down by mistake. With any luck, Bess and I would be popping along there later.

My current situation was a disaster, but I was still enjoying myself a bit. I'd never been in a helicopter before, so I figured it was okay to make the most of the opportunity. Also, I couldn't help feeling a little curious about my private island paradise. I wondered how big it would be, what facilities it would have. And since we were going there whether I liked it or not, I reckoned I may as well check it out and *then* get whizzed back to my friends and family, as soon as these officials had realised their mistake. The caravan wasn't booked in for crushing until 10 a.m. tomorrow. There'd be time to find Quince and fix the Portals of Doom and travel along the Path of Heroes and complete the Twelve Tasks . . .

No, it was too much. I didn't stand a chance!

'Here we are!' shouted the co-pilot. Below us, an enchanting archipelago, awash with blue lagoons and lush green vegetation, stretched out peacefully in the sun-sparkled river. We descended towards one of the larger islands, touching down on a big flowery H in a forest clearing. As the rotor blades slowed to a standstill, a group of people approached from the trees. One of them opened the helicopter door and invited me to step down on to the springy ground.

'Welcome to paradise, Harley Lenton!' declared an official with a clipboard. It took me a moment to realise it was *the* official with a clipboard, the same one who'd tutted at me and threatened me with Deletion last time I was down here. This was the Acting General Secretary of the Hero Welcoming Committee, and he was surrounded by those same colleagues who'd ganged up on me until Olly had talked them round. I hadn't recognised them all immediately – firstly because they were smiling; and secondly because they were wearing new uniforms that made them look just like the staff in Chicken Town, only with MANAGEMENT printed across the pockets of their stripy shirts. I had to admit, those outfits were making me hungry. I could almost taste the sizzling . . . But this wasn't Chicken Town, it was the Hero Welcoming Committee. And they were all here, apart from Big Moustache who'd appeared on the big screens earlier. Clearly, *he'd* moved on to bigger things.

'Hello,' I said, looking sheepishly at the Acting General Secretary's shiny new clipboard. (I'd accidentally broken his previous one when I knocked him over on the beach, so I was worried he might bear a grudge. Fortunately, he seemed to have forgotten all about it.)

'Beverage?' he said, nodding at a colleague, who held out a silver tray with an enormous multicoloured drink on it in a glass like a vase.

'Thanks,' I said. The rainbow drink was tall and chilled, and it had a swirly straw and tiny umbrellas and segments of orange and lime and pineapple glistening juicily round the rim.

'Enjoy your retirement, Harley Lenton,' said the Acting General Secretary. 'You've earned it.' Then the entire Hero Welcoming Committee shuffled past me and squeezed into the helicopter as the rotor blades chugged into life and began spinning round.

'Wait!' I called out. 'I'm not dead!'

'Oh, we know,' the Acting General Secretary called back, still smiling.

'I'm here on a quest!' I shouted. 'I need to get back. I just wanted to see the island for a moment –' I approached the helicopter, but it was fuller than a bus at rush hour.

'Just to be clear,' said the Acting General Secretary, 'we cannot endorse any further Heroic quests from you, Harley Lenton.' He was still smiling, and only now did I realise it was a smile of revenge.

He *hadn't* got over me breaking his clipboard at all!

'Your Heroism is DONE,' he continued, in his infuriatingly officious manner. 'You are not eligible for a Heroic Picnic. You do not have permission to set foot upon the Path of Heroes. You do not qualify for Inlightenment. Your tales of Heroism have been recorded for posterity. You've had your moment. Now you RETIRE!'

He slammed the door shut with the sort of self-satisfied smile that only someone with a clipboard could muster. Then they flew away, and I was left standing there, all alone in the breezy sunshine with a massive, fruitily-edged drink.

As I watched a giant tortoise wandering slowly across the helipad, I realised how much I'd messed up. If only I'd listened to my grandparents, I wouldn't be stranded on this beautiful tropical island.

I tensed, half expecting a big slobbery parasite to jump on my head. In *Beyond*, Doubts and Regrets had a physical form – a very slimy, sloppy, spiky physical form. Whenever you started to doubt yourself and regret things, they leapt on you, getting their claws into your hair and wrapping their tentacles round your legs. Luckily, there didn't seem to be any here right now – just this chilled-out tortoise and a few parrots. I guessed Doubts and Regrets were banned on these Luxury Islands, same as they were banned in most of the Back of Beyond. (Just not at the Front of Beyond or on the shores of the River Betwixt or Beyond the Back of Beyond – I'd spent a lot of time covered in Doubts and Regrets last time I was down here.)

The ice in my cocktail was melting rapidly, along with my chances of avoiding Eternal Damnation. Even if, somehow, I managed to get the Portals fixed, Bess and I would still have to get all the way to the Archive at the end of the Path of Heroes. And whatever happened, the Archivist would be writing it down – just as she wrote down every detail of every Heroic quest in the Land of the Dead (along with a few embellishments of her own). She'd even be writing *this* down! I could picture her now, sharpening her ancient pencil to record my epic failure: *Having abandoned her friends and family, Harley stood around feeling sorry for herself . . .*

That was no good! I'd have to change it up, do something Heroic.

Somewhere nearby, a parrot squawked. The giant tortoise had nearly reached the other leg of the big H and my last ice cube was a tiny marble. I slurped up the final dribbles of my rainbow drink and shook myself into action. Clearly the appropriate thing for a young Hero abandoned on a deserted island to do, was *explore* – not stand around getting depressed. I put the empty glass carefully on the ground and set off into the trees.

Dappled sunlight danced across the lush forest floor. Cute furry animals skittered among the leaves –

A stick snapped behind me and I swung round. Somewhere through the dense foliage, eyes were watching. I stared into the undergrowth, edging slowly backwards . . .

And fell down a hole.

'Ow,' I said. It wasn't a massive hole, but it was deep enough for me to wish I hadn't fallen into it. I rubbed my elbow and looked up to see four familiar faces peering down at me. Four faces that were strangely recognisable, even though I'd never met them before. Four majestic faces set atop mighty bodies, silhouetted against the evening sun like statues.

One of them leaned in closer. His chiselled jaw looked like it had been carved out of antique marble; his confident eyebrows looked like they'd been sculpted by a grand master; his piercing eyes, full of depth and mystery, were like eyes in an oil painting, flickering in the flaming torchlight upon the cold, stone wall of an ancient castle . . . And that's when I realised *exactly* where I'd seen these faces before – in a bunch of old paintings on the Path of Heroes!

'Bilbamýn the Bold?' I gasped. Bilbamýn the Bold grinned heroically back at me. I looked from face to face. 'Vileeda the Valiant! Craemog the Intrepid! Hallyria the Unrelenting! But you're . . . legends!'

'And so are you, Harley Lenton,' said Vileeda the Valiant in a voice like molten gold.

Bilbamýn the Bold, Vileeda the Valiant, Craemog the Intrepid and Hallyria the Unrelenting were four of the Legendary Heroes whose epic adventures my grandparents used to tell me over and over and over, during long cosy evenings in the caravan. I used to *love* these Heroes when

I was little! And even though no one in the Land of the Living had heard of them, down here they were mega-celebrities. They looked the part too. Each of them was toned and muscly and attractive and confident, and they were wearing Heroic armour and carrying Heroic weapons. I really couldn't see how I was going to fit in here. It was like being back at school.

Vileeda the Valiant reached out a hand. 'Allow me to help you out of this hole,' she said, in her rich, silky tones.

'Thanks,' I mumbled, staring at the shining spikes on her armoured fighting boots as she pulled me out. 'I didn't see it there. I guess it's an animal trap . . .'

For some reason, this made the Legendary Heroes guffaw like warriors at a merry banquet. But they quickly composed themselves, becoming solemn and dignified again.

'You have justly won your place upon these islands, Harley Lenton,' declared Craemog the Intrepid, in a voice that seemed to rumble from the rocks below.

'Indeed,' said Hallyria the Unrelenting. 'The Archivist regaled us with the wondrous tale of your epic adventures. I trust the Hero Welcoming Committee honoured your arrival with due reverence?'

'Oh yeah, they did, thanks,' I said. 'They gave me a drink with four umbrellas in it.' The Legendary Heroes smiled, and I felt like such a child. They had armour and weapons and so much confidence. This was nearly as awkward as this afternoon's maths lesson. Why had I come here? I was meant to be rescuing my best friend and saving an eternity of Restless Souls from being trapped forever in the Land of the Living!

'Your Loyal Sidekick, Oliver Polliver, has also spoken most eloquently of your heroism,' said Vileeda the Valiant.

'Oh, right,' I said. 'Yeah, that sounds like the sort of thing he'd do.' I wished Olly was here now. He'd know how to make the best of this situation. 'Actually, I kind of need to get back to him,' I said. 'See, I'm not quite ready to retire –'

'We all felt that way once,' boomed Bilbamýn the Bold. 'You must not feel guilty about enjoying your prize, Harley the Legendary Hero. Come now, let us feast!'

With a sweep of his big Heroic arm, a great dining table laden with sumptuous treats appeared before us. At least, I assumed they were sumptuous treats, but I didn't really recognise much of the food, apart from a staring pig's head with an apple in its mouth. Also, there was way too much cutlery. The other four Legendary Heroes each sat upon a golden throne, then gestured for me to sit on the shiniest golden throne of all, at the head of the table.

'Thanks, but I'm not really hungry,' I said, glancing at the silver platters covered in complicated-looking food.

'Very well,' said Bilbamýn the Bold. With a thunderous clap of his hands, the table and chairs disappeared. 'Let's go to the beach!'

# 10

## 8:29 p.m. MONDAY

### 13 hours and 31 minutes until Eternal Damnation

We stood on the golden beach, staring across a vast stretch of the wide River Betwixt at four neighbouring islands. They weren't miles away, but they weren't swimmable either, although the water here did look very appealing – so different to downriver where the Happy Shore faced the gloomy gateway to the Path of Heroes. There, the river was murky and the beach was stony; here, the water shimmered in a deep, enticing blue that ran crystal clear as it lapped gently at the sandy shore. In fact, it was so appealing that Hallyria the Unrelenting had taken off her armoured fighting boots and stepped in for a paddle, and Craemog the Intrepid was unstrapping his battle sandals to join her. Even the sparkly unicorns that had towed us through the forest in a golden carriage were frolicking playfully in the shallows. (Yes, sparkly unicorns and a golden carriage. That's the kind of place this was.)

'Over there is the island home of Craemog the Intrepid,' declared Bilbamýn the Bold, pointing to the first of the small islands – a rocky outcrop covered in landscaped lawns and manicured hedges, topped off with a big, shiny beachside mansion that reminded me of Barbie's Dream House. 'And that palatial dwelling belongs to Vileeda the Valiant,' said Bilbamýn, pointing to the next island along, which had a fairy-tale castle on it, with towers and flags and a fleet of jet skis moored at a stone jetty. 'Hallyria the Unrelenting lives in peaceful luxury upon *that* charming rock.' Hallyria's island was an exotic wonderland full of surprising fountains and secret gardens and tree houses and waterfalls and magical hedges. Brightly plumed birds perched upon a thatched cottage with roses round the door and a little chimney that puffed out smoke in a cosy welcome. 'And this little place,' said Bilbamýn, dismissively shaking his wrist at the island on the far right, 'is my humble abode.' His was the most ridiculous island home of them all. It was basically a car park with a skyscraper sticking out of it.

'I bet you've got a lovely view,' I said.

'Indeed,' Bilbamýn replied proudly. 'I have a panoramic

view of the entire archipelago. From Big Musclius the Confident's High Security Fortress in the south, all the way round to Count Kloog's Cloud Citadel in the north. Sometimes I sail around the islands on one of my yachts, looking at other people's homes from a distance.'

'What do you plan to do with *your* island, Harley the Legendary Hero?' asked Hallyria the Unrelenting. 'The builders will be here soon. They'll build anything you can dream of.'

I looked around me. *This* was *my* island. It was pretty awesome already, but I'd need somewhere to sleep. And eat. It seemed a shame to concrete the whole place like Bilbamýn the Bold – but at the same time I might not want quite as much nature as Hallyria had gone for. And I'd want something a bit more *tasteful* than Craemog's shiny monstrosity. I suppose a couple of jet skis would be cool, but I wouldn't necessarily need a whole fleet . . .

What was I on about?! I wasn't even dead yet! This Legendary Hero thing was going to my head! Looking at my heavily armoured future neighbours with their massive homes, I could see how easy it would be to get carried away with your own Heroic self-importance out here, miles away from any normal dead people, and without any actual Heroics to be getting on with. No doubt about it, I needed to get back to my quest as soon as possible, for my own sanity. I needed a plan. So I took off my shoes and socks and strolled along the beautiful sandy beach to help me think.

Wandering along the seashore, I marvelled at the size of everything. These Luxury Islands were so big and there was so much space between one Heroic mansion and the next – could there *really* be a population crisis? Big Moustache had announced that *Beyond* was dangerously overcrowded, yet my own private island was *massive*. Thousands of Souls could rest up here. There was something dodgy going on, and clearly my grandparents and friends had thought so too. I had to get back to them.

I strode back along the beach to where the other Legendary Heroes were paddling and relaxing in the sand. I had decided to trust my Heroic peers with the whole truth and ask for their advice. After all, what was the worst that could happen?

'I need to get back,' I announced. 'I'm not dead. I'm on a quest.'

At first, none of them looked at me, and I wondered if they'd heard. Craemog the Intrepid, who'd been skimming stones on the river, picked up a boulder and hurled it into the water with a ferocious splash. Hallyria the Unrelenting punched the sand, burying her fist up to the shoulder. Finally, Vileeda the Valiant turned to me with a forced smile. 'Stay here, Harley,' she said through gritted teeth. 'Relax. Enjoy your retirement.'

The atmosphere had suddenly become very tense.

Craemog and Hallyria and Bilbamýn couldn't make eye contact with me, and Vileeda was smiling so hard it looked painful.

'I can't stay,' I said. 'I'm not dead. If I stay, I'll get older and older and waste away into a mushy pile of jellied bones and my brain will go sloppy and I'll fall apart – and so will my friend Bess. You Dead Souls are all right – you can just chill out all healthy and solid for eternity. Me and Bess can't. I need to get us Back to Life. Sorry.'

Craemog the Intrepid and Hallyria the Unrelenting scowled at me and stormed off down the beach, angrily kicking sand and shells as they went. Bilbamýn the Bold was gnashing his teeth and clenching and unclenching his fists. He reached for his sword – but Vileeda the Valiant reached out and grabbed his arm.

'No!' she commanded. 'Not like this.' She led him away and they whispered intensely. I seemed to have really annoyed them. So much for our Heroic community.

Luckily, whatever Vileeda the Valiant had said seemed to have calmed Bilbamýn the Bold, and now they were striding up to me, smiling heroically.

'My apologies,' boomed Bilbamýn. 'It is natural, of course, that as a Legendary Hero your instinct is to rescue your friend. Any of us would do the same . . .' He trailed off, as the insistent growl of a pair of speedboats cut across his speech. Craemog the Intrepid and Hallyria the Unrelenting were zooming back to their islands in a sulk. Why were my fellow Heroes so upset about me not wanting to stay here? It was nice to feel wanted, but still . . .

'Craemog the Intrepid and Hallyria the Unrelenting have got a lot on at the moment,' explained Vileeda the Valiant in her silky, honey tones. 'I expect Craemog suddenly remembered he had to finish drawing up the plans for his fifth swimming pool. And I've no doubt Hallyria was rushing home to oversee some urgent topiary . . . Please don't take it personally.'

I knew she was lying – they'd blatantly left in a strop. But I reckoned she knew I knew she was lying, and she didn't care, as long as I played along and didn't accuse her of lying. So much for asking my Heroic peers for advice. This lot were more into home improvements than Heroism.

'You really must stay,' said Bilbamýn the Bold, who was standing so close to me now that his bulky frame was blotting out the sun. As he breathed over me, his right arm kept jerking uncontrollably towards the hilt of his massive sword. I stepped back.

'This hot weather,' said Vileeda. 'It puts us all on edge.' A gentle breeze ruffled her hair majestically as she spoke.

Looking up at them, silhouetted imposingly against the sun, I wondered if for some strange reason they were going to keep me here against my will, trapped on this island forever. It seemed to me that anyone whose friendliness felt this unnerving was almost certainly a kidnapper. Perhaps Vileeda the Valiant saw the fear in my eyes, because at that moment she smiled again, more gently.

Then she squatted.

And Bilbamýn the Bold squatted beside her.

'We do understand,' said Vileeda the Valiant kindly.

'We really do,' said Bilbamýn the Bold sweetly.

Vileeda leaned in closer, which was a real testament to the Heroic strength in her thighs because she was still squatting. 'First and foremost, us Legendary Heroes have to take care of our *reputations*. We understand that. You're concerned about the impact this Bess situation might have on your Legacy – and you're right to be concerned. What self-respecting Hero wouldn't be? After all the hardships you suffered on your Noble Quest, it would be a tragedy if a little thing like the accidental murder of your friend were to damage your Heroic Legacy. But fear not – we can help.'

I stared at her, but I didn't say anything. A crab scuttled over my toes.

'We can help you to clear your name,' said Bilbamýn the Bold. 'All we need is a story. An elaborate tale to prove your innocence and protect your reputation. Don't worry, Harley, we've all done it – accidentally murdered one of the good guys. Heroism always involves a bit of collateral damage. It's no big deal, really it isn't. Just leave it with us:

we'll arrange a cover story to protect your Heroic Legacy, so you can just lie back and relax. There really is no need for you to worry about getting Bess Back to Life.'

'This way, everyone wins,' said Vileeda in her silky voice. 'After all, I'm sure Bess is happy here.'

Now I *knew* these two were nuts. I mean, yeah, Bess was happy here. She'd be happy anywhere, making new friends, being brave and fun and easy-going.

'But I still need to get her out,' I said, thinking aloud. 'Just as soon as we've got the gloop flowing and fixed the Portals.'

'A *third* quest?' spluttered Bilbamýn the Bold, wobbling slightly despite his sturdy squat. 'Think of the damage ***that*** could do!' he hissed at Vileeda.

'Just like the Management warned us,' muttered Vileeda the Valiant, clearly ruffled, but sustaining an impressively solid and secure squat despite her discomposure.

'She's too keen,' growled Bilbamýn.

Vileeda forced a smile back on to her face. 'And how do you plan to go about completing this Portal of Doom fixing quest, Harley Lenton?'

'Well,' I said, no longer in any doubt that these people were *not* on my side, but somewhat distracted by their squatting prowess. 'I thought I'd start by finding Quince from the Dead Plumbers Society.'

Bilbamýn the Bold let out a great sigh of relief. 'The

Dead Plumbers Society is a myth,' he declared. 'It doesn't exist. It never has existed. And as for Quince . . . Pah! In the *stories,* Quince was a terrible Villain! A cruel, heartless maniac! She was irresponsible and, and, and . . . lazy!'

I seemed to have touched another nerve.

'Quince was evil, and she used the Pipe Wrench of Destiny to further her wicked ends!' announced Vileeda the Valiant. 'And that is why the Pipe Wrench was taken from her and hidden! According to the stories . . .'

'No point trying to find Quince,' said Bilbamýn the Bold. 'She doesn't exist.'

'That's a shame,' I said, fairly convinced she really must exist for anyone to go on about her not existing this much. 'I do love a myth, though. I'd love to know the *story* of where the totally made-up, fictional character Quince used to hang out . . .'

'Oh, you'll never track her down,' said Bilbamýn the Bold.

'Shhh,' said Vileeda the Valiant.

'Because she's not real,' said Bilbamýn pointedly. 'Besides, even in the made-up not true stories, she dwelt deep within the nastiest, most crooked lanes of the smelliest slums in the Badlands of the Back of Beyond – on Evil Street, of all places! Just think of that: Evil Street! That ought to give you an idea of what sort of person she is – *was*!'

It was amazing how rattled some people got whenever

Quince was mentioned – she really must be worth meeting! And now, thanks to Bilbamýn's incompetence, I had her address.

# 11

## 8:50 p.m. MONDAY

### 13 hours and 10 minutes until Eternal Damnation

I needed to get off this island. Squinting at the sun-soaked bay where Hallyria and Craemog had moored their speedboats, I wondered if there might be any more I could borrow. For a moment, I considered making a run for it. I'd get a head start because I wasn't squatting, but running through sand would be tough. And even though Bilbamýn and Vileeda had been squatting for ages, their Heroic legs were showing no signs of fatigue. I bet they could squat all night. I didn't think I'd ever be able to squat like a true Legendary Hero.

I decided to play it cool. 'I'm just going for a stroll,' I said.

'We really must insist you stay here with us,' said Vileeda the Valiant, in a voice like treacle laced with arsenic.

'Okay,' I said, as Bilbamýn the Bold's sword flashed in the sun, a warning to steer clear of the perilous rocks.

'Relax!' he commanded. 'Enjoy your retirement. We shall attend to your Heroic Legacy. We shall deal with the Bess situation. We shall contact some Dead Plumbers and get them to fix the Portals so that an eternity of future Restless Souls can rest in peace *if that's what you really want*. But we must insist you stay here and RELAX.'

'You've done your Noble Quest, Harley,' said Vileeda. 'Why risk another one, when you've earned the right to lounge around in the lap of luxury for eternity?'

And then Bilbamýn the Bold lost it. He launched out of his squat like a coiled spring. 'You CAN'T do another quest!' he boomed. 'We can't allow it! How do you think it will make US look if YOU do *another* quest? Let alone TWO more quests?!'

'Look at how you've upset Bilbamýn the Bold!' snapped Vileeda the Valiant, rising to her full height and staring down her Heroic nose at me like a headmistress in armoured fighting boots. 'Well? What have you got to say for yourself, Harley Lenton?'

'Erm,' I stammered. 'My first quest wasn't really that impressive . . . I mean, the Twelve Tasks were just a load of household chores and DIY . . .'

Turned out this was the wrong thing to say: Bilbamýn and Vileeda erupted.

'Don't EVER say that!' gasped Vileeda. 'How dare you break the Heroic Code? We NEVER talk about the true nature of the Twelve Tasks! What possible advantage is there to all the normal people knowing THAT? Just think of our Legacies, Harley Lenton! Think of *your* Legacy! What kind of Legendary Heroes would we be if everyone knew our Epic Quests merely required us to tidy up, mop the floor, change a light bulb, or replenish a loo roll? It is CLEARLY much better for EVERYONE that they think we've slain dragons and leapt over flaming chasms and wrestled poisonous laser sharks! It's not just about us, Harley – you're killing people's DREAMS!'

Vileeda and Bilbamýn were in a total panic and it finally made sense why they were so desperate to keep me here – and why they wanted to keep *all* the Legendary Heroes here, locked up in their fancy towers away from the rest of *Beyond*. It was so everyone could carry on believing the stories of their epic deeds, and their Legacies could remain intact. This whole Luxury Island retirement set-up was a conspiracy to keep the truth hidden! These "Heroes" were nothing but vain liars . . .

On the other hand, Bilbamýn the Bold and Vileeda the Valiant were very big and very strong – and now they were very angry too. So, I pretended to agree with everything they said, to ensure they didn't chop me up and bury me in the cool shade of a swaying palm tree.

Luckily, I was much better at lying under pressure than they were. 'I understand now,' I said. 'You're right, of course. I should relax and enjoy my retirement. From now on, that's what I'll do.' I sat down on the sandy shore to prove I meant it.

'Excellent!' boomed Bilbamýn the Bold, who was obviously so used to getting his own way, he didn't find my sudden change of heart suspicious. He clapped his hands imperiously and a pole with a ball on a string appeared.

'Swingball?' he said, offering me a plastic racket.

'Sure,' I said. And there I stood, playing Swingball with a Legendary Hero whose courage and fortitude (in the stories) had inspired and entertained me for years.

'You know what?' I said. 'Maybe those Portals don't even need fixing.'

'That's the spirit!' boomed Bilbamýn, gleefully hitting the ball round and round and round.

Vileeda sat apart from us and I wondered if she might take a little more convincing that I was sincere about abandoning my quests so easily. But I wasn't too worried about her. I was busy thinking about how awful this blissful retirement in paradise would be, even if I *was* dead. Because while I was here, my friends and family would be back on the mainland having fun without me. Being a Hero sucked.

'Aha!' boomed Bilbamýn the Bold. 'The builders are here!'

A little boat sped across the river towards us. The pilot anchored it in the shallows just offshore, then leapt out and waded over to me.

'Good evening, your Legendary Heroicness,' she said, bowing so low her hard hat fell off. 'I'm your project manager. Got quite a team with us today!' She gestured at the river behind her, where a landing craft was chugging up to the shore. Its ramp was lowered, and bulldozers and diggers drove up the beach, heading towards the trees behind me.

'Wait!' I shouted.

'Hold up!' the project manager yelled, and the vehicles stopped. She turned to me. 'We're just clearing a patch to lay foundations for your mansion, your Legendary Heroicness. Then you can talk us through what you fancy.'

'Okay,' I said. 'I just need to think. Could you hold off on chopping down trees and digging things up for a bit?'

'No problem,' said the project manager. 'Take your time. You can get your island kitted out to any specification you like. We can knock you up a mansion, a castle, a fortress or a skyscraper. And we can do it in the shape of a carrot, or an onion, or a cucumber, or an artichoke, or a building –'

'Could you take me out in your little boat, please?' I asked. 'I'd like to have a look around the whole island –

you know, to get a feel for the overall shape of it.'

'Sure, that makes sense,' said the project manager. 'After you.'

Vileeda the Valiant was watching suspiciously, so I skipped into the river pretending to be excited about my island designs. 'I can't wait to see my dreams engineered into reality!' I said (because really, of course, I was planning to escape).

'We'll create your perfect fantasy home,' said the project manager as we waded out to her little speedboat. 'We did a lovely fairy-tale castle for Hallyria the Unrelenting a few centuries ago. It's over there – do you like it? Not sure? Perhaps you'd prefer something more secure? I know some of you Legendary Heroes can get a touch paranoid out here. Big Musclius the Confident, for example. He used to get very anxious about intruders, so we built him an impenetrable fortress. And he *loves* it in there! As far as we know.'

The boat was anchored offshore at waist depth. I didn't mind getting wet because the water was warm, and brightly coloured fish darted around my knees beneath the sun-dappled surface. We clambered aboard and set off on our tour of the island.

But as soon as we were out of my Heroic companions' earshot, I said, 'They're trying to kidnap me. We need to go back downriver to the Happy Shore.'

'I beg your pardon, your Legendary Heroicness?'

'Please can you take me away from here?' I said. '*Please.*'

The project manager looked unsure. 'Doesn't sound right to me –'

'But you're supposed to do whatever I say, aren't you?' I pointed out. I didn't like pulling rank, but these were desperate times.

'I'm supposed to *build* you whatever you like, not drive you wherever you like,' she replied huffily. 'I'm a professional engineer, thank you very much, not a chauffeur!'

'I demand you drive me to the Happy Shore!' I said – because that seemed like the sort of thing your Classic Legendary Hero would say.

'No,' she said.

Now at this point, your Classic Legendary Hero would probably push her overboard and steal the boat. However, the project manager looked pretty solid, so I didn't fancy my chances of tipping her out – plus I'd never driven a speedboat before and stealing made me feel guilty. Then I had another idea.

'Hey, listen. I'm on a Noble Quest. Seriously. It's top secret and very important. And if you help me now, I can make sure you get a really good mention in the Legendary Tale of my adventures.'

The project manager's eyes lit up at the prospect of fame. 'Can you really do that?' she asked.

'I know the Archivist,' I replied. 'We've chatted *a lot.*'

(I didn't mention the fact that most of our chat had been the Archivist telling me off.)

'Remember to mention how brave I was, will you?' said the project manager, opening the throttle and steering us rapidly downriver.

'Sure thing,' I said.

'Yee-ha!' she yelled, as the wind swept over her hard hat. 'I'm going to be a Legend!'

Unfortunately, we'd only gone halfway down the River Betwixt when Bilbamýn the Bold and Vileeda the Valiant caught up with our little boat. Bilbamýn was on one of his massive luxury yachts and Vileeda was on a jet ski. She looked awesome with her hair and her cape streaming out behind her – but it was completely annoying that they were chasing us.

'Turn around and return to your island!' boomed Bilbamýn the Bold through a megaphone. 'If you persist with your escape, we shall have no choice but to – what the jiggins!?'

Suddenly, a great scaly beast leapt from the water in front of us, its massive fins flashing in the sunlight as it arced through the air. Then it dived into the river with a splash that echoed against the distant mountains like an explosion. Its tail fin smacked into the water, sending a tidal wave that nearly capsized our little boat.

'What was that?' asked my pilot, as we held on tight. 'It looked like a . . . big fish.'

A really big fish. A fish the size of a whale – and here it was again. And this time the tip of its scaly head broke the surface as it swam towards us . . . And now it was opening its great jaws – it wanted to swallow us! The project manager was frozen with fear. I grabbed the steering wheel and sent us out of the fish's munching path. It dived again – but suddenly its tail swished up, and I saw Vileeda the Valiant knocked off her jet ski,

moments before our boat capsized and we were hurled into the water. I swam towards the floating jet ski and grabbed on to it.

The fish had disappeared for now, but I had a feeling it was still down there, biding its time. I watched the project manager clamber on top of her capsized boat, while further upriver, Bilbamýn the Bold had thrown a rope to Vileeda the Valiant and was pulling her up on to his yacht.

'Welcome aboard, Vileeda the Valiant!' he boomed – for some reason he was still talking through his megaphone. 'Look, we have been gifted a Noble Quest! Let us hunt the Big Fish! A noble encounter twixt man and beast . . . Yes, and woman. Let us slay it with our bare hands – by pulling the triggers on this torpedo and this harpoon and this cannon!'

And here was his chance – for the beast was back. It was further away now, as if it had gone off to get a long run-up – and now it was storming towards us. The project manager was in the direct line of its charge, and she was a sitting duck on the capsized boat. As the Big Fish swept nearer, I closed my eyes – then opened them again, to see that the fish had swum straight *past* the project manager and was heading towards *me*, its fishy jaws opening –

Some survival instinct kicked in at that moment, enabling me to power up the jet ski and ride it pell-mell out of there. I sped to the Happy Shore without once looking back. I had no idea what became of those Heroes on their big yacht, but

I was pretty sure the fish had no interest in bothering them. That fish had been going for me. No, that was ridiculous – it was a fish! It didn't care who it swallowed . . . I was being paranoid; this wasn't personal.

I just couldn't shake the feeling that in the split second before I made my escape – that fish had *winked* at me.

# 12

## 9:08 p.m. MONDAY

### 12 hours and 52 minutes until Eternal Damnation

I hid Vileeda's jet ski among some reeds on the banks of the River Betwixt, then headed straight up the beach to the Happy Meadow. When I arrived back at the compound, it was deserted. My friends and family had gone off without me.

I slumped into an armchair.

Then a voice came to me on the breeze . . . a ghostly, ethereal voice.

'Harley!' it cried. 'Harley!'

It was Nana! Her words floated gently over to me like a spirit guide from another realm. But which realm? Where had she gone this time?

'Up here, dear!' she called.

I looked up and saw her step out of the caravan and climb down the tree it was in.

'We weren't sure what time you'd be back,' she said, hugging me. 'The others are at J-Wolf's workshop, but I had to pop back for my reading glasses.' (This was classic Nana; she did get in a muddle. Not long ago, she'd accidentally taken my little brother to the Land of the Dead in her wheelie bag – and look how that had ended up.) 'Everyone's going to be ***very*** excited to see you!' she continued. 'We've missed you. And we *need* you, Harley! We need your Heroic skills . . . Come along. All will be revealed!'

They'd missed me! They *needed* me! It was such a relief to be back at Nana's side as we set off to join the others. 'We've all been very busy since you took off,' she said, hurrying along. 'Grandpa and J-Wolf have come up with a clever scientific solution to the population crisis. I'll let them explain it when we get there. And the rest of us have been helping out – well, you'll see.'

We wound our way through strange streets towards J-Wolf's workshop on the edge of the Techno District.

'Having come up with their genius master plan, Grandpa and J-Wolf have been eager to return to the docks,' Nana continued. 'They've been very secretive about whatever they've been doing down there. All we know is that they've been working on something BIG. Something *to throw enemies off the scent and protect the truth.* Very mysterious!'

Well, that all sounded pretty weird to me. Then we saw something even weirder, which made me temporarily forget about my grandpa's secret project at the docks. We were walking down an alleyway between two tall buildings and there was a band of cats hanging around some bins. A dazed-looking long-haired cat was tuning a banjo, while a chilled-out tabby was struggling to blow a few notes out of a battered saxophone. When they saw us coming, the drummer cat – a sleek tortoiseshell in a trilby – tapped out a rhythm and they all played together. They weren't

very good, and it wasn't exactly a tune, but they were *cats*, so I had to stop and watch. And actually, they weren't much worse than the busker who played his guitar outside Meg's Mini Mart in Kesmitherly – and he was a human. I applauded when they'd finished playing, but they took no notice – just turned away and washed themselves. Typical cats.

'That's not something you see every day,' said Nana, as we continued down the alley. 'One of the wonderful things about eternity is there's always time to learn new skills. It's amazing what you can do if you put your mind to it.'

The musical cats made me think of Mr Purry Paws. I hoped he was all right up there, holding my place in the Land of the Living. I felt bad swapping his Soul out when he could've been down here, learning the harmonica or something. Then again, I wasn't sure he'd be as motivated as these cats.

'So, how have you been, Harley?' asked Nana. 'What happened downriver?'

And here it was – confession time. I wanted to tell Nana how awful the Legendary Heroes were and how I wished I wasn't one because all this Heroism stuff was dishonest and misleading. And I wanted to tell her about my plan to find Quince so I could fix the Portals and impress everyone with my Heroism. But when I thought about it like that, I realised there was a bit of a contradiction here – I'd need to get my thoughts in order about this Heroism business. Also, I still felt embarrassed that I'd left the compound and ended up in that helicopter when there was important stuff going on here that I should've been helping with.

'I've got an island,' I said. 'But I didn't like it there.'

Nana smiled. We turned a corner, and another corner –

'Those Legendary Heroes LIE!' I blurted out, unable to contain myself. 'They don't want anyone to know the Twelve Tasks on the Path of Heroes are just household chores and DIY, so they hide away on their Luxury Islands and let everyone *believe* all those fake stories about their epic deeds and monster slaying! It's all so dishonest – and they make out like I'm one of them! What should I do, Nana? Should I tell everyone the truth about those Heroes and their stories?'

Nana slowed her pace, but she kept walking. She seemed thoughtful. 'People like to believe in Heroes,' she said. 'We like to imagine the possibility of excitement and adventure and triumph. Existence can be tiring. Perhaps we need stories to believe in, to dream about, to be inspired by. Like you used to.'

She smiled at me, and suddenly I was back in the caravan in those long-ago happy times before my grandparents passed *Beyond*. Those cosy nights when I used to curl up and enjoy their crazy tales of Brave Heroes and Scary Monsters without worrying whether the Heroes were lying, or the monsters were miserable. Back then, I imagined Bilbamýn the Bold and Hallyria the Unrelenting and Vileeda the Valiant and Craemog the Intrepid and all those other Legendary Heroes were as great as the stories made them out to be. I imagined the monsters deserved to be destroyed. I imagined the cosiness would last forever . . .

And now my friends and family were waiting for *my* Heroic skills. What did that even mean? What *were* Heroic skills? Lying? Chasing children on jet skis? Playing Swingball for eternity to stave off boredom?

But . . . what if I could be like those Legendary Heroes as they were *back then*, in the stories? Not like they were now, with their stupid island mansions and yachts and lies and bullying – but the impressive, made-up, Heroic versions of them? What if *I* could be an inspiration to others like they had been to me?

'Thanks, Nana,' I said, and smiled back.

Entering the Techno District was like stepping inside a computer, but with more diamond rainbow fountains and frozen yoghurt stalls. The ground-level hatchway to J-Wolf's workshop recognised Nana's ankles as we approached. It slid open to reveal an escalator that led down to an underground bunker. The workshop looked like a hi-tech laboratory in a space station. Strange tools and mysterious gadgets lay around on sleek metal worktops. I recognised some of the gizmos. A dismantled moon buggy J-Wolf had been tinkering with, a couple more of those hover-capsules like he'd arrived in earlier, a few jetpacks, a mood-sensitive toothbrush. Pops was sitting in the corner, scowling at a pile of Digital Soul Adjusters. Like the Self-Service Tea Machine, these were designed to replace the Gatekeepers of Portals of Doom; Pops strongly disapproved.

'Hey, Harley!' said Elektra, peeping out from behind a big shiny flashy thing. 'Hey, Harley's nana! We thought you might be Grandpa and J-Wolf when we heard the hatch opening.'

'Yeah, they been gone ages!' said Frazzle. 'How long does it even take to buy crisps?'

'Probably down at the docks again,' said Nana, rolling her eyes.

'Working on their top-secret project,' said Sparky mysteriously.

'While the rest of us are *starving*,' muttered Pops.

'Harley! You're here! Brilliant!' said Bess, her head peeping round the other side of the big shiny flashy thing.

'Hi, everyone,' I said. It was great to be back.

'What you been up to, Harley-arley-arley! Vroom! Vroom! VROOM!?' asked Olly.

'I got an island,' I said. 'But I didn't like it.'

'Cool,' said Frazzle.

'Come on, let's show Harley the presentation.' Elektra came over and pointed towards a silver disc in the middle of the floor. 'Grandpa and J-Wolf recorded this for you before they popped out.'

'Yeah, go on, play it, Sparky!' said Frazzle. 'Harley must be dying to know the master plan!'

Sparky turned some dials and pressed a few flashy buttons until a light shone out of the silver disc on the floor. Flickering, faintly transparent versions of J-Wolf and Grandpa appeared.

'Hello, Harley!' said Grandpa.

'Hello,' I said.

'They can't hear you,' whispered Frazzle.

'We can't hear you,' Grandpa continued. 'Because we're not there. This is a pre-recorded hologram. Clever, isn't it?'

'So, like, we done this to get you up to speed with the master plan, you get me?' said J-Wolf. 'Your grandaddy had a idea of how to deal with this overcrowding situation.'

'Shrinking!' said Grandpa, looking pleased with himself in a flickering electric way. 'We're going to build a machine that will very, very gradually shrink the entire population of *Beyond*. All of us, all the time – we'll all be constantly shrinking. That way, we'll continually be making more space for the arrival of new Souls.'

'This is a much more humane solution than the Management's eviction proposal,' said J-Wolf, impressed by his old techno-protegee. 'And the mathematical principle is sound. Because like the amount of space for all the Dead will grow exponentially in objective correlation with the arrival of fresh Dead for infinity, you get me?'

I did get it – and it was kind of clever in a totally bonkers way. But was it actually necessary? Was *Beyond* really overcrowded? I wanted to point out how much space there was on the islands – but the presentation was still going on.

'Now this is where YOU fit in to the master plan, Harley,' said Grandpa, pointing at the wall next to me. 'It is very important that we promote this Shrinking Solution. People need to know this Shrinking Solution is on its way, and that'll stop them from panicking –'

The hologram disappeared.

'That's the end,' said Sparky. 'I mean, I accidentally stopped recording then, but they'd basically finished anyway.'

Gran turned to me. 'Slowly shrinking everyone may sound peculiar,' she said, 'but it does make sense when you think about it. And like your grandpa was saying there – people need to KNOW it's coming. Then they'll put pressure on the Management to stop this dangerous Eviction of Undesirables plan they've been talking about.'

'And *this* is what we need your Heroic expertise for, Harley,' said Nana, beaming proudly at me. 'Leafleting!'

'Sorry, what?' I said.

'We've all been working on an intensive leafleting campaign to spread the good news about the new Shrinking Solution!' said Gran.

'Oy! Oy! Oy!' said Olly, spinning his yo-yo round his head. 'We've been going mad for it on the leafleting, Harley-arley-arley! Vroom! Vroom! VROOM!'

'Leafleting!' said Frazzle, grabbing a handful of leaflets and waving them. 'Elektra delivered a thousand! I did eight hundred. And Bess has given out about a trillion!'

'Yay, leafleting!' said Bess, who I now noticed was kneeling on the floor behind the big flashy thing, sorting leaflets into piles.

'Bess is an epic pamphleteer!' said Sparky, passing her a fresh batch of leaflets.

Bess grinned from ear to ear at that compliment, and I couldn't help smiling too, even though everyone seemed to have gone completely crazy.

'Everyone's been doing a great job,' said Gran. 'Well, nearly everyone.' She glanced over at Pops, who remained in his corner, sneering at the Digital Soul Adjusters and muttering crossly. 'While Oliver, Elektra, Frazzle and Bess have been rapidly distributing, Sparky has kept the printer running at top speed, spewing out batch after batch,' Gran continued. 'And now, with our very own Legendary Hero on board, we'll be unstoppable!'

I smiled weakly, wondering how to break it to them

that I would *not* be getting involved in this nonsense. Firstly, I wasn't convinced there even *was* a population crisis – and my grandparents hadn't seemed to think there was before I'd flown away either. There was tons of space on those islands, and in other parts of *Beyond* too – so why did we even need a Shrinking Solution? Secondly, even if **AN EXCESS OF FOULNESS DESCENDING** *did* refer to population overcrowding, the prophecy said the solution was **AN ALMIGHTY SURGE** – which didn't sound like *shrinking* at all. And thirdly, *leafleting* was *not* what I'd had in mind when I was getting all inspired about Legendary Heroism just now.

Overall, this master plan seemed pretty much ridiculous. It would take *weeks* to spread the word about the Shrinking Solution through leafleting and the Management was planning to begin the evictions *tonight*. Plus there was the little matter of Bess and me getting Back to Life by 10 a.m. tomorrow – I could not face having to remind everyone about the dangers of Eternal Damnation *again*.

'Hey, shall we get back out there?' said Bess, jumping up with a stack of leaflets as thick as a breeze block.

'Nice one!' said Olly, tucking his yo-yo away and grabbing a wodge. 'Come on, Harley-arley-arley!'

All this team spirit stuff did make for a fun atmosphere, so I could see why they'd been getting carried away with it. But *leaflets*? They were just so old-fashioned and wasteful . . .

'Come on, Harley!' said Bess. And before I had a chance to burst the bubble of her leafleting zeal, she stepped on to the escalator that led up to street level.

But as Bess rose towards the exit hatch, someone banged on it from the outside. It was an aggressive, urgent banging that made Bess turn and run back down the escalator. She ran and ran and ran and ran . . .

And she was still running down the up escalator when the hatch was smashed open by a squad of soldiers with wheelie bins.

# 13

## 9:37 p.m. MONDAY

### 12 hours and 23 minutes
### until Eternal Damnation

The heavily armoured soldier at the front of the squad wedged a bayonet into the escalator to stop it from moving, then the others marched down and stood to attention on either side of the workshop. Each soldier was holding one of those electro-stabby-laser-poking-sticks. I knew from my last visit that these weapons were worse than deadly. They had the power to *Delete* us – to make it so we didn't exist and never *had* existed, dead or alive. The Deletion wands buzzed and crackled at us menacingly. No one moved. No one spoke. Not even Pops.

Behind the soldiers, a group of serious-looking

Management officials was struggling down the escalator with four wheelie bins brimming with leaflets. Behind them, struggling to make a dramatic entrance past four wheelie bins brimming with leaflets, was Big Moustache.

'Good evening,' he said, his eyes shining cruelly as they scanned the room. 'The Management would like to speak with a certain "J-Wolf", and his accomplice who goes by the alias "Grandpa".'

'They're not here,' said Pops defiantly from his grumpy corner. 'They're buying crisps.'

'Oh, how convenient,' said Big Moustache sarcastically.

'We'll let them know you dropped by,' said Olly. 'Thanks for calling.'

Big Moustache thrust his moustache into Olly's face. 'Do you know who I am?' he asked menacingly.

Olly grinned back at him. 'Yep,' he said. 'D'you remember who *I* am?'

Big Moustache's superior sneer melted as he recognised Olly. 'You're that urchin who humiliated me in front of my colleagues!' His face contorted into such viciousness I thought he might grind all his teeth out. He stared at my dead friend with a look of pure hatred – just like Ambary's mum had stared at me earlier. Then the sinister smile crept back on to his face. 'I ought to thank you, young man,' he said, like someone who didn't mean it. 'Your behaviour inspired me to set up the Management and redesignate the Hero Welcoming Committee as a subsidiary operation. Indeed, you are exactly the sort of young man who exemplifies how important our work is.'

'Do you mean that Olly saving me from Deletion before was what led to us being threatened with Deletion today?' I asked in dismay. Sometimes bad stuff felt so unavoidable!

Big Moustache turned to me and his eyebrows nearly popped off their perches. 'YOU!?' he snarled. 'Harley Lenton the Undeserving Legendary Hero?!'

A silence followed. The only sound was the violent crackling of the Deletion wands. Then one of the soldiers sneezed, which helped to break the tension a bit.

'Bless you,' said another soldier.

Big Moustache composed himself and continued in his confident dictator mode. 'It has come to the attention of the Management that these *missing persons* – "Grandpa" and "J-Wolf" – have been spreading dangerous misinformation about the current population crisis. Their so-called "Shrinking Solution" is unauthorised, unscientific and silly. Therefore, the Management has voted unanimously to insist that they stop doing it.' He nodded to the soldier nearest the printer. 'Seize the remaining pamphlets.'

'Excuse me!' said Nana defensively. 'That's my husband you're talking about. And he's not silly!'

'Yeah!' said Pops, rising to his feet. 'And you're fooling yourself if you think you can scare us with your moustache!'

Big Moustache was unfazed. '**WHEN AN EXCESS OF FOULNESS DESCENDS, ONLY AN ALMIGHTY SURGE SHALL CLEANSE THIS PLACE**,' he declared. 'We WILL be conducting **AN ALMIGHTY SURGE**. And anyone who objects, may well find themselves *going on holiday*.' He turned on his heels and marched up the escalator, his colleagues scuttling along behind him, dragging the wheelie bins with them.

'Looks like this leafleting has got them rattled,' said Gran.

'Yeah, but why?' I asked. 'Why would the leader of the Management turn up in person just to confiscate some leaflets?'

'It is pecoooooliar,' said Olly, toying thoughtfully with his yo-yo.

Nana was pacing up and down nervously.

'Do you think Grandpa and J-Wolf are in danger?' asked Elektra.

'I thought they were buying crisps?' said Frazzle.

'The *going on holiday* comment was a threat,' I explained to Frazzle. 'Remember those messages J-Wolf got earlier about the opposition scientists who'd mysteriously *gone on holiday?*'

'Yeah, and that Moustache geezer made *holidays* sound proper sinister the way he said it,' said Olly.

Nana looked worried. I wasn't sure what to say to comfort her, so I just went and stood next to her.

'We should go down to the docks and look for them,' said Pops. 'They need to be warned.'

'They won't be easy to find,' said Nana, hugging me. 'They'll have kept their top-secret project well hidden.'

'And a search party would lead Management straight to them,' said Gran. 'They're bound to have put spies out there, watching our next move. We might be better to wait it out. J-Wolf and Grandpa can look after themselves. They'll have a plan.'

Everyone paced about, getting cross and anxious.

'This is no good – we have to do *something*!' I said after a few moments.

'We could do another leaflet campaign to protest against the leaflet ban?' suggested Frazzle.

'Hey, I've got an idea,' said Bess. 'What if we ALL go out in different directions to throw the spies off the scent? We pretend we've split up to search for them, but really we'll send those spies on a wild goose chase, anywhere but the docks. Meanwhile, ONE of us secretly waits behind to go to the docks as soon as we've led all the spies away. Then later, when we've shaken the spies off, we meet back here and eat crisps.'

'That's brilliant!' said Pops.

'Oy! Oy! Oy!' said Olly.

'Yes!' said Sparky.

'Harley should be the one to wait here then sneak off,' said Bess. 'Because she's the Legendary Hero, so she'll be best at it.'

Everyone nodded and murmured their agreement.

'Yeah, Harley the Legend.'

'Harley-arley-arley! Obviously.'

I felt a bit choked up. They'd all chosen *me*!

'Let's go in pairs,' said Gran, pushing her specs up her

nose like she always did when she was organising people. 'Bess and Elektra; Sparky and Frazzle; me and Pops; Nana and Olly.'

As everyone got ready, tightening shoelaces, polishing glasses and winding up yo-yos, I tried not to grin ecstatically about how good it felt being chosen to do the main part of the mission. This was my chance to be a proper Hero! Not like those lying, glory-seeking Heroes on the islands – but a proper, sneaky, spy Hero, warning the goodies they're in danger, doing something useful!

And it was all thanks to my new best friend with her sensible master plan. I felt so proud!

# 14

## 10:00 p.m. MONDAY

### 12 hours
### until Eternal Damnation

I watched through a periscope as the Management guards and spies set off in pursuit of my noisy friends and grandparents. They did a great job of fooling those baddies, with a lot of loud talk about going to warn Grandpa and J-Wolf in their secret hideout – while *really* they were leading them away on random journeys to anywhere and everywhere but the docks.

When they'd all cleared off, I snuck out through the smashed-up hatch, my hood pulled low. Heading away from the brightly lit Techno District, I realised night was drawing in. The eerily starless under-sky of *Beyond* was a glowering purple, and spooky shadows danced through the streets. As I was ducking down an alleyway towards the docks, I spotted something. Further along the main road, Big Moustache was having a heated discussion with a squad of soldiers and admin assistants. I slipped into a doorway and peered round to watch them. A moment later they set off at a rapid pace.

Now I was torn about what to do next.

I wanted to follow Big Moustache, to see where he was going and what he was up to. And it did kind of make sense to do that, because while I was watching him, I'd *know* he wasn't finding Grandpa and J-Wolf and I'd know they were safe. On the other hand, the others had entrusted me with the specific mission of going to the docks, and I didn't want to let them down. But was going to the docks the best thing to do right now? Grandpa and J-Wolf would be so well hidden . . . I had to decide quickly because Big Moustache and his cronies were disappearing down the road. Curiosity got the better of me; I followed them. I figured I could always run over and check out the docks when they stopped for a coffee or something.

I hurried to catch up with them at a sneaky distance, hiding behind lamp posts and bus shelters like a proper spy. They turned down another street. I ran to the turning, looked down it – they were nowhere to be seen.

'Doh!' I said, kicking a wall. 'Ow!'

I shouldn't have kicked that wall. And I shouldn't have hesitated just now, worrying about whether following my instincts was the right thing to do or not. That wasn't the way for a Legendary Hero to behave. Action – that was what counted – not *thinking*!

I sighed deeply, as the plaintive sound of a lone harmonica filled the cobbled street. Looking down, I saw that it was being played by a cat – one of the same cats I'd seen earlier. It was the chilled-out tabby who'd had a go at the saxophone, and he was doing an even better job with the harmonica. I mean, it wasn't exactly a tune, but it sounded great for a creature without lips. I applauded spontaneously, forgetting my troubles as that cat played. When he'd finished, he looked me straight in the eye and nodded meaningfully.

Then he set off down the street and I followed him. He had something to show me. At least, I was pretty sure that's what he'd meant. I crawled after him through a tiny door into a walled garden full of frightening vegetables. Past the spooky cabbages, the cat slipped under a rusty gate and paused, waiting for me. I pushed the gate and it creaked open.

He padded on.

I followed that cat down street after street, through parks and subways, as dusk gave way to night. After a while, it began to drizzle. The neighbourhood we were in was quite different now. Narrow, filthy lanes, full of holes and despair, glowing eerily in the blue light of the gas lamps. It was the gloomiest place I'd been on this side of the river. The chilled-out tabby led me along Desolation Row, down Misery Lane . . . then he stopped. He sat on the muddy cobblestones and washed himself.

Why had we stopped here? I looked up at the grimy street sign.

Quince! The cat had led me to Quince's street! He'd helped me!

I recognised the Dead Plumber's home immediately. I didn't know why I knew, or how, but something told me it was hers. Quince's shack wasn't the smallest dwelling, or the dirtiest, but it was the saddest.

'Thanks for bringing me here, cat,' I said. 'I guess you appreciated my appreciation of your music. It just goes to show – cats care. Everyone cares. Kindness is never forgotten.'

The cat ignored me and washed itself. I stroked its head – then dived for cover behind a spooky tree.

Big Moustache had just stormed out of Quince's shack.

He was so angry that his cronies had to jog through muddy puddles to catch up with him. I waited until they were out of sight, then approached the shack and knocked on the corrugated iron door.

A pair of eyes appeared at the letter box. Then the door opened, and there she was. Quince. The legendary ex-leader of the Dead Plumbers Society. At least, I felt pretty sure it was her.

'Yeah, it's me, kid,' she said, as if she could read my mind. 'I'd invite you in, except I don't want you to come in.'

She looked kind of amazing. Strong, unstoppable, almost glamorous in a rough and raggedy, unwashed kind of way. She looked like someone who rarely smiled, but when she did, it would mean everything. Or maybe she used to smile, and it had just been a long time.

'Hi,' I said, standing in the rain on the mud-soaked cobblestones. 'I've come to ask you a favour.'

'Course you have,' said Quince. Her voice was gruff, but she sounded kind. Though that may have been wishful thinking. 'What's in it for me?' she asked. 'If I do you this "favour", what do I get in return?'

'Erm, satisfaction?' I suggested. 'Maybe I should explain what the favour is. Then you might want to do it when you understand how important it is.'

'I know how important it is,' said Quince. Then she laughed and I wondered if I'd guessed wrong about the rarity of her smile – though I'd been right about its effect. It was a strong smile. Powerful, generous, slightly crazy. 'You know, it's a funny thing, kid,' she mused. 'You ain't the first to come round here today. Seems there's been a *spike in demand* for my services this evening. Some "important people" dropped by just now, begging me to get my tools out *one more time*.'

'The Management,' I said. 'Yeah, I know. I saw them. I followed a cat –'

Quince looked confused, and I worried I might be coming across as crazy in front of this famously crazy person. I decided to leave the cat out of it.

'We need your help,' I said.

'You want me to fix the Portals and get the gloop flowing,' said Quince.

I nodded.

'*Everyone* wants Quince to get the gloop flowing!' she said. 'Question is: which way do you want it to flow, kid? The right way, or the wrong way?'

'I'm with the goodies,' I said. 'We want it to flow the right way.'

'That's what everyone says.' She took a nut out of her top pocket and bit into it without removing the shell.

'I've been told you're the only person who can fix the Portals of Doom,' I said, hoping to win her round her with flattery.

'They're right about that,' she said, crunching slowly. 'Ain't easy, you know, being the greatest transcendental plumber in the Land of the Dead. They all say I'm mad, bad and dangerous.' She smiled strangely. 'Maybe I am. What do you think, kid?' I opened my mouth to say something polite, but she just carried on. 'I work for cash, gold, diamonds. Ain't interested in reputation or glory or getting my name in lights.'

I watched a rat run up to her door, turn its nose up in disgust and scurry off again. I wondered how the cash, gold, diamonds approach was working out for her – but I didn't ask. She did seem at least *slightly* mad, bad and dangerous.

'There's been a prophecy,' I said.

**'WHEN AN EXCESS OF FOULNESS DESCENDS, ONLY AN ALMIGHTY SURGE SHALL CLEANSE THIS PLACE**,' said Quince. 'I'll tell you something about that prophecy, kid: I've seen those words before. Long ago. Seen them written, I have. Far from here, in a place of monsters. Those words ain't new, kid.'

'Do you know what they mean?' I asked, excited that we might finally be getting somewhere. But Quince said nothing. Just crunched her nutshell mysteriously. 'The Management claims it's about population overcrowding,' I said. 'They say they need to evict Souls from *Beyond* in an **ALMIGHTY SURGE** . . .'

Quince laughed. 'You're too smart to fall for that, ain't you, kid? Yeah, I can see you're too smart. Sure, I know all about the Management's REVERSE FLOW plan. They wanted my services, but they didn't like my price. Still, they'll find other Dead Plumbers who'll do the job – or who'll *say* they'll do the job. Seems to me they already recruited some of my former associates. That gloop ain't stopped itself from flowing.'

She paused, crunching, as the rain hammered on the metal roof.

'Yeah, I reckon some of my old colleagues stopped that flow,' she continued. 'And they'll be tempted to claim they can fix up this **ALMIGHTY SURGE** too. Can't say I blame them. I'd have done it myself if they could've afforded me. Job's a job – no sense getting sentimental about it. That's something you got to understand about me, kid. If I do this job for you, you got to understand what you're getting into. I'm a maverick. A lone rider. I got skills, but I ain't got principles.'

She took another nut from her pocket and peered at it thoughtfully.

'Let me tell you a story, kid. Long ago, us Dead Plumbers built those Portals of Doom, and we've maintained them ever since. We plumbed in the pipework, rigged up the flumes. Before we did that, there was no way down for Restless Souls. That's why there were so many ghosts in the old days.'

'Yeah, my teacher told me,' I said.

'Your teacher?' Quince looked impressed. 'School sure ain't what it used to be.'

'It wasn't at school,' I said. 'It was in a cafe – anyway, never mind that. What I don't get is, you did a good thing setting up those Portals and flumes. So why do people say –' I stopped myself. Quince didn't need to know what people said about her.

She smiled. 'What bad stuff you heard about me?' she asked.

'Oh, erm,' I stumbled. 'Apparently you used to be the

leader of the Dead Plumbers Society, but then . . . something about a Legendary Pipe Wrench of Destiny?'

Quince looked away. For someone who claimed not to care about her reputation, she seemed to have a lot of pent-up emotions about all this. 'They don't like my methods, kid,' she said. 'Got my own way of doing things. And it don't come cheap.'

'How much?' I asked.

'One billion caskets of gold,' she said.

At first, I didn't say anything. I assumed she was joking.

'One billion caskets of gold,' she said again. 'That's my fee. Take it or leave it.'

'But what's the point of having a billion caskets of gold?' I asked. 'What would you spend it on?'

'Ain't particularly looking to spend it,' she said. 'You just gotta know your value, kid.'

'Could you maybe do this job out of kindness?' I tried.

Quince laughed uproariously. When eventually she stopped, she looked at me, a stillness in her eyes like the unbroken surface of a pond. 'What's your name, kid?'

'Harley,' I said.

'Good luck, Harley,' she said. Then she closed the door and left me standing in the rain.

What had I been thinking? Following a cat, trying to employ a transcendental plumber without any gold – I should've stuck to the plan, not gone off on this *lone rider* nonsense! I'd behaved just like mad, bad and dangerous Quince and look where it had got me. Wallowing in a puddle, trying to be a maverick Hero instead of doing the one important thing my family and friends were relying on me for. Grandpa and J-Wolf still needed to be warned of the danger they were in. I needed to get to the docks.

# 15

## 11:14 p.m. MONDAY

**10 hours and 46 minutes until Eternal Damnation**

The docks were busy and noisy and smelly. Although it was night, nobody seemed to be sleeping. Everywhere I looked, people were rolling barrels up gangplanks or shouting about ropes. All along the wharf, enormous cranes raised and lowered shipping crates like giant metal fingers playing with cuboid yo-yos. The whole world was loading and unloading; everything was creaking and banging and clanking beneath the light of a million swinging lanterns. I had no idea what any of these mysterious cargos were, or where any of the ships that sailed along the River Betwixt and lay anchor here came from, and right now I was too distracted to care.

I walked out along the harbour wall to get a wider view of the quayside as I looked back inland. I was hoping to spot some clue about where Grandpa and J-Wolf might be hiding, though I had no idea what I was looking for. Then, before I'd even begun my search, I *did* spot something – but it wasn't Grandpa, and it was in the opposite direction.

It was that fish. The Big Fish that had tried to swallow me earlier! I could see it way out in the middle of the eerily glowing river, thrashing its tail and leaping in and out of the water.

And now it was heading inland.

Towards me? No, it couldn't really be targeting ***me*** – could it?

It was skimming through the water at a terrifying speed, getting closer by the second. Now its great scaly head was cresting the surface, and there were its huge, lifeless eyes –

And it winked at me. Just like last time – it WINKED at me!

And because the Big Fish had winked at me, I was too shocked to run, too slow to react. It leapt out of the water, its mouth open wide – and launched itself straight at me!

I threw myself to the ground. The fish's slimy bottom lip slobbered over me, its scaly belly brushing against my back and rolling me along until I fell off the harbour wall and into the river. Splashing about, I kept my head above water as the fish dived below the surface and disappeared. I swam to a length of rope hanging loose from a mooring and dragged myself up the damp stone wall. Then I ran round the harbour to the quayside. When I looked back, there was no sign of the creature. No one else seemed to have noticed that a rust-coloured winking fish the size of a whale had just tried to swallow me.

Maybe it hadn't happened. Maybe I was losing my mind.

I slumped on to a crate to get my breath back. And while I sat there, sopping wet on a busy dockside in the Land of the Dead, my own giant face appeared on an advertising screen opposite me – proving, without a doubt, that I had gone mad. And this was the worst kind of madness, the kind where you think the whole world revolves around you – that Big Fish are out to get you, that everyone's looking at you . . .

I closed my eyes to try and make me go away. But when I opened them again, I was still there.

Beneath the photo of my massive face were the words:

WANTED FOR HEROISM.

I sat on the crate and pulled my soggy hood low over my eyes, wondering how long it would be until someone spotted me. I thought about running away, but everyone on the quayside seemed too busy to notice and I figured it would attract more attention if I moved. Besides, I needed to see what would happen next.

My big face was soon replaced by a bigger, hairier face. Big Moustache. After a thunderous throat clearance, people stopped what they were doing to watch.

'Welcome to the Management's second update on the population crisis,' he announced. 'From tonight, we will be redoubling our efforts to round up those Undesirables whose eviction from *Beyond* will allow decent Souls to rest in peace. Our scientists have identified two main categories of Undesirable Dead. The first category is the monsters. Generally, we know where these monsters are to be found. They are lurking Beyond the Back of Beyond, either *Beneath* or on the Path of Heroes. Although there have been some recent sightings of monsters that have ESCAPED *Beneath*.'

The image on screen cut away from his sneery face to a distant, blurry video of some sort of river creature . . . the Big Fish! So *that's* where this thing had come from! Until now, I'd pretty much rejected the idea that my scaly nemesis had swum across from *Beneath*. I guess the winking had made it seem slightly less monstrous in an odd, creepy way. But it made sense that this fish was one of those Resentful Beasts, hell-bent on revenge against humanity for our destructive behaviour in the Land of the Living. (Humanity probably deserved it, but I didn't feel like taking all the blame myself.)

'The second major category of Undesirable Dead,' Big Moustache continued, as his face reappeared, 'is the Villains. Locating the Villains will be a far greater challenge. Villains are all around us. Villains hide in plain sight. The person standing next to you might be a Villain. Any one of YOU could be a Villain.'

People around me began shooting nervous glances at each other. I hunkered down, keeping my face hidden. Then the image on screen cut to a wide shot. Big Moustache was standing in a fancy-looking room in a castle, flanked on either side by – no, I couldn't believe it – Bilbamýn the Bold and Vileeda the Valiant!

'The Management is pleased to announce that in order to achieve our targets for rounding up monsters and Villains, we have enlisted the support of some well-known Legendary Heroes who will be joining the fight to save *Beyond* from overcrowding.'

Everyone on the quayside was as surprised as me to see Bilbamýn and Vileeda. But they were excitably starstruck, whilst I was seriously worried. These were the so-called "Heroes" who not long ago had been chasing me in a yacht with a harpoon.

'We would like to take this opportunity to appeal to other Legendary Heroes to join the cause!' boomed Bilbamýn the Bold.

'In particular, we would like to implore the Land of the Dead's most recent Legendary Hero to do the right thing, and join our fight to protect *Beyond*,' said Vileeda the Valiant. 'Harley Lenton,' she declared, staring directly at me as the camera zoomed in for a close-up. 'Join us, Harley. Join the Heroic Alliance. It is your duty. It is your destiny. Help us to capture monsters and Villains. You are a Legendary Hero, Harley Lenton. For the good of All Souls, step forth at this time of crisis.'

Then the screen cut to another big picture of me. It was that embarrassing one from the Heroic Picnic when my head was stuck in a fence. Could they really not have found a better photo? I scrunched myself up on to my crate so that no one would identify me – but of course, no one was expecting to spot a sopping-wet Legendary Hero at the docks. So, while Big Moustache and his Heroic partners stood around looking intense as a stirring anthem blasted out of the speakers, I skulked away down a gloomy alleyway.

I had no idea what to do next. It would be hopeless trying to find Grandpa and J-Wolf now, with my face plastered over every screen in the Back of Beyond. And what was all this about a Heroic Alliance? Why were Bilbamýn and

Vileeda collaborating with the Management? Everything was so confusing, and I was so soggy. I wanted to run back to the workshop and see if the others had returned. But then I'd have to admit that not only had I failed to find Grandpa and J-Wolf, I'd barely even tried. I'd have to explain why I'd thought it was a better idea to follow a cat with a harmonica –

'Hey, look! There she is! There's that Hero girl off the telly just now! The Wanted Legendary Hero!' A group of excited dockers was pointing at me from the end of the alleyway.

'I'm not her,' I said. Then I turned and ran.

Seconds later, the dim alleyway exploded with light.

'Stay where you are, Harley Lenton!' boomed a voice from on high. 'We're coming to get you!'

I looked up at the outline of an enormous airship, silhouetted against the dazzling searchlights that had picked me out. A rope ladder was lowered, and Vileeda the Valiant came sliding down it like a superhero, her boots and her cape and her hair looking more impressive than ever as she came gliding towards me. What a waste! If only she'd been one of the good guys. Although, technically, she was.

On either side of me, crowds of random Dead were closing in. I had nowhere to run.

'What a pleasure it is to see you again, Harley Lenton,' said Vileeda, smiling as she grasped my arm in her vice-like grip, while holding the ladder with her other hand. We flew away, swinging below the airship as crowds of ordinary Dead pointed up at us.

After we'd been reeled into the cabin, I was shown to a comfy armchair and given another one of those rainbow drinks. Bilbamýn and Vileeda were being smiley and friendly again, like when we'd first met, and I was almost taken in. They sure knew how to win people round, these Legendary Heroes.

'So marvellous to have you back on board,' boomed Bilbamýn the Bold, whose voice wasn't much quieter without the loudspeaker. 'What a splendid time we shall have, hunting down those monsters! The Many-Limbed Optimugoon, the Razor-Elbowed Glockenpard, the Dreaded Polyops of Eastleigh, Old Gobbo Mawjaw and the Serpent of a

Thousand Nightmares – not to mention the Spikanik, the Sporgle and the Spifflemucus. You're going to have such a lot of fun, Harley Lenton!'

I almost choked on my fancy drink. 'But those are the Beast Guardians of the Twelve Tasks!' I said. 'You *know* they don't deserve to be rounded up and evicted. They're just doing their jobs –'

'They are monsters,' said Bilbamýn the Bold uncompromisingly. 'And we are Heroes.'

It was no good trying to reason with these two. They'd been very clear about their desperation to have everyone believe us Heroes were in an eternal battle with those monsters. Though I still didn't fully get why they'd teamed up with the Management.

'If you must insist on a second quest, Harley Lenton,' said Vileeda the Valiant, '*this* is a noble one. Join our Heroic Alliance and we can all look good. This *Management*,' she said, with a derisive wave of her hand towards the airship's cockpit, 'it'll be gone soon enough. Little committees like this pop up every now again: they come; they go. But us Legendary Heroes, we're here forever. So it's important that we *look good*. The Management is of small consequence, but they've got big screens. They can help us to remind people how great we are – as we rid the underworld of monsters and Villains!'

Okay, so now I got why they'd teamed up with the Management.

I accepted a second rainbow cocktail and sat slurping in silence. These drinks were the only nutrition I'd had for *ages* and my stomach still hadn't got over the disappointment of those crisps that never turned up. My hunger was a reminder of how much time had passed since Bert climbed into my maths lesson and kicked this crazy adventure off. Now only ten hours remained until the crushing of the caravan – and I still hadn't found Grandpa and J-Wolf *or* made any progress towards getting the Portals of Doom fixed. Obviously, the last thing I needed right now was to take on *another* quest. But at the same time, I felt a strong urge to *warn* those poor Beast Guardians that a bunch of glory-seeking Heroes were about to come after them with swords and spears. It seemed so unfair!

'You will be handsomely rewarded for your Heroism,' declared Bilbamýn the Bold. 'For every monster you capture, the Management will pay you . . . ONE HUNDRED CASKETS OF GOLD!'

That made me sit up. Ordinarily, it'd be hard to see what use a hundred caskets of gold would be in the Land of the Dead. But *today* . . . I wondered if Quince might accept a hundred caskets as a down payment. You know what? I bet she would. A hundred wasn't a billion, but 'a job's a job' and all that. I bet she would! This could be an opportunity for getting that Portal of Doom fixing quest sorted. If only there was some way of earning the gold without harming any monsters. Or even better, earning the gold while *protecting* the monsters . . . Yes! That's what I needed to do. Here was a perfect chance for a Heroic double whammy!

A plan was forming rapidly in my head, like a sped-up film of a tadpole growing into a frog. I'd cross the river to the Path of Heroes and secretly persuade the Many-Limbed Optimugoon and the Razor-Elbowed Glockenpard to return with me as fake prisoners – then I'd get the gold, pay Quince a deposit to fix the Portals, and release the monsters. I'd have to be quick to squeeze all that in *and* find Grandpa and J-Wolf *and* get me and Bess Back to Life before the caravan was crushed in the morning. But it was better than floating about sipping rainbows all night.

'I'll do it!' I said.

# 16

## 12:18 a.m. TUESDAY

### 9 hours and 42 minutes until Eternal Damnation

I was speeding across the River Betwixt on the jet ski I'd borrowed from Vileeda the Valiant earlier. Luckily, she and Bilbamýn had agreed to my going on ahead while they polished their swords ready for the big hunt. I guess they felt they could trust me on my own again, now that there was gold involved. So, here I was, surging towards the far shore where the Path of Heroes lay hidden in icy swirling mists.

The jet ski was looking good as it glimmered in the moonlight. I'd kitted it out with medieval jousting lances – three in the bows, three in the stern, three to port and three to starboard. There was no way that pesky fish could swallow me now: I was spikier than a stickleback, pointier than a puffed-up pufferfish, pricklier than a porcupine on a surfboard. This was the kind of lo-fi upgrade J-Wolf would've fixed up for me if he hadn't been hiding with Grandpa, working on their top-secret project. (Though actually, my armoured jet ski was a lot better than that shopping trolley with a bit of tinsel and a wonky wheel I'd been given last time.)

I'd chosen the jousting lances from an array of medieval weaponry that had been offered to me, including a suit of armour which was too heavy to lift, and a lot of shiny sharp things which looked too dangerous to play about with. I knew I had to take some kind of weapon with me, to prevent the other Heroes from suspecting my plan of not attacking anything – and these lances made a perfect defence against the vengeful fish.

As the wind and spray chilled my knuckles, I wondered about my friends and grandparents. What must they have thought when they'd seen the big screen announcement of my Heroic assistance to the Management's eviction scheme? I just hoped they'd guessed my plan and didn't think I was really intending to slay innocent monsters. The idea that any of them might believe I was *that* sort of Hero made me feel sick. Still, at least they'd be pleased when I returned to them having fixed the Portals *and* saved the monsters. As long as Grandpa and J-Wolf were okay. And the rest of them . . .

I glanced in the jet ski's wing mirror to see the Happy Shore receding behind me – and I noticed I was being followed. It was a rowing boat, so whoever it was had no chance of catching up with me. Now they were waving – two Souls were standing in the boat and waving and calling out to me . . .

I nearly fell overboard when I realised who it was. It was my grandparents! Nana and Pops waving, and Gran at the oars! Now they were beckoning, like they wanted to tell me something –

Then the Big Fish leapt out of the water and swallowed them, boat and all.

I blinked spray out of my eyes and adjusted the wing mirror. Had that just happened?

My spiky jet ski floated aimlessly on the eerily calm water, as I stared at the place where a moment before my grandparents had been waving at me. The whole thing had been so sudden. Had I imagined it? The fish was nowhere to be seen.

But neither were my grandparents.

They were gone, leaving only the slightest ripple. Nana, Gran, Pops – gone. And now I couldn't imagine Grandpa was anywhere other than in the fish's belly too.

This fish was out to get me. It was punishing me.

A fin broke the surface. Here it was again, charging towards me, despite my spiky defences. The top of its scaly head crested the water as it unhinged its massive jaws –

I opened the throttle and zoomed off. In my spray-soaked mirror, I could see it gaining on me. It was too huge and powerful to outpace – but I could out-manoeuvre it. It launched out of the water, open-mouthed – and I spun round and jetted off in the other direction, ducking my head as its glistening belly swept over me. And now I was heading back to the Happy Shore –

But what was this? Elektra, Sparky, Frazzle and Bess, paddling bravely towards me in four little kayaks!

'Noooo!' I yelled. 'Turn round! Go back! It'll get you –'

But already, it was too late. The fish swept through the water, swallowing one, two, three, four . . .

When would the nightmare end!?

As it came for me again, I zigzagged towards the shore. Running the jet ski aground, I leapt off and sprinted up the beach. When I was more than a big fish's length away from the river's edge, I collapsed and looked out to the water. For a moment, it was so strangely silent and empty I couldn't believe any of the carnage had happened. Then it reared its head one final time . . . and WINKED at me!

Did it wink at me? Yes, it *did* – it winked at me, evilly! Like it had *enjoyed* itself!

I guess some monsters really *were* monstrous.

Further along the beach, a lone figure was staring at the water. It was Olly, arrived just in time to see his friends swallowed. Swallowed by a giant, vengeful fish while they were paddling out to *me*! A giant, vengeful fish that I'd led straight to them, when I should've been at their side, fighting the forces of evil together – not off on my own glory-seeking monster rescue. If only I'd gone straight to the docks. If only I hadn't got into that helicopter, or followed that cat, or set off on yet another stupid quest on a spiky jet ski –

They'd all still be here!

After what felt like an eternity, but was probably only a minute, Olly turned his back on the river and walked up the beach. Our eyes met, but neither of us could speak. This was a whole new Olly, an Olly I'd never known before. Gone was the cheery Soul who no calamity could shake. Gone was the happy-go-lucky, yo-yo-spinning loon who'd helped me and kept me going through every adversity. Olly was gone – and I'd driven him away.

He walked past me. Walked away.

I couldn't blame him. He was better off without me; that was for sure. Whenever people tried to help me, they got hurt. I'd lost my grandparents for a second time. I'd lost Bess for a second time. I'd lost Elektra and Sparky and Frazzle. They'd only been out on the water because of me. I'd put them in danger, and I'd lost them all. I lay down on the stony beach, just below the high-tide mark. The Regrets piled on, crushing me into the Happy Shore.

# PART THREE

# 17

## 12:37 a.m. TUESDAY

### 9 hours and 23 minutes until Eternal Damnation

Squashed beneath a blubbery mound of Regrets, I tried to seek comfort in the fact that at least things couldn't get any worse. Then things got worse.

'Gotcha!'

Flicking an oily tentacle out of my eye, I glanced up to see a pair of shifty-looking chancers holding the handle of a giant fishing net they'd just ensnared me in.

'Why d'you do that?' I asked miserably.

'For the reward, of course!' said the first shifty-looking chancer. He was wearing several jackets and shirts, and a variety of frocks and pantaloons – like a model who hadn't bothered to undress between photo shoots. But he didn't look like a model.

'What reward?' I asked, wondering if they'd misunderstood the WANTED FOR HEROISM adverts.

'Haven't you heard?' said the second chancer, who was wearing so much jewellery she was sinking into the shingle. 'Hasn't she heard?' she said, turning to her excessively clothed companion.

'I don't think she's heard,' said the first chancer, polishing a shiny button on one of his tunics.

'Heard what?' I asked, getting frustrated.

'We're bounty hunters,' he said. 'We've caught you in a net because there's a price on your head. Because *you*, Harley Lenton – wait! You are Harley Lenton, aren't you?' He peered at my face, suddenly unsure. And at this point I could so easily have denied it – but I was just too depressed to care.

'Yeah,' I said.

The bounty hunters chuckled gleefully. '*You*, Harley Lenton, are an official Villain! It has been announced by the Management that you are in league with monsters over the river and a known associate of villainous Quince! Do you deny it? Ha! No, I didn't think so. You stand accused of *glory-seeking*. You betrayed the Heroic Alliance! And worst of all, you sent the Innocent Soul, Bess Macadamia, into *Beyond* on purpose, just so you could rescue her!' He shared a look of disgust with his bejewelled accomplice, as if they couldn't believe anyone could be so immoral. 'And when Bess didn't *want* rescuing,' he continued, 'you got that Big Fish monster to *swallow* her! And all those other people too! You can't deny it – we just saw it. Absolutely shocking behaviour . . .' He shook his head.

'All that Hero fame has made her too big for her boots,' said his companion, who couldn't even bring herself to talk directly to me. 'Just like the Management said – she's got so big-headed, she's gone villainous. At least the Management is doing something about people like her. It's a relief to know that she'll be in the first batch of Undesirable Souls to get evicted from the Land of the Dead.'

'Yeah,' said the first bounty hunter. 'And they've offered a very generous reward for her capture –'

'A whole casket of gold!' declared his companion, rubbing her hands in greedy rapture.

'Only *one?*' I asked.

'*Only one?*' she said, mimicking my voice like I was a spoilt princess.

'That's a lot of gold for us ordinary Souls, little miss high and mighty,' said her snaggle-eared accomplice. 'We've netted ourselves a valuable little Villain, and only an hour after the reward was advertised!'

*Only an hour*? Then I realised: I'd been set up. The Villain reward had been out since the moment I'd been airlifted into that blimp. Bilbamýn and Vileeda and Big Moustache had planned to frame me as a Villain all along; they'd never had any intention of making me look Heroic. And that was what my grandparents and Bess and the pylon kids had been coming to warn me – that I was a Wanted Villain. They'd been swallowed *believing* I was a Villain!

And I bet those Heroes never had any intention of encountering any dangerous monsters either. Sending me over the river was all part of their ploy to set me up as a villainous monster-sympathiser! They knew they could get the glory for monster-hunting without taking any of the risk. They knew the public wouldn't need any *proof*. We were Heroes – what else would we have been up to?

Except that now I was a Villain.

Or was I a victim? 'That Big Fish was trying to swallow me too!' I yelled at my captors. But it sounded like a lie. The sort of lie a Villain would tell.

'How we gonna shift her with all those on her?' asked the bejewelled mercenary, pointing to the mountain of slobbery Regrets pinning me to the ground.

'You'll have to cheer me up,' I said miserably. 'Seriously. It's the only way. I'll be honest, I don't fancy your chances.'

Her friend stroked his chin thoughtfully. 'What do you like then?' he asked. 'What are you into? What kind of thing might cheer you up?'

I smelled an escape plan – and at the very thought,

I felt a small Regret shift its weight off my ankle and slither away, unnoticed by my two captors.

'There is one thing,' I said, peering up at them through the netting. 'Freedom.'

'How do you mean?'

'Well,' I said. 'I love freedom. I love the idea of freedom, and I love being free. So, if you were to release me from this net, that'd cheer me up. Then, once I'm free, I *promise* I'll come along with you and you can get your reward.'

He stroked his chin until it was as smooth as an otter's back. 'How do we know you won't just run away?'

'Well, that's a tricky one,' I said. 'I mean, I *promise* I won't run away, but of course I might be lying.' (I was.) 'Trouble is, if you don't let me go free, I won't cheer up, so you can't move me, and you won't get the reward.'

'I've got it!' said the bejewelled chancer. 'Let's take her shoes. Then she *can't* run away! *And* we get another pair of shoes!'

Her mate danced a jig, or something that might've been a jig if I'd known what a jig looked like. 'Brilliant!' he squealed. 'I love shoes! I love shoes!' I believed him; he was already wearing three shoes on each foot.

They pulled my trainers off and the man with too many shoes struggled to put them on over his other shoes while the woman with too much jewellery heaved the big net away. Gradually, a few Regrets slid off into the shingle, allowing me to crawl slowly along.

'Hey, where are you going?' she asked.

'I'm just experiencing freedom,' I said. 'To get rid of these other ones so that we can go and collect your reward.'

She peered at me suspiciously, as I eased my way slowly up the beach. And now I was less than a metre from the high-tide mark – beyond this point, Doubts and Regrets were banned in the Back of Beyond. And sure enough, as soon as I dragged myself over the boundary, the remaining parasites popped and shrivelled. I stood up, brushed myself down, and ran away.

'Hey!' yelped the woman, limping slowly after me. But she was too weighed down with jewellery, and he was too weighed down with clothes and shoes, and I soon left them behind.

I ducked through alleyways, sticking to the shadows and keeping my head down. I was a fugitive now; I needed somewhere to lie low while I worked out my next move. I kept walking until I'd left the inhabited places behind. I walked on, over the hot, dusty terrain, wishing I had my shoes. On I walked, until I reached a vast, barren emptiness. Here, the dead trees gave no shelter. But there was a rock, a red rock, and there was shadow under this rock. I squeezed into the shadow of this red rock. I shuffled under, I hugged my knees, I buried my face, and I cried.

Olly's friends and my friend and my grandparents were gone. All of them, swallowed by a Big Fish because of me. If only I'd stuck to the plan! All that time I'd been afraid of losing Bess to Orlando and Ambary and that lot – and now I'd lost *everyone*! I'd lost Bess *twice*!

Perhaps the Management's campaign to paint me as a Villain wasn't so far from the truth. In life, and in death, I'd been the worst possible friend I could've been. I'd let Bess get swallowed by a toilet and then a fish.

At least no one would find me out here. Perhaps I could shrivel away in peace without ruining anyone else's life or death.

It turned out I was wrong about that too.

'Harley-arley-arley! Vroom! Vroom . . . whatever,' said Olly, slumping down on to the stony ground beside me. He sighed, got his yo-yo out, stared at it, then put it away

again. I'd never seen Olly like this. Never. Not up in *Before*, not in the Back of Beyond when he was running away from his dad, not when he fell *Beneath*. The truth was, those of us who hadn't been swallowed by a big, angry fish were no better off than those who had. I'd ruined Bess's life and Olly's death.

'You found my epic hiding place then,' I said. 'Makes sense. I can't even hide heroically.'

'Look, Harley-arley,' said Olly, running his fingers through the sand. 'I've just come to say bye.' He wasn't going to say he blamed me, but it felt like he did. And fair enough. I couldn't bring myself to say bye, though, not yet. 'My dad's been on at me to get a job,' he said. 'And I think he's right. It's time. I know I'm only eleven, but I've been eleven for more than thirty years now. It's time for me to grow up.'

'But you love skiving and messing about and being a burden on society,' I said.

'Yeah, well . . . maybe that was the old me.' He stood up. 'I'll see you around, Harley-arley-arley! Vroom! Vroom! VROOM!'

And then he was gone.

I couldn't believe it. I'd made Olly so depressed he'd decided to get a job.

Maybe he was right. If I'd have done my Gatekeeper duty properly, instead of entrusting it to a machine that needed winding up, none of this would've happened. Bess, my grandparents – they'd all still be here. Well, not here. Just not in a Big Fish.

Olly had become more responsible than I was.

But actually, that made sense, seeing as I was a Villain now. I mean, I hadn't chosen to be a Villain, but I'd become one anyway. I'd made selfish choices and left a trail of destruction in my wake . . .

All the evidence suggested that Villainy was my new destiny.

In which case, I should try and make the best of it. I mean, if Villainy was my future, I should at least give it my best shot. I should be the best Villain I could be.

And now I felt bad because, up to now, I hadn't put any effort in to my Villainy. And that wasn't like me. I was a hard worker – Miss Delaporte had always said so. I needed to up my game on this Villainy. And I should start immediately.

So, here I was, skulking under a rock. What sort of thing should a Villain be working on while skulking under a rock? Plotting her bloodthirsty revenge perhaps? Yeah, that sounded about right. In fact, that was perfect. My friends and family hadn't deserved to be swallowed. I should *definitely* be seeking vengeance against the monster that took them from me!

I must hunt down and destroy that fish.

# 18

## 1:22 a.m. TUESDAY

### 8 hours and 38 minutes until Eternal Damnation

As I marched back to the shore, I scowled villainously. At the beach, I stared defiantly at the water where I'd lost everyone. Gathering all the grief that lay deep within me, I tried to convert it into vengeful fury. A tear trickled down my cheek . . . But that was no good! Not boo-hoo self-pitying *tears*! I needed hard-hearted rage, merciless anger! I tried snorting like an irate bull, hunching my shoulders, clenching my fists. I summoned fiery vengeance –

Then I realised my jet ski was gone. I'd left it right over there – I bet those bounty hunters stole it after I ran off! I suppose it would've been some compensation for not getting a casket of gold. I mean, it was definitely *worth* stealing. It was a jet ski souped up with medieval jousting lances. *I* would've stolen it, especially now that I was a Villain.

Yeah, I was really into stealing now. In fact, it was surprising I hadn't stolen anything in the last few minutes.

I looked around for something to steal. A small child was playing with a bucket and spade, shovelling shingle, tipping it out, shovelling it in. Beside him was a box of sweets. I wanted a sweet – and now that I was a Villain, there was nothing to stop me from having one. Like taking candy from a baby! I mean, exactly like it.

I sauntered over and grabbed the box of sweets. The little boy looked up at me and smiled. 'Would you like a sweetie?' he said, in a gentle sing-song voice of pure innocence.

I took one and handed him the box. 'Thank you,' I said and strode away to stare angrily at the water again.

Turned out I was as hopeless at Villainy as I was at Heroism. I couldn't even steal sweets off a kid!

I tried again to reignite my anger, staring at the River Betwixt in an intense stance of unquenchable rage. But it was no good. I didn't feel angry; I just felt sorry for myself, and grateful to the kid who'd given me a sweet. A pair of squelchy Doubts oozed their way over the shingle and leapt on to my shoulders.

Villainy was hard. But I'd have to get better at it

because it was all I had left. Villain was who I was – it had been declared, announced, officially proclaimed – and all my selfish, stupid actions and decisions had confirmed it. Villainy was my destiny. I'd have to get less rubbish at it.

Several families were playing on the beach, paddling and swimming and giggling. I watched them, young and old, joyfully frolicking together, so happy and carefree – and it occurred to me that here was a perfect opportunity to summon up some feelings of bitterness and envy. Why should they be enjoying themselves when I was so miserable? Unfortunately, seeing them having fun didn't make me feel bitter or envious. If anything, it kind of cheered me up.

Conjuring up villainous feelings was just so hard!

The beach was getting busier, and more and more people were going into the river. A boy was paddling about on a yellow lilo. One family was a long way out in a rowing boat – at this distance, it could almost have been my parents and Malcolm. Of course, it couldn't *literally* have been them. It was just my imagination playing tricks because I was missing them. If only they were here now! I should never have set out on a quest to the underworld without their help. A slippery Regret slimed its way on to my foot and squelched up my leg. I looked down at its greasy, knobbly tentacles as they clung to me.

And when I looked up again, there it was. My old enemy had reared its great, scaly head, and was heading this way.

It was a long way out, even further than the rowing boat, and from this distance it looked the size of a normal fish – until it got nearer to that little boat. My heart was in my throat and for a moment I couldn't cry out – not that they would've heard me. And even though they couldn't actually be my family, panic gripped me as if they were – as if I was about to see my parents and little brother swallowed by this terrible creature that wouldn't leave me alone!

But the fish swept straight past the little boat, diving again as it headed towards the shore. Towards the hordes of swimmers and innocent, frolicking families!

'Get out of the water!' I yelled. 'There's a fish! A great big fish! Quick, get out of the water!'

They couldn't hear me above the happy din of their splashing and giggling. I wanted to run to the water's edge, to wave at them, to dive in and swim to their rescue – but I was pinned down by Doubts and Regrets, and all I could do was drag myself slowly down the beach.

'Get out of the water!' I shouted, sliding across the shingle under my blubbery load. 'FISH!' I yelled. 'FI—' Then a Doubt's rubbery tentacle slipped down my face and across my mouth, muffling my shouts (which had gone unheard amidst the splashing and screams of delight anyway).

The fish's slimy fin broke the surface of the water once more. It was close now, getting closer. It passed the boy on the yellow lilo, passed the swimmers, gliding unseen between them. And on it came, towards the shore – towards ME!

But it *couldn't* be coming towards me! *Why* would it be swimming at *me*? How self-absorbed could I get, to believe that this strange creature of the deep was singling me out? Perhaps this was part of my Villainy, this crazy sense of self-importance, of victimhood? Yes, it must've been – for the monster continued to swim towards me, licking its lips, its great mouth slowly opening . . . Then it *winked* at me! This time I was certain – my fishy nemesis was winking at me!

It was coming for me and it was relishing the moment of my terror. Desperately, I tried to drag myself up the beach, away from my scaly adversary. The Doubts and Regrets were weighing me down and I knew I needed to *look on their bright sides* – only by seeing their shiny bellies could I get rid of these pesky parasites.

I spoke aloud, desperately trying to conjure up reasons to be hopeful. 'At least the fish didn't eat any of those innocent people,' I said to the stony beach beneath me. 'At least the family in the boat are safe, the ones who looked like my parents and brother. And at least my actual parents and brother are safe at home. If I can just drag myself away from this Big Fish, I can still try and get those Portals fixed, helping gazillions of future Restless Souls . . .'

It was working! A couple of Regrets plopped off, so I could just about stand. I made my way slowly up the beach.

Away from the fish. Nearer and nearer to the Banned Zone.

As soon as I crossed the high-tide mark, the Doubts and Regrets popped and shrivelled. Then I turned to see the Big Fish winking crazily and waving its fin – taunting me still! It had swallowed everyone I cared about, and it KNEW I was too cowardly to summon the vengeful rage I needed to destroy it . . . Why wouldn't it leave me alone? Now the fish was nodding towards something behind me – then it flipped on its back and swam off.

Behind me, a group of Management officials were marching past with their clipboards and their stripy shirts. This fish was messing with my head – why had it been pointing to this lot? Had it been warning me? Helping me?

The officials were deep in conversation and hadn't noticed me. They looked like they were in a hurry. Maybe here was my chance to find out what was really going on with these Portals of Doom. And maybe, if I found out more, I could still persuade Quince to help. Sticking to the shadows, I followed them.

# 19

## 1:44 a.m. TUESDAY

### 8 hours and 16 minutes until Eternal Damnation

Passing through the backstreets of the Back of Beyond, I lurked in the shadows, hoping these clipboard-wielding officials would lead me to some kind of clue. I needed to find out what the Management was up to, and why they'd set me up. Anyway, I had nothing better to do now that everyone I cared about had been swallowed or got a job – and Villainy just wasn't working out for me.

Suddenly, a man called out from the side of the street. 'Hello, fancy seeing you here!'

I flattened myself against a wall in case the Management officials turned round and saw me. They didn't, so

I whispered, 'Hi, Bert. Everything okay?'

'Everything's *brilliant* down here, Harley – thanks very much for asking,' said the cheery maths lesson intruder. 'As soon as I arrived *Beyond*, I set up my new business,' he continued, even though I'd only asked out of politeness. 'And I've been loving every minute of it! No customers yet, but it's only been a few hours. Look – here's my office!'

He pointed to a desk on the pavement in front of a derelict building with a sign on the wall:

**BERT'S THEFT RECOVERY SERVICE**

**STOLEN GOODS RETURNED TO THEIR RIGHTFUL OWNERS. NO COST. NO CATCH. BRING ANYTHING YOU'VE NICKED TO ME, AND I'LL GIVE IT BACK**

***SO YOU DON'T HAVE TO!***

'That's great, Bert,' I said. 'But I'm in a massive hurry, so . . . good luck. See you later!' I ran off after the stripy-shirted officials.

After a few more twists and turns, we arrived at the foot of a small hill. A wide driveway led up through dense woodland to a castle surrounded by a moat. I hid behind a bush and watched as the drawbridge was lowered and the portcullis raised to let the admin team in. There'd be no way of getting in the front entrance without being spotted, so I circled the ancient fortress at a distance, looking for a ventilation shaft I could crawl through. Obviously there wasn't one, because no sensible Villains would be so carefree about the security of their lair. However, what I *did* find round the back of the castle was a young Management official who'd gone for a dip in the moat during her break. I tiptoed up to her pile of neatly folded work clothes and stole her Chicken Town inspired shirt and cap. Thank goodness gaining entry to high security locations really was like the movies sometimes!

I ducked behind some bushes and got changed. I'd nearly stolen her shoes too – which would've been useful because I'd given mine away ages ago – but hers weren't the right size and I felt mean enough about taking her clothes. I wanted to leave my hoodie as a swap, but I thought it'd be too risky sneaking back over to the moat's edge a second time. Also, my hoodie was so stinky and soggy from the river, I wasn't sure she'd want it.

I waited until the drawbridge was lowered to let a few stripy-shirted workers out, then I crossed into the castle with the confidence of someone who definitely worked there (and definitely didn't need shoes). But as soon as

I was inside the fortress, I lost my nerve. There were guards with Deletion wands everywhere, and my face had been advertised throughout the Back of Beyond with a reward for my capture. What was I thinking? A stripy shirt and cap weren't going to fool anyone!

'Look lively, colleagues,' said a Management official, shaking her clipboard authoritatively. 'The boss is coming, and he's got those VIPs with him.'

There was a bustle of movement as stripy-shirted workers straightened rugs and polished doorknobs. In a blind panic, I ran into the nearest room and hid in a wardrobe, pulling the doors shut behind me.

'Let's go in here,' came the unmistakable voice of Big Moustache. I knelt down to peer through the keyhole . . . and here he was! Here! He'd meant *here*! This room! What were the chances of that?

And he wasn't alone – Bilbamýn the Bold and Vileeda the Valiant were here too. Both Legendary Heroes were nonchalantly holding an extra-large and extra-scary-looking Deletion wand in one hand and a glass of wine in the other.

My heart was pounding in my ears. I tried to breathe silently.

'Leave the nibbles and show our visitors in when they arrive,' said Big Moustache to an assistant, who nodded, placed a tray of food on a fancy table, and left, shutting the room's large doors behind him. Shutting me *in*, with these three!

'Personally, I'm not at all surprised that people believe our story about *Beyond* being overcrowded,' Big Moustache continued, pouring himself a glass of wine and topping up his guests. 'You have to remember that most people don't have their own castle or island. And as for whipping up fear against some imaginary enemy . . . it's the oldest trick in the book.'

'I must admit, it's very clever,' boomed Bilbamŷn the Bold, his armour glistening in the light of the chandelier. 'But cleverness is no good without the courage and strength of the Heroic Alliance.'

'Here's to our mutually profitable arrangement!' said Big Moustache, and they all clinked glasses.

I *knew* it! Just as I'd suspected all along, *Beyond* wasn't really overcrowded. This whole population crisis was yet another conspiracy. Another *story* to fool people into thinking we needed the Management to protect us from a bunch of so-called Villains and monsters. I thought of my grandparents with their Shrinking Solution campaign – it was depressing to think that even *they'd* been fooled. I guess it was because of the prophecy. It was so hard to argue against a prophecy.

'Once we've got the reverse flow set up,' said Big Moustache, 'we'll be able to evict anyone who stands in our way. Anyone who disagrees with me, or annoys me, or insults my moustache –'

'But *first*, we have to get the reverse flow set up,' interrupted Vileeda the Valiant, calmly but firmly.

'Yessss,' said Big Moustache, wringing his hands. 'And this requires some rather advanced technical knowhow. But fear not, my Heroic accomplices, I have hired the greatest Dead Plumbers in the land –'

'Oh, so you managed to persuade Quince, did you?' asked Bilbamýn the Bold.

Big Moustache hesitated before replying. 'Not Quince herself,' he said, clearly bitter about her refusal to work for him. 'But we have her former associates. Anyway, everyone knows Quince is mad, bad and dangerous . . .'

'These Dead Plumbers,' Vileeda interrupted. 'Can they be trusted?'

'No one can be trusted,' replied Big Moustache. 'And that is why we shall evict them as soon as the job's done. There's one in particular whose eviction will give me considerable pleasure. A youngster recruited within the last hour on a training scheme. One Oliver Polliver –'

I stifled a gasp. Olly!

'Oliver Polliver,' said Bilbamýn the Bold, thoughtfully. 'Don't I know that name from somewhere? Wasn't he –? Yes, I believe he was – the official Loyal Sidekick to that troublemaker, Harley Lenton?'

'But we don't need to worry about *her* any more,'

chuckled Big Moustache. 'If she hasn't already been torn to pieces by those monsters Beyond the Back of Beyond, she'll soon enough be captured by gold-hungry bounty hunters and delivered to us for an even nastier ending!' Then they all enjoyed a bit of evil cackling with their wine and nibbles, until they were interrupted by the demonic clanging of a gigantic doorbell.

'Speak of the devil!' said Big Moustache. 'That'll be them – our Dead Plumbing associates. Now when they come in, *don't say anything*. Remember: just act normal!'

Bilbamýn the Bold giggled.

But as soon as the Dead Plumbers entered the room, those Legendary Heroes greeted them with fake smiles and lying handshakes. The Dead Plumbers were a motley crew, not like any of the plumbers I'd ever met. They were more like a band of scurvy pirates who'd swapped their cutlasses for pipe wrenches. As they lingered self-consciously in this palatial room with its tapestries and candelabras and golden furniture, I could easily imagine them being led by Quince. And there, skulking at the back of the group, like a shiftless kid who'd fallen into a bad crowd, was Olly.

Of all the youth training schemes in all the Land of the Dead, he'd joined this one. Olly had enrolled in an apprenticeship with a team of plumbers who were enabling the eviction of countless innocent Souls, including themselves. Why now, Olly? Why this? All those years doing no work at all – why start tonight?

My dead friend was wearing an oversized tool belt, which made him look younger than ever among this crew of old-timers. I wanted to warn him of the danger he was in. I wanted to warn them all that they were at the top of the eviction list. As soon as they'd rigged up that reverse flow, they'd be ejected into an eternity of miserable lingering in the Land of the Living! But if I burst out of my hiding place now, armed only with a wet sock, it would end badly for all of us. I had to be patient.

Unfortunately, as I leaned in to get a clearer view, I knocked a coat hanger against the door –

'Did you hear something?' Bilbamýn looked towards the wardrobe and I froze. 'Who's there?' he boomed, raising his supersized Deletion wand menacingly.

'Calm yourself, my Heroic colleague,' said Big Moustache soothingly. 'I'm sure it's just a rat. You know what they're like, these old castles. Full of dirty rats.' Then he too looked towards the wardrobe, and it felt as if his eyes were burning through the wooden doors, into the safe darkness of my cubbyhole.

'Not for much longer, though,' he murmured under his breath. 'Soon we shall **CLEANSE THIS PLACE** of all the filthy vermin. We'll get rid of them. One rat at a time.'

# 20

## 2:29 a.m. TUESDAY

### 7 hours and 31 minutes until Eternal Damnation

I shuffled deeper into the wardrobe between rows of fur coats. At every step, I expected to bump into the back. But as I continued to edge away from the door, there was still nothing behind me. Retreating from the sinister gaze of Big Moustache, I passed more coats until I noticed something crunching under my feet. A moment later, I felt snowflakes falling on to my hair . . .

I couldn't believe it – I'd gone through the wardrobe to Narnia! Wow, this was so magical – I wished Bess could've been here with me.

When I'd blinked a few times and my eyes had adjusted

to the light, I realised this wasn't quite Narnia – although it *was* snowing. The backless wardrobe had led into another room in the castle. It looked like a grand dining hall, but the chairs and tables had been moved aside to make space for people to lounge about on beanbags and deckchairs. Those who weren't asleep were just lying around murmuring contentedly to themselves. Apart from the snoring and happy mumbles, the only other sounds were the dreamy tinkling of wind chimes and the gentle bubbling of a huge aquarium in which a troupe of performing terrapins in spangly leotards rode unicycles and juggled. Chandeliers and glitter balls sparkled, their soft light refracting through flurries of snow, creating a miniature snow rainbow that arced over the snoozing inmates.

I held out my hand to catch a snowflake and was unsurprised by its warmth. Lovely warm snow, drifting peacefully through the delicious smell of an unseen barbecue. Glancing around at the blissed-out residents, I had a pretty good idea what was going on here. These happy Souls were prisoners, trapped by pleasure. I knew, because it had happened to me when I was rescuing Malcolm.

But who were they, these contented prisoners lounging about in the warm snow? I approached the nearest one, an elderly man in a lab coat. He was slumped on a beanbag staring at the glittery disco ball with a mindless grin on his face.

'Hi,' I said, stepping between him and his light show.

'Mmmm,' he said, reaching out to a tray of sliced fruit, which was floating past.

'You know the doors are open?' I said.

He waved his papaya at me. 'I know,' he said. 'I'm leaving soon.' He closed his eyes.

'Sit down and have some pizza,' said the young woman beside him. She clicked her fingers and a slice of pizza floated teasingly towards my mouth. 'We've all got to build our strength up before the big fun begins.'

I noticed she was also wearing a lab coat. And hers had a name badge: Professor Yaxis. It was a name I thought I'd heard before, but I couldn't think where. Glancing around at the other inmates, I felt like a few of them were giving off a scientific vibe. Was this some kind of conference?

'What big fun are you waiting for?' I asked. Professor Yaxis smiled and waved towards a screen hovering over the fireplace. It was playing an advert for a flashy holiday resort, which boasted 'The Land of the Dead's first ever UPWARD FLUMES!'

'They've told Doctor Radar and me that we're going to be at the front of the queue,' she explained, looking very pleased with herself. 'Because of all our clever research.'

And then I remembered where I'd heard her name before. Professor Yaxis and Doctor Radar were the scientists who'd texted J-Wolf. These prisoners were the missing scientists who'd unexpectedly *gone on holiday.* No wonder they'd messaged J-Wolf seeming so blissed-out and carefree: they'd been here, lounging uselessly in the lap of luxury. Tempted away from their research, which would have disproved the Management's overcrowding claim. Holed up here while Big Moustache spread lies about a fake population crisis to justify the eviction of innocent Restless Souls! And now these scientists – and the Dead Plumbers – were going to be sent up first. And they thought it was a treat!

I had to warn them of the danger they were in. But for some reason I couldn't be bothered.

'You mustn't go,' I mumbled. They ignored me, and as a comfy-looking beanbag sidled over, I realised how exhausted I was. All that walking and hiding and jet-skiing. All the stress and worry of failed Heroism and failed Villainy. I needed to sit down.

But I resisted. This was an evil beanbag, tempting me to delay my quest! This had happened to me before; I couldn't let it happen again. The pizza, the warm snow, the sweet sounds and the soft smells – it was all conspiring to make me give up and enjoy myself when I was meant to be suffering. Yes, suffering! For a moment, I couldn't remember why. But I knew I mustn't sit down; I knew I mustn't eat the evil floating pizza or any of the other evil floating snacks. I knew I was meant to be miserable and exhausted . . .

My head felt fuzzy. What was going on? Where was I?

Who was I?

'Harley Lenton!' a voice called from across the room.

That was it: Harley Lenton. Something like that anyway.

I heard a loud bubbling behind me and turned to see a mobile jacuzzi sliding over the warm snow towards us. A smiley head was bobbing about on the frothy surface. A smiley bobbing head in a policeman's helmet –

'Sergeant Polliver!' I gasped. 'What are you doing here?'

'Even the police deserve a holiday,' said Olly's dad, as the bubbles tickled his chin. 'And so do Legendary Heroes, Harley Lenton!'

Sergeant Polliver's jacuzzi bumped gently into my knees, knocking me into the soft embrace of my beanbag.

As I fell, I reached out to steady myself and grabbed a slice of evil floating pizza, which I quickly ate before it had a chance to tempt me. Then I got rid of all the other snacks floating about my head, trying to stop me from leaving. Now everything felt better. It was lovely to be here with Olly's dad. So good to see him relaxing, taking time off from his policing duties now that his son had finally got a job. I felt my eyes flickering shut.

'Olly's in danger,' I mumbled, struggling to stay awake.

Sergeant Polliver sipped his pina colada. 'Again?' he said.

'Yes,' I said, forcing myself to speak even though I wanted to sleep. 'And so are you. I don't know why they've chosen you, Sergeant Polliver, but everyone here is going to be evicted from the Land of the Dead and splurged back out for an eternity of miserable restlessness.'

'Oh, that,' said Olly's dad, sliding back into his bubbles. 'Don't worry about that, Harley. It's just a rumour. The Management isn't evil – it's just people who are good at organising stuff. Sit down. Relax. No one's getting evicted. We're going on holiday.'

'No!' I said. 'It's not a water park – it's the Flume of Infinite Terror and they're going to set it to work in reverse, to launch you back out through the Portal of Doom.'

'But the Management loves us, dearie!' said Doctor Radar, waltzing around with a cello that was playing itself for him. 'They don't want rid of us; they want to reward us for our contributions to science and technology. All of this is a great big thank you!' He bit a grape off a vine that had lowered itself to his mouth.

'I'm being rewarded for my policing duties,' said Olly's dad, his head lolling deeper into the warm bubbles. 'The Management has always valued keyworkers.'

'I don't think they have,' I said. 'In fact, I bet you're getting evicted for being too good at your job! I bet Bilbamýn and Vileeda want you out of the way because you keep investigating stuff on the Path of Heroes – I bet it's because you know the truth about the Twelve Tasks –'

'What you're saying isn't logical,' said Professor Yaxis. 'Surely no one could be so cruel as to deliberately deport a Soul away from their eternal rest? The idea's preposterous! It's unnatural! There'd be rioting in the streets . . .'

'No one's rioting against our evictions because they think *we're* the baddies,' I explained. 'They think the Management is doing them a favour by getting rid of all the monsters and Villains –'

'Quite right too!' said Doctor Radar, as he danced through the snow. 'We ought to get rid of those monsters and Villains. I think that's a jolly sensible idea.'

'But that's *us*!' I repeated, exasperated. '*We're* the monsters and Villains! The Management tells us we're Heroes to keep us quiet, but meanwhile they're putting

WANTED posters up, telling the rest of the population we're Villains –'

'No, no,' said Doctor Radar. 'We're not Villains. We're the good guys, and that's why we have all this!' He did a sweeping gesture with his arms, then rolled over and closed his eyes.

I still felt woozy, but my head was clear enough to see this carnival of laziness for what it was. It was like being back on the Luxury Islands. These were some of the cleverest people in the underworld, but they didn't want to see the truth because they were too comfortable. The truth was inconvenient – it required us to leave all of this behind and walk out that door into whatever fresh misery awaited us. Lying here and believing we were about to go on the best holiday ever was infinitely more appealing.

But it was a lie.

'I'm leaving,' I said, standing up and kicking my beanbag away.

'There's the way out, dearie,' said Doctor Radar. 'But why would you leave? We have cupcakes, you know!' He held out a plate of delicate, brightly coloured cupcakes. For a moment, I perused the sweet treats, wondering which one to choose . . . then I shoved the whole lot in my mouth and left.

# 21

## 3:24 a.m. TUESDAY

### 6 hours and 36 minutes until Eternal Damnation

Leaving the sleepy scientists behind, I wound my way along tapestry-lined stone corridors until I reached the front of the castle. Luckily, the portcullis was up – but I quickly ducked behind a barrel as Big Moustache came sweeping across the lowered drawbridge, leading a group of officials and the Dead Plumbers.

'We meet here,' he said, stopping just in front of the barrel I was hiding behind, 'in forty-five minutes. Have you got that?'

'Aye, aye, Cap'n!' said a plumber. Big Moustache eyed him warily, perhaps unsure if he was taking the mick or not.

'Well, you'd better have. Because if you're late, we'll leave without you. And that'll mean no gold for you!'

'Right,' said the plumber to his mates, as Big Moustache strode away dramatically. 'Let's get a drink and a bite at the canteen. Just make sure we're all back here in forty-five minutes. That includes you, Jonah.' This made them all laugh, and they went chuckling down the corridor.

Forty-five minutes until they'd be setting off on this reverse flow job. I checked my phone. I had until 4:15 a.m. to persuade Quince to do the right thing and stop them. I felt sure they'd listen to her – well, about sixty per cent sure – that they'd turn down the job and fix the gloop to flow naturally again if their old leader came up here and told them to.

When everyone had cleared out of the entrance hall, I ran over the lowered drawbridge. The castle was on top of a hill with a clear view all the way to the River Betwixt. I could make out Quince's neighbourhood, and it would take too long to walk there and back. So I ran down the hill, stopping at the bike sheds. And there it was – Big Moustache's majestically shining bicycle from the first film they'd showed us. This sleek machine looked like it could get any non-wobbly-baked-potato rider wherever they needed to go super quick. Unfortunately, it was securely locked to the rack. I tried several others, and they were all locked – apart from one. The only bike available to borrow for my crucial life and death mission was a penny-farthing – one of those clunky old contraptions with one giant wheel and one tiny wheel. It was ridiculous, but it was unlocked. So I took it.

Obviously, I was only borrowing it – same as I was only borrowing this Management worker's uniform. I definitely wasn't *stealing* it. But it was interesting how much easier I was finding it to borrow stuff since I'd given up Villainy.

Freewheeling down the hill, I steered off the main track on to a path through dense woodland. Bumping over bracken and slaloming between giant fir trees, I thought about how awful it would be to get lost in these woods – to be stuck here at the mercy of wolves and bears while the Management succeeded in their evil scheme just because a girl forgot to check her route before setting off on a penny-farthing . . . I stopped and leaned against a tree. I was completely lost. Every direction looked the same.

What had I done? Don't go into the woods – that was a basic rule for adventuring! I'd messed everything up again . . .

Something howled nearby and I shuddered, hoping the height of my stupidly tall bike might offer some protection from the snapping jaws of any leaping wolves . . . The howling continued, getting nearer, and I realised it wasn't exactly a howl. More a screech, a squeal, kind of melodic . . . It was a trumpet! And there he was – my chilled-out tabby cat, blowing his horn like a jazz fairy godmother. Beside him, his two bandmates struck up a walking bassline on a double bass. They had one end each. (Obviously a cat couldn't play a double bass by itself.) The sleek tortoiseshell in a trilby was on the ground plucking, while the dazed-looking long-haired casually lowered a paw from the branch he was lying on to reach the neck of the instrument. Once again, I found myself applauding spontaneously at the ingenuity of these cats. My penny-farthing wobbled against the trunk I was leaning on, so I had to cut short my applause and grab on to stop myself from falling.

The tabby put his trumpet down and pulled a lever on the tree behind him. Immediately, a row of lights lit up through the forest like an airport runway. I smiled at the cats, who continued to pretend they didn't care, then I followed the light trail out of the woods to a street I recognised.

Pedalling along the same route I'd taken when I followed the cat earlier, I soon reached Quince's neighbourhood. On arrival at the Dead Plumber's shack, it was raining again. Everything in Evil Street was so damp and rusty and miserable, I wondered if it ever stopped raining here.

I banged on the corrugated iron door.

No reply. I banged again. Still no answer.

I knelt in the mud and shouted through the letter box.

'The Management is planning to evict anyone who annoys them!' I yelled, not even caring if the neighbours heard. 'Your old colleagues are going to set up the reverse flow, just like you said they would! And my friend Olly's with them. I upset him and he joined a training scheme . . . Please, Quince, you've got to help! You're the only one that can stop them! And I *know* you can get the gloop flowing again – the RIGHT way! Please, Quince? You could be a Legendary Hero –'

'Who'd want *that*?' came a shout from within.

Ha! I *knew* she was in there!

'You're right,' I said. 'Look, forget the Hero thing. I know the stories are lying about those brave warriors who saved the day. But here's something I think might be true –' I paused, feeling suddenly embarrassed about acting all wise in front of this famous plumber. Luckily there didn't seem to be anyone around and the noise of the rain drumming on the metal roof would've drowned out my shouts anyway. Also, I kind of *believed* what I was about to say. So, I said it. 'Good things happen when people stick together.'

There was a moment's silence. 'I was like you once, kid,' Quince replied quietly. 'But when you've been around as long as I have, you'll understand that you can't rely on people. You're better off on your own –'

'Actually, I was like YOU, once,' I said, interrupting her. 'I thought I was better off on my own – that's *exactly* what I thought. But you know what? People proved me wrong.' I felt a lump in my throat. 'My grandparents,' I said.

'Elektra, Sparky, Frazzle . . .' I took a deep breath. 'All of them, swallowed by a Big Fish while trying to help me. And Olly, my Loyal Sidekick, who's given up everything and got a job . . . And Bess . . . Bess, who stood by me, and didn't go off with Ambary and Orlando and that lot . . . Bess! Dragged into the Land of the Dead while protecting the Portal of Doom –'

'You know, that's an interesting situation,' interrupted Quince, 'from a technical point of view. Sounds to me like a sudden vacuum in the system must've sucked the Portal open when the gloop was turned off, pulling your friend in before sealing it shut . . .'

'That's what Grandpa reckoned too,' I said, choking back the tears. 'Now he's gone . . . The point is, I'm hopeless without my friends and family – even though they're complicated and ridiculous. You can't give up on people, Quince. People are all we've got. They'll save you – suddenly, unexpectedly . . . And even when they get it *wrong* – and start playing with their yo-yo or *leafleting* – just seeing them *try* to get it right can be enough. Enough to make you want to try . . .' By this point I was crying like a baby and the rain was mingling with my tears like in a movie.

I listened at the letter box.

Silence.

Then . . . the door slowly opened, just a crack, and Quince's watery eyes peeped round. She looked tired.

'Okay, kid,' she said. 'You've inspired me. I'll fix that pipe. I'll get those Portals working. I'll help you save an eternity of Restless Souls.'

'Yes!' I pumped the air and danced the Victory Shuffle in the mud. I *knew* she'd come good! Quince had turned down the Management's offer of gold and glory because she wanted to *do the right thing* –

'And you know what, kid?' she said, opening the door a little wider. 'Because you've inspired me, I'm going to offer you a special discount deal.' She looked at me seriously. 'Half a billion caskets of gold!'

Then she burst out laughing and slammed the door, cackling manically to herself as the rain fell.

# 22

## 4:03 a.m. TUESDAY

### 5 hours and 57 minutes until Eternal Damnation

As I pedalled back along the mud-soaked cobblestones of Quince's neighbourhood, I still couldn't believe she'd said no. I'd put my heart and soul into that speech! I honestly thought she'd come along and help us for free.

It was totally miserable that Quince hadn't gone for it, but one thing was certain: I couldn't give up now. After all my big talk about believing in people, it was clear that I'd have to continue my quest with the help of . . . *people*. And as I sped towards the castle on my ridiculous stolen bicycle, I thought of the ideal person to help me right now. Someone perfectly placed to create a distraction while I slipped back into the castle to follow the Dead Plumbers to their reverse flow job.

I bounced and bumped my way through the woods, following the light trail past the lazily snoozing cats. When I emerged on the other side, I turned left and freewheeled *down* the hill, away from the castle. I had to see a man about a bike.

After dropping off the penny-farthing with Bert, I circled round and went up the side of the hill on foot, avoiding the main approach. Peeping out from behind a bush, I watched as an angry official with a monocle waved furiously at another official. The second official was presumably more important because she had *two* clipboards and a walkie-talkie, which she now spoke into. A moment later, Big Moustache came out, accompanied by a whole troop of guards armed with Deletion wands. Together, they marched down to the bicycle shed where Mr Monocle pointed dramatically at the rack his penny-farthing had disappeared from.

Big Moustache grabbed a telescope from his assistant and raised it to his eye. He swept it across the horizon and I ducked as his gaze swung towards me. Then I peeped out again to see him lower the telescope in surprise. He'd spotted Bert, striding enthusiastically up the hill, wheeling the penny-farthing. While they gathered round to listen to Bert's bewildering explanation of his Returning Stolen

Goods business, I slipped over the drawbridge unnoticed.

In the entrance hall, I hid behind the same barrel, seconds before the Dead Plumbers assembled.

'Oy! Oy! Oy!' said Olly. 'Who fancies a sing-song while we wait?'

I didn't dare peep over my barrel for fear of being seen, but Olly was clearly very close. If only there was some way to get a message to him.

'There will be no singing here,' said Big Moustache, arriving with his soldiers just in time to spoil the fun. 'And before anyone asks, I am one minute late because I had to deal with a serious theft. The Management takes theft *and* punctuality very seriously. We will depart as soon as our transport is ready.'

'Will we be travelling in the same coach as the Undesirables?' asked one of the plumbers nervously.

'Don't be daft, Boz!' said another plumber. 'Those Undesirables are vicious monsters and Villains! They'll be chained up in armoured tanks with loads of guards.'

I peeped over to see Big Moustache smiling deviously. 'Indeed,' he said. 'You will be doing the decent Souls of *Beyond* a great service by helping to get these dangerous Undesirables evicted.'

Just like the sleepy scientists, these Dead Plumbers had no idea what was really going on. I wanted to leap up and shout at them: *There ARE no dangerous Undesirables! It's just*

*YOU and ME and some professors and a police officer in a hot tub. WE'RE the ones getting evicted – followed by ANYONE ELSE these tyrants feel like getting rid of!*

And the idea of Professor Yaxis and Doctor Radar chained up in armoured tanks was laughable. They'd been so brainwashed they didn't even need guarding. More likely, they'd be sharing snacks and enjoying the sort of jolly sing-song that Olly had been hoping for. Anyway, the guards were *here*. Bilbamýn the Bold and Vileeda the Valiant were standing on either side of the Dead Plumbers, their massive Deletion wands buzzing ominously.

'We will be travelling separately to the Undesirables,' said Big Moustache's assistant. 'You won't have any dealings with them. Now, we're almost ready to leave, but I notice we're one Dead Plumber short –'

'Jonah,' chuckled Boz. 'He'll be here. Probably just in the –'

'Sorry I'm late!' came a breathless voice that must've been Jonah's, his footsteps echoing down the stone corridor. 'I hate getting stuck on a long journey when you need a –'

'Yes, yes, yes,' said Big Moustache impatiently. Jonah stopped talking and dumped his tool bag down on the floor. He dumped his tool bag on the floor *right beside my barrel.* Jonah had a particularly large tool bag. Almost large enough . . . I wondered. It was worth a try. I reached out and grabbed the end of Jonah's bag, and pulled it slowly towards me, behind the barrel. It was heavy. Perhaps nearly as heavy as me.

At that moment, Olly cracked a joke, which made the other Dead Plumbers guffaw. While they were laughing, I unzipped the bag and removed some of the tools, hiding them inside the barrel. Then I squeezed into the bag and zipped myself in.

'Transport's here!' announced an official, and a moment later I was hefted up on to Jonah's shoulders. As I settled into the journey, I noticed the inside of the bag smelled of cherries. It was very cramped and cosy, and overall, I felt that being a stowaway in this bag was a pretty good arrangement. Judging from the shine on his pipe wrench, Jonah was a man who looked after things; I felt I could trust him to get me there safely.

Where *there* was, I had no idea. Nor did I have a clue what I intended to do once we got there. But at least I was near Olly. As soon as Bilbamýn and Vileeda were out of the way, I could warn him, and we could do something.

After a while, the atmosphere inside the bag felt strangely different. I unzipped it a crack and peeped out. There was nothing there. Not darkness or emptiness or quiet – just Nothing. Pure, total Nothingness. And that could only mean one thing: we were heading away from the Back of Beyond, towards the arrival point – where the Portals of Doom opened above the Flumes of Infinite Terror. I zipped the bag shut and waited.

As we travelled, I managed to learn some of the Dead Plumbers' names by listening to snippets of their conversation. There was Boz, of course, who'd done a lot of the talking earlier, and Jonah, whose bag I was in, and Nell and Mel and Rik – as well as Olly and a few more whose names I hadn't caught. The more I got to know them, the worse I felt for them. These Dead Plumbers had no idea they were first in line for eviction – their Souls whooshed up the Flume of Infinite Terror and out into an eternity of miserable restlessness in the Land of the Living! As far as they were concerned, they were just part of the workforce: do the job, take the gold, ask no questions. They didn't deserve eviction. And Olly *really* didn't.

I was just dropping into a snooze when the journey became bumpier and the voices of the Dead Plumbers more echoey. Peeping out, I recognised where we were. This was the Front of *Beyond*, at the bottom of the Flumes of Infinite Terror which launched newly arrived Souls into gloopy splash pools. The Portals of Doom were way, way above us, out of sight beyond the clouds. I knew now there were thousands of these flumes and pools, but this one did look pretty much identical to the one I'd arrived in at half-term – except that today the place was full of people drilling and hammering and painting. They seemed to be sprucing the place up, giving it a makeover. There was scaffolding up the sides of the flume –

Someone looked in our direction, so I quickly zipped up the bag. A moment later, it felt like we were going underground. The air became humid. Finally, I was set down on the ground.

'So, this is where it all happens?' said Boz in awestruck wonder. 'The nerve centre of the whole operation!'

'Correct,' came the voice of an official. 'We are currently below the flumes, in one of the pump rooms. Remember, this is a closed loop system. Purgatorial gloop flows in to the reservoir, which is located beyond this wall, before being pumped to the top of the flumes –'

'Okay, okay, that'll do!' said Big Moustache impatiently. 'They don't need a guided tour! We're not on a school trip.'

I cautiously zipped open the tiniest crack and peeped out. We were in a brightly lit underground bunker full of pipes and tanks and cylinders. At one end of the room stood Big Moustache, flanked, as ever, by Bilbamýn the Bold and Vileeda the Valiant. The Dead Plumbers were standing in a group, awaiting orders, while officials in hi-vis jackets flicked switches, twiddled dials and ticked boxes on clipboards.

'All we need you to do,' said Big Moustache, addressing the Dead Plumbers, 'is to set the system to run in reverse. We simply need the gloop to flow *upwards* to carry unwanted Souls up and out.'

The Dead Plumbers looked around at the mass of intertwined pipes and tubes lining every wall, shaking their heads and exhaling doubtfully.

'What you're looking at here,' said Boz, pursing his lips and sighing dramatically, 'is a HIGH-PRESSURE REVERSE FLOW. Now a high-pressure reverse flow isn't your standard, everyday kind of a job. A high-pressure reverse flow requires *transcendental plumbing*.'

'I'm sure you'll rise to the challenge,' said Big Moustache. 'And in case anyone needs a little encouragement, I think this ought to help.' He stepped over to what I'd assumed was a pile of specialist equipment with a huge sheet draped over it. Big Moustache whipped off the sheet to reveal –

'A billion caskets of gold!' Rik gasped, his eyes like saucers as he gawped at the shiny treasure.

'That ain't a billion,' said Olly. 'More like twenty.'

'Twenty-four,' grinned Big Moustache. 'Twenty-four caskets of shiny, shiny gold. But of course, if that's not enough to persuade you, there's always this.' He clapped his hands and Bilbamýn the Bold and Vileeda the Valiant stepped forward, brandishing their supersized Deletion wands. It still astounded me, how these Legendary Heroes had been reduced to minions, mindlessly following the orders of a power-hungry dictator! Just because the Management could bring them more fame and glory.

'Give us half an hour,' said Nell, and her colleagues

nodded. Between the promise of gold and the threat of Deletion, the Dead Plumbers had been persuaded to get on with the job.

'Fifteen minutes,' said Big Moustache in his annoying got-to-have-the-last-word way. Then he stood there, arms folded, watching. Nell glanced up at the closed hatch at the top of the ladder. Clearly the Dead Plumbers had expected them to leave. But still Big Moustache stood there, and Bilbamýn the Bold and Vileeda the Valiant stood with him.

Rik stared hungrily at the gold. Mel reached out to stroke it, hesitantly, as if it were a tiger cub. Boz and Jonah kept flitting their eyes nervously between the piled-up caskets and the crackling wands.

By this point, my arms and legs had been squashed up for so long, I wondered if they'd ever unfold again. But it wasn't time to reveal myself yet. Not while the threat of Deletion hung in the air.

'Who's going up them flumes?', said Olly.

'What?' snapped Big Moustache. He really couldn't stand Olly. It made me so proud. 'Villains go up it. Monsters. *Undesirables.*'

The Deletion wands fizzed menacingly.

Olly stepped in front of them.

The Dead Plumbers gasped in unison. They must've thought Olly was a right daredevil. I mean, he was – but I'd seen him do this a couple of times now. It was like he had a death wish. Except he was already dead, and these devices promised a fate worse than death. Deletion. A complete termination of existence, past and future.

Olly got his yo-yo out and spun it casually.

'How do we know you'll only send up the proper Villains?' he asked, looking at Big Moustache suspiciously. 'Who's to say you won't start trying to get rid of any old Souls you don't like? Anyone who *you* think is "Undesirable"?'

'Shhh,' said Boz, nodding towards the pile of gold. 'Dead Plumbers Apprenticeship Lesson One: take the cash, don't ask questions. Customer's always right.' Boz turned towards Big Moustache apologetically. 'Sorry, sir, but this lad's new to the business. First day on the job. He'll learn.' He threw Olly a warning look.

'No need to apologise,' hissed Big Moustache. 'We were all young once.'

'Seriously, though,' said Olly, unperturbed. He turned to address his professional colleagues. 'I don't reckon this job's moral. Reverse flow ain't natural, and I ain't sure I trust this lot not to use it to get rid of whoever they want.'

Bilbamýn the Bold raised his weapon, and the Dead Plumbers flinched. Not Olly, though. I guess I should've felt proud of my friend's courage, standing up for what he believed in in the face of grave danger. And I suppose I did, but the timing of Olly's resistance was pretty annoying. I'd been hiding in a bag for literally hours, patiently awaiting my moment to sneak out and do something cunning to outwit Big Moustache and his cronies. Now they knew their motives were under suspicion, they'd be on their guard. Olly might've ruined my whole plan! Not that it really was a plan.

Perhaps the real reason I felt so annoyed, was that Olly was being reckless. And not his hilarious whoopee-cushion-on-the-teacher's-chair kind of reckless. This was the far more dangerous, getting-exterminated kind of reckless. I just couldn't bear the thought of watching another friend disappear.

A slippery Doubt oozed itself up Rik's leg. 'The boy's right,' he said. 'This job's immoral. We shouldn't be tempted.' He looked wistfully at the caskets of shiny gold. 'We should do the right thing,' he said.

Big Moustache's eye began to twitch, then his other eye, then his moustache. He looked like he might bite someone.

'Let's be honest about this,' said Mel, 'we couldn't do the job anyway, even if some of us wanted to. Face it, colleagues – we haven't got the skills. We haven't got the knowhow. We haven't got the tools.'

The other Dead Plumbers nodded, murmuring their reluctant agreement with this assessment of the situation.

'There's only one Dead Plumber who could do a job like this,' said Nell.

'Only one Dead Plumber who *would* do a job like this,'

said Rik. The others laughed. 'Only one mad, bad and dangerous enough – only one *skilled* enough – to transcendentally plumb against Nature. There's only one Dead Plumber out there with enough courage, grit and experience . . .' He trailed off, staring thoughtfully at the pipes.

All the Dead Plumbers were absorbed in their own memories. Obviously they were talking about Quince, but it was as if they were too afraid or too angry or too in love to say her name. I couldn't tell which.

'Only one,' said Boz, shaking his head wistfully – and again, I couldn't be sure if this was love or anger. Maybe he wasn't even sure himself. 'Nothing to be done, though,' he went on. 'Don't reckon she'll be showing her face round here any time soon, after she let us down so badly . . .'

The others nodded.

'There you go then,' said Olly, turning conclusively to Big Moustache. 'Looks like it's game over for you lot. There's only one Dead Plumber brave or mad enough to take on a job as tricky and immoral as what you've got planned – and she ain't here.'

At that moment, a blinding light burst on to the scene – a pair of lights – headlights – beacons of Hope in the darkness. A white van, older than Time and grubbier than Truth, roared out of the darkness and came screeching to a halt in front of us.

The driver's door flew open, and the greatest transcendental plumber in the history of Death stepped out.

'I'll do it,' said Quince. 'But I can't do it alone. Now who's with me?'

# 23

## 6:20 a.m. TUESDAY

### 3 hours and 40 minutes until Eternal Damnation

Quince waited expectantly. Nobody moved. Nobody spoke. The Dead Plumbers' bewildered heads swung back and forth between their ex-leader and the dark corner where her van had magically appeared, like meerkats at a Swingball match. It had been an impressively dramatic entrance and I really felt Quince deserved a cheer – but she didn't even get a polite hello.

'Who's with me?' she asked again, as a blobby Regret leapt on to her shoulders.

Still nobody responded, and now I felt bad because I'd given her that pep talk about working together and asking for help – and here she was, doing just that, and no one was stepping forward. Of course, she'd missed the conversation about the job being immoral. But she'd also missed whatever years of longing and betrayal the others felt.

'It's not right,' said Boz finally. 'Fixing that pipe. It's not natural. We've had a meeting and we've all agreed we're not doing the job.' The others looked at their feet.

Big Moustache smiled. 'Looks like that's twenty-four caskets all for you, Quince.'

Quince looked at the gold and nodded. 'That's a hefty pile you got there,' she said. 'And today, I'm prepared to split it – that's twelve caskets for one of you. I just need . . . an assistant. A mate. A helping hand.' Quince scanned the faces of her ex-colleagues expectantly. One by one, they lowered their eyes. Quince held her nerve.

'What about you, kid?' she said, turning to Olly. 'Be good learning for you, this would. I need a mate to hold the torch and pass the tools. Whaddya reckon? It'd be solid experience for you, kid. Let's get this gloop flowing!'

Olly stared defiantly into Quince's face. 'I ain't doing it,' he said. 'And you shouldn't do it neither. They're sending up "Undesirables". How d'you know you ain't one?'

'It's a job, kid,' said Quince. 'You don't turn a job down.'

Their eyes locked like rival stags in an underground wilderness. I knew Quince would never back down. I knew Olly would never back down.

But I also knew – thought – *hoped* – that Olly had got it wrong. He'd misjudged Quince. They all had. And Quince knew that, and she'd done it on purpose. Hopefully. 'Let's get this gloop flowing!' she'd said – but she hadn't said in which direction. Olly and the other Dead Plumbers had *assumed* Quince was intending to fix up a reverse flow like the Management wanted. But I had a feeling this was a trick. I had a feeling Quince was double-crossing the Management. Really, she was here to get that gloop flowing in the *right* direction – downwards. And she was relying on her villainous reputation to fool everyone into thinking she was here to reverse the flow and take the gold – because if anyone guessed she was here to do the right thing, she'd get Deleted.

Of course, I might've been wrong. She might've been about to use her transcendental plumbing skills for evil. She might've been about to set up the reverse flow, causing untold misery for an eternity of Restless Souls and so-called Undesirables. But I didn't believe she was the Villain her reputation made her out to be. I had a feeling she was going to risk her neck to save an eternity of future Restless Souls, and all she needed was a mate to help her.

'Here's my final offer,' said Quince. 'I'll take one casket of gold for expenses. The other twenty-three go to my assistant. Now, for the last time – *who's with me?*'

'You're crazy, Quince!' said Mel. 'Mad, bad and

dangerous, just like everyone says! No one here could be villainous enough to join you now!'

Two seconds later, the tense silence was slowly torn apart.

*ZZZZIIIIIPPPP!*

I emerged from the tool bag like a gangly duckling hatching from a plumber's egg.

'I'll join you,' I said. 'I'll carry the torch.'

# 24

## 6:31 a.m. TUESDAY

### 3 hours and 29 minutes until Eternal Damnation

I knew that to make this work, I'd have to appear convincingly villainous. If anyone suspected I was here for anything other than gold and glory, I'd be Deleted. Even Olly had to believe I'd turned proper bad. But on the day when I'd got his best friends swallowed by a Big Fish, I reckoned that shouldn't be too hard.

'What you playing at, Harley-arley-arley?' asked Olly. He looked hurt, betrayed. My plan was working. 'Only a Villain would work with the notorious Quince!'

'Well, I *am* a Villain now,' I said, staring up at the pipes to avoid meeting Olly's eye. 'Everything you've heard about me is true. I used to pretend to be good. But I'm not. I'm only here for the gold and the glory. Setting up this reverse flow will provide me with a quick and convenient route Back to Life. I don't care about the consequences for others – I'm just doing it for my own personal gain. I was only waiting in that tool bag until there was enough gold on offer to make it worth my while. For twenty-three caskets, I'd do anything. Because I'm a Villain, just like they said.' I scowled and sneered and distorted my face into the most villainous expression I could muster.

'She really *is* a Villain!' gasped Boz. 'Look at her face!'

'But if you do this, Harley Lenton,' boomed Bilbamýn the Bold. 'You shall once again be a true Legendary Hero!'

'Indeed,' declared Vileeda the Valiant. 'A true Legendary Hero. Just like us!'

'Er, yeah, okay,' I said. As long as everyone believed I was on the same side as the people with the big extermination weapons, I didn't care what they called me – Villain, Hero, whatever. Right now, they just had to think that Quince and I were going to fix up a reverse flow so that we could get up there and do the opposite.

'She's not a Hero!' said Rik in disgust. 'She's a lowdown Villain! Let's stop them!' He lunged at Quince, but was blocked by the electric swoosh of Vileeda's wand barring his way.

'The tale of our Heroic adventure shall be told

forevermore!' declared Vileeda the Valiant.

'*Our* adventure?' I said, suddenly panicked. If Vileeda and Bilbamýn and their supersized Deletion wands came up the pipes with us, they'd make sure we set up a reverse flow. My plan to prevent the suffering of an eternity of future Restless Souls would be ruined! 'Are you two gonna help?' I asked nervously.

'No, of course not,' boomed Bilbamýn. 'Vileeda and I are very busy dealing with all the important Heroism down here.'

Phew, that was close. Luckily, these Legendary Heroes were too lazy to climb up the perilous network of spaghetti pipework and do any real work.

'How dare you call yourselves Heroes!' exclaimed Boz. 'This is Villainy! Pure Villainy, I tell you!'

'Heroism, Villainy, Shmeroism, Shmillainy,' laughed Quince. 'It's a *job*, cash in hand, that's what it is. Come on, kid. Let's get plumbing.'

'You have made the right decision, Harley Lenton,' said Big Moustache, who had been silently rubbing his hands in triumph ever since I'd announced my Villainy.

'Yeah,' I mumbled, turning away.

Quince grabbed a grappling hook from her epically equipped tool belt and swung it into the darkness above, where it clanged into position around an unseen pipe. Then she scrambled up the rope and called out for me to follow. I could feel Olly's eyes on me as I clambered up the tangled nest of pipework, but I couldn't bring myself to look at his disapproving face. From a few metres up, I glanced down and saw him whispering with the other Dead Plumbers. I tried not to imagine what they must be saying about me.

But I'd realised now that doing the right thing was more important than looking like I was doing the right thing. I kept picturing Bess, shutting herself in the caravan toilet. She hadn't cared what Ambary thought at all – she'd just instinctively tried to protect the Portal of Doom. Anyway, I couldn't control what other people thought about me – but I could control what I chose to do next. And the thing to do next, the right thing, was to help Quince get the gloop flowing and foil the Management's evil plan.

Yes, this was definitely the right thing, as long as I hadn't completely misjudged Quince's motives. Because if she *hadn't* been lying to the Management just now, then I was about to assist in an act of pure evil that would have tragic consequences for eternity. And that would be seriously bad.

I was taking a big risk here – not my style at all. As I followed Quince into a dark tunnel, I felt a small Doubt splodge on to my shoulder.

'Erm, Quince, can I just double-check something please?' I said, as I crawled along behind her. 'We are going to *fix* the pipes, aren't we? I mean, like, back to how they were? For the good of All Souls?'

Quince didn't reply. All I could see was the torch-lit soles of her boots, but I had a feeling she was smiling mysteriously. She crawled on in silence, and I began to panic that I'd made the wrong choice . . .

What had I done? Quince was famously crazy! Mad, bad and dangerous – everyone said so! I was up a dark pipe with a Legendary Maniac! She was here to set up the reverse flow, not to save the day! And she wasn't even doing it for the gold – she was just doing it to be controversial and annoying and to show off her transcendental plumbing skills!

From out of nowhere, a bigger, sloppier Doubt squelched on to my leg, as a slimy Regret hooked its talons into my hair.

'No point trying to convince people we're not Villains, kid,' said Quince. 'Makes no difference what people think of us, anyway.'

'Yeah,' I said, struggling under the extra weight of the blobby parasites. 'We're not though, are we? Villains, I mean.'

'Dunno about you, kid. I sure ain't no Hero.'

The sloppy Doubt gripped my leg firmly.

'I get what you're saying,' I said, as we crawled out of the pipe on to a rocky ledge. 'But just to clarify: we *are* going to fix the Portals, aren't we? Properly, I mean. We're not going to set up a reverse flow . . .?'

'I noticed something back there,' said Quince. 'That

pump was still working. Listen.' She paused and we both listened. I wasn't sure what we were listening to, but whatever it was, she could hear it and I couldn't. 'ALL the pumps are still working,' she continued. 'And that means the gloop *should* still be flowing like normal. Up the pipes, down the flumes. This is an intriguing situation, kid. Fixing this'll be the greatest professional challenge of my long and distinguished career. A perfect opportunity to reveal the true power of my legendary transcendental plumbing skills . . .'

Why wouldn't she answer my question? This was driving me crazy! Was Quince going to set this gloop flowing the RIGHT way – or was I about to assist her in an act of pure evil? Suddenly, her face lit up like a spectre in the gloom, as she flashed the torch on under her chin. 'BOO!' she shouted, and I nearly slipped off the ledge. 'I'm just winding you up, kid,' she laughed, clapping me on the shoulder. 'We'll fix those Portals.'

My heart was hammering in my chest. Quince had really strung me along there. I guess she *was* mad, bad and dangerous – but in kind of a fun, annoying way, a bit like Olly.

As the slippery Doubt oozed itself off my leg, Quince swung the torch round, revealing a tiny crevice in the rocky wall. 'D'you reckon you can fit through there, kid?'

'Don't think so,' I said.

'Hmmm.' Quince looked thoughtful. 'As a

transcendental plumber, you've got to be able to get places others can't. That's why I've got a magic van. Come on, kid – you hid in a tool bag. We can get through here.'

The gap was about the size of a weasel's burrow. I couldn't see how this was going to work.

'I'll turn the torch off,' said Quince. 'Some things are easier when you're not in the spotlight.' Darkness descended, and I heard a scrabbling, like a fox going up a fence. Then I heard a violent squeal, like a badger defending its set. Finally, I heard a disappointed sigh, like a human who'd given up trying to squeeze through a gap that was blatantly too narrow. The torch flashed back on.

'I've got a better idea,' said Quince. 'Let's go this way.' She shone the beam over to our right, where a wider tunnel opened into the rock. We crawled through it. Moments later we arrived in an enormous cavern containing an eerily shimmering lake of purgatorial gloop.

'This ain't right, kid,' said Quince. 'The reservoir shouldn't be full. This here is why the gloop stopped flowing – someone left the plug in.'

Quince shone the torch across the smooth surface of the reservoir. Last time I'd seen purgatorial gloop, it had been gushing and frothing in a wild torrent. But here, its greenish-yellow surface was so still, I could almost imagine walking across it.

'Usually, the plug should only be left in for a few

minutes,' said Quince. 'Just long enough to regulate the system. But this plug's been in for too long – since yesterday afternoon, judging from the depth. Over there –' Quince directed the torch beam across the lake to an opening high on the opposite side of the cavern – 'fresh gloop *should* be flowing in. But the whole system's run dry because it's all backed up here. Sabotage, kid! After centuries of running smoothly to get Restless Souls safely down from the Land of the Living, our system has been deliberately messed up.'

Quince swung the beam upward to the cavernous ceiling, where great stalactites hung like green icicles.

'So, here's what we do,' she continued. 'See that chain going up to the pulley in the roof, then over to that capstan? We gotta edge our way round the cavern to turn that capstan and pull the plug.' She swept the torchlight around the edge of the lake, where a pair of gutter-sized parallel pipes snaked round the rocky wall, a few metres above the surface. 'Follow me, kid. Feet on the lower one, hands on the higher one. And make sure you hold on tight. Nobody wants to fall into the Lake of Lost Souls.'

'The Lake of Lost Souls?' I asked nervously.

'That's what I'm thinking we should call it,' said Quince. 'Sounds more epic than gloopy reservoir.'

As we clambered gingerly round the edge, I kept my eyes fixed on the pipe in front of me, clinging on with my hands while sliding my feet along the lower pipe. At places, the fittings attaching the pipe to the rocky cavern wall had worked loose. The pipe creaked and shook as we clung to it. But it held us up, and after a while, my fear of the pipework being wrenched from the wall gave way to muscle fatigue. Eventually however, I found a rhythm and we edged steadily on.

Pausing for a moment, I looked over my shoulder at the great lake. As I looked, its glassy surface rippled, ever so slightly, and a sound came to my ears on the breeze. A sort of whispered, gurgling song; a simmering, bubbling melody, half breath, half music rose softly from the reservoir and hovered in the air around me.

'It doesn't matter what other people think,' Quince declared, cutting through the mesmerising effect of that bubbling murmur as she dredged up our earlier conversation.

'Yeah,' I said, though I wasn't sure either of us completely believed that.

'Right now, my old colleagues and your old mate, they think we're Villains. But who cares, eh? As long as we're *doing the right thing*,' she continued, unconvincingly. 'Always better to do the *right thing*, instead of the popular thing.'

'Yeah,' I said, wondering if we were both slightly lying to ourselves.

'Those so-called Legendary Heroes back there,' Quince

continued – more to herself than to me, 'all they care about is their reputations. Their Legacies. They're only worried about the stories that'll be told about them, not the story they're in. But this thing we're doing is the *right thing*. We're sacrificing *our* reputations for the good of others. And as long as *we* know we're Heroes, it doesn't matter if everyone else thinks we're Villains –'

Suddenly, a great, bristly, flubbery Doubt leapt out of the reservoir with a squelchy plop. It was a big one, about the size of a newborn manatee or a fully grown otter. As it attached itself to Quince's back, the extra weight shook her, but she kept a firm grip on the pipe.

'Try not to think too much about it,' I suggested. It wasn't brilliant advice, but it felt like the best I could do in the circumstances. If Olly had been here, he'd have tried to lift Quince's spirits with one of his "cheery songs" to make the Doubts and Regrets go away. The memory made me smile – but I wasn't about to start any of that nonsense myself.

Quince breathed deeply. 'You're right, kid. Just keep going, get the job done.' She edged cautiously onwards. 'Only, if we *don't* fix up these Portals,' she continued, as that hefty Doubt lashed its tentacles round her shoulders. 'If we *fail*, and someone else comes along to set up that reverse flow . . . no one will ever even know we *tried* to do the right thing.' A leathery Regret burst out of the gloop and latched on to Quince's thigh. She held firm, but I could see her straining under the extra weight. 'We'll *always* be known as the Villains, forever more. Everyone, for all eternity, will think it was us, that *we* did this –'

'Not everyone,' I said, gripping the pipe as I scanned the reservoir for more of the squelchy parasitic blobs. They'd be coming for me soon. But as the anxious seconds passed, no Doubts surfaced, and no Regrets. I breathed deeply, trying to work out why. It was almost as if I believed what I was saying.

With great difficulty, Quince craned her neck round to look at me. 'Whaddya mean, kid?'

'I'm not sure,' I said, surprised by my unexpected burst of hope. 'Maybe our friends will realise we're not Villains? Because . . . they're our friends?'

'Not in my experience, kid. Everyone thinks I'm mad, bad and dangerous – everyone! Even my old colleagues in the Dead Plumbers Society. And the trouble is, you can get too used to what other people think you are. I'd got so used to being that crazy, unreliable loner everyone said I was, that I started playing along with it. That's why I demanded stupid amounts of gold and laughed like a loon and sent you away earlier – even though your soppy speech had completely won me round. I'd got so used to being mad and bad, I couldn't really picture myself doing the right thing. But you'd got me *so* fired up, I had to come and find you in my magic van . . . And now I'm not sure again. Got a lot of Doubts, kid. A lot of Regrets. Because even though most of that stuff about me is rumours and lies, some true stuff did happen too –' Another pair of particularly slippery Regrets slimed their way up the wall and slid on to Quince's ankles.

'Yeah, the true stuff,' I said – and one of the slimy Regrets reached out a tentacle and wrapped itself round my leg. 'My best dead friend thinks I'm a Villain because I let my best living friend get swallowed by a Resentful Big Fish. That's the truth and I can't escape it.'

Quince stopped to catch her breath. 'You know, I ain't so sure about this Big Fish vendetta,' she said, shaking a tentacle off her cheek. 'I ain't convinced it *is* deliberately targeting you. Don't seem to me like the sort of thing a fish would do. Same goes for all those creatures in *Beneath.* People make out they're vengeful, but I reckon there ain't no such thing as a Resentful Beast. Fish don't hold on to the bad stuff. They let it go.'

It was a pretty persuasive speech and Quince seemed to have made her mind up, so I decided not to mention the winking.

By this point, we'd finally reached the capstan. Together, we turned it – each heaving the wheel slowly round with one hand, while we held on tight to the pipes with the other. The weird singing was getting louder, but it was less melodious now. The gently bubbling harmony had given way to a deep, throbbing gurgle, as we pushed and heaved, turning that wheel until –

POP!

The plug was out. There was a gushing roar and the gloop bubbled like lava. Steam rose from the surface of the reservoir – and suddenly, a towering geyser erupted out of the lake! We clung to the pipe desperately, as hot waves battered us. The mountainous fountain of gloop surged out of the reservoir. And surfing on top of it was my slimy-finned arch-enemy – the Big Fish that had swallowed everyone I cared about! My scaly-gilled nemesis shot out of the lake, then dived into the broiling gloop and swam towards us.

We had nowhere to hide. The Big Fish leapt from the bubbling surface of the reservoir, scraping my toes with its scaly back, and flew open-mouthed towards Quince, snapping at her ankles! With razor-sharp reflexes, the Legendary Dead Plumber swung aside, and those gnashing jaws came clamping down on empty air. The fish crashed into the gloop with a tremendous splash that nearly knocked me off my pipes. I held on, but Quince's legs had been swept away, leaving her swinging wildly. Weighed down by Doubts and Regrets, she couldn't regain her footing on the pipe or get a grip on the slippery rock.

I looked over my shoulder and saw that the gloop was in retreat. Where the giant plug had been removed from the centre of the reservoir, where just now a fountain of Big Fish had jettisoned upwards, the purgatorial gloop was circling round and round before being sucked down into an unseen hole. The Big Fish was caught in this swirling vortex, and was being whisked round the cavern, ever closer to the eye of the whirlpool – until it was dragged under and disappeared. The gloop continued to swirl violently, bubbling and steaming in the cavernous space.

Quince had finally managed to get her feet back on the lower pipe. We both clung on, buffeted by hot spray, our faces pressed against the slimy rock as we stared into one another's eyes.

'Now do you believe me?' I yelled. 'That fish came straight for us!'

'It's a red herring, kid!'

'I don't care what kind of fish it is, Quince! All I know is that it's massive and it keeps trying to swallow me and everyone I like!'

'You just gotta – whoa!' Suddenly, Quince was struck by a falling rock dislodged by the waves of gloop. She slipped and fell – but I reached out and grabbed her hand.

'I've got you!' I called, grinding my teeth with the effort, and wondering how long I could hold on. My other arm gripped the upper pipe – but now it was coming loose, the fittings working their way out of the rocky wall.

'Leave me, kid!' Quince yelled. 'Save yourself!'

I held on, but the pain was excruciating. I couldn't talk, could barely think.

'Go on without me!' Quince called. 'You've got to do this, Harley –'

Below her, the gushing gloop gurgled violently. If she fell, she wouldn't stand a chance – she'd be swept away and sucked under like a spider in a bathtub.

I closed my eyes and channelled every atom into holding on to Quince's hand as she dangled perilously over the swirling vortex. As I strained, it felt as though time and reality were evaporating. Quince's words floated up to me as if in a dream.

'I'm not really a maverick loner, kid,' she confessed. 'I never *wanted* to work alone. The truth is, I lost the knack. I can't plumb transcendentally any more! I haven't summoned a magical tool in years! That's why I drove the others away and broke up the society – because I couldn't admit that I was no longer the transcendental plumber they used to respect . . .'

I wanted to reassure her that those Dead Plumbers still respected her – I knew, I'd seen it in their eyes. But I couldn't talk, the strain of holding on was too much. It was taking every last drop of energy, and I was running out.

'And I'll tell you another truth,' yelled Quince, crying and laughing at the same time. 'If a person DID want to set up a reverse flow, they wouldn't do it *here*. Anyone seriously interested in the Legendary Reverse Flow would want to follow the prophecy to its source –'

She winked and blinked and laughed and I wasn't sure if she was trying to tell me something or was becoming delirious.

**'WHEN AN EXCESS OF FOULNESS DESCENDS** – tee-hee-hee!' she giggled crazily, **'ONLY AN ALMIGHTY SURGE** – ha ha ha! – **SHALL CLEANSE THIS PLACE** – ho ho ho! People got no idea, kid! The Management got no idea! Tee-hee-hee, ha ha ha!'

Quince was slipping from my grasp. Any second now she'd drop into that whirlpool of gloop, to be swept around and swallowed into its depths like dirty dishwater down the kitchen sink. She was slipping, slipping, slipping – I shut my eyes – and then she was gone.

As the weight of the Dead Plumber was released, my aching arm immediately felt the relief. Through closed eyelids, I sensed a shadow pass over me, as though an avenging angel had risen from the purgatorial gloop to place a curse upon my Soul.

# 25

## 7:18 a.m. TUESDAY

### 2 hours and 42 minutes until Eternal Damnation

'Mind out, darling.'

Opening my eyes, I discovered it wasn't the shadow of an avenging angel after all; it was a chain of Dead Plumbers, swinging from the pipework beside me. At the end of the chain, dangling above the swirling vortex, Mel had caught Quince's arm and was pulling her away from a gloopy doom. Mel was held by Boz, who was held by Nell, who was held by Jonah, whose toes were hooked over the lower pipe beside me, his ankles held firmly in place by Rik, whose other hand was gripping the upper pipe. Beyond Rik, the chain of Dead Plumbers stretched back around the

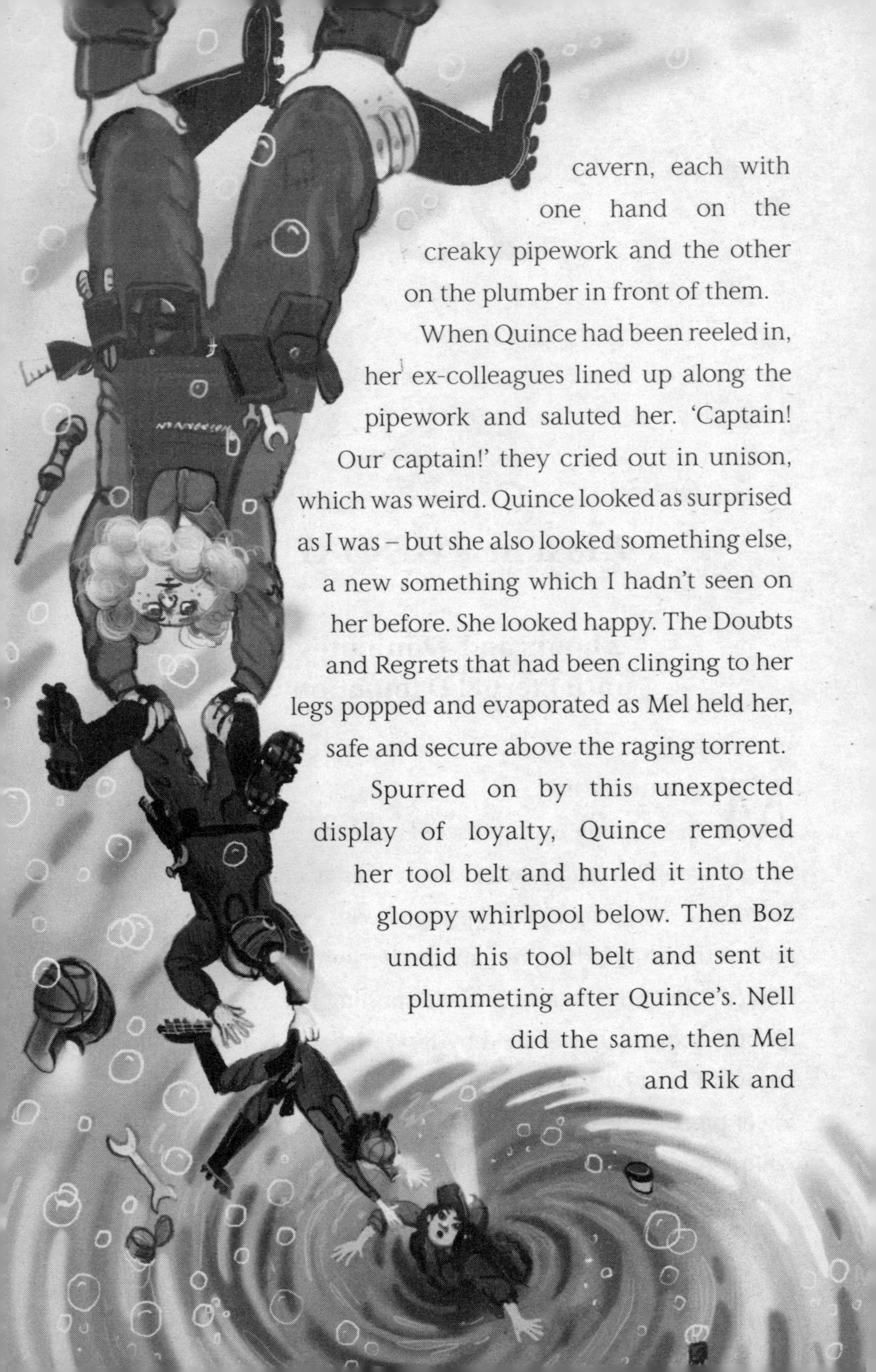

cavern, each with one hand on the creaky pipework and the other on the plumber in front of them.

When Quince had been reeled in, her ex-colleagues lined up along the pipework and saluted her. 'Captain! Our captain!' they cried out in unison, which was weird. Quince looked as surprised as I was – but she also looked something else, a new something which I hadn't seen on her before. She looked happy. The Doubts and Regrets that had been clinging to her legs popped and evaporated as Mel held her, safe and secure above the raging torrent.

Spurred on by this unexpected display of loyalty, Quince removed her tool belt and hurled it into the gloopy whirlpool below. Then Boz undid his tool belt and sent it plummeting after Quince's. Nell did the same, then Mel and Rik and

Jonah – and each of the Dead Plumbers, on and on down the line.

'What're you all doing that for?' I asked.

'I reckon it's symbolic, kid,' said Quince, beaming proudly at her loyal band of Dead Plumbers. 'A gesture of solidarity. We're abandoning conventional tools and relying on each other and our shared knowledge and experience.' The gesture of solidarity continued to pass on down the line as one after another they removed their tool belts and hurled them to the slimy waves below. It really was an impressively moving ritual, as tool belt after tool belt was flung ceremoniously to the frothy depths – until it came to the turn of a smaller Dead Plumber near the back whose trousers fell down.

'Oy! Oy! Oy!' he said, in case anyone hadn't noticed.

'Olly!' I called out.

'Harley-arley-arely! Vroom! Vroom! VROOM!' he yelled back. 'Brung you some reinforcements, didn't I? Managed to talk this lot round, persuade them to come and save the day. Why not, eh? I would usually get my yo-yo out in a situation like this – but my trousers have fallen down, so pardon me if I save it for later. Oy! Oy! Oy!'

Olly! Of course – Olly! That's what he'd been whispering to the other plumbers as I'd climbed up the pipe nest; he'd been persuading them to rally round their old leader. He must've seen, like I had, that Quince was here to do the

right thing. Somehow, I'd known Olly would come. I'd had a feeling Quince had to be wrong about *everyone* believing in our Villainy. I guess at some level I knew that Olly trusted me – I'd trusted him to trust me. And now, these loyal Dead Plumbers had come to their mighty leader's aid at this time of Pipe Crisis – all thanks to Olly, the work experience boy with his trousers round his ankles.

(To be honest, there was no reason for his trousers to have fallen down. It was a tool belt for carrying tools, not a hold-your-trousers-up belt. He must've done it on purpose. Classic Olly.)

As my best dead friend scrabbled to regain his dignity without falling off the pipes, Quince surveyed her tooled-down troops like a proud general. If only Bess and my grandparents and Olly's friends could've been here. It was a truly majestic, triumphant scene. While Mel held her securely round the knees, Quince reached out with a firm grasp of confident leadership and took hold of an invisible object that hovered in the air before her – an object which slowly materialised and solidified, emitting a warm glow of Hope that shone magnificently, lighting up the gloomy cavern like a new dawn.

'The Legendary Pipe Wrench of Destiny!' gasped Boz.

'The ultimate tool of the transcendental plumber!' gasped Nell.

'This tool is *our* tool!' Quince declared. 'Together, we

shall get a firm grip on Evil. From this day forth, we shall protect those Portals of Doom that, long ago, our ancestors plumbed in for the good of All Souls. We few, we happy few! With our firm, collective grasp upon this transcendental pipe wrench – this beacon of Hope – this proud symbol of the leverage we can have when we work together! Yes, together, we shall protect this system from abuse . . . We shall . . . fix leaks . . . replace washers . . . investigate drain smells . . .' Quince had the look of someone who'd accidentally launched into a longer speech than she'd intended. I think everyone was relieved when she cut her rousing monologue short. 'Let's get plumbing!' she yelled, and the others cheered in response.

By this time, the lake of gloop had nearly emptied. The final dregs of purgatorial slime trickled down the giant sinkhole in the centre of the cavern and dribbled away. Following Quince's lead, the Dead Plumbers climbed down the slippery wall of the empty basin. Cautiously approaching the sinkhole, they peered over the edge into the darkness.

'The gloop goes down here and gets pumped up to the top of the flume,' Boz explained to Olly.

'And will that fish be going with it?' he asked.

'Reckon it will,' said Boz. 'It's a long way up, mind. Be at least fifteen minutes till it's back down. Then another hour to get round the whole system.'

'Meantime, we got some unfinished business to take care of,' said Quince, her face set into a grim smirk of retribution. 'Time to have a word with the client.'

# 26

## 7:45 a.m. TUESDAY

### 2 hours and 15 minutes until Eternal Damnation

We left the empty reservoir and went back through the tunnel to the pump room, then up the ladder and out the hatch to the poolside. The place had been transformed. The scaffolding was down, the painting was finished and there were balloons and bunting everywhere. Big Moustache and his entourage were on a small stage beside the still empty splash pool at the bottom of the flume. There were TV cameras, and a gaggle of journalists was assembled for the glitzy opening of the underworld's FIRST upward flume! Forming an orderly queue in their swimming costumes and flip-flops were the soon-to-be-evicted scientists and other Undesirables I'd met at the castle.

The Management looked nervous as they fake-smiled at the TV cameras in an attempt to downplay the blatant absence of any upward-flowing gloop. As soon as Big Moustache spotted us in the corner by the hatch, he hurried over.

'What's going on?' he hissed.

'All done, boss,' Quince lied. 'We've set up the reverse flow. You'll have gloop splurging up that flume any minute now. There'll just be a slight delay while the system recalibrates. You know, the pressure's just balancing. Spigots and isobars. I could explain the technical stuff to your guests if that'd help?' Quince nodded towards the waiting TV crews.

Big Moustache thought for a moment. 'Yes,' he said. 'Let's do that. I could introduce you as an "expert". People like experts.'

'She *is* an expert,' I said, but Big Moustache ignored me and strode back to his little platform. I couldn't wait to see the look on his face when that gloop came flowing DOWN the flume in a few minutes. As long as the Management had no idea what we'd really done in there, by the time the gloop was flowing it'd be too late for them to stop it.

Someone shouted, 'Quiet on set! Going live in five, four –' And then I saw yet another terrible Soul from last time I came *Beyond*. It was the smarmy silver-haired host who'd interviewed me at the Heroic Picnic. He'd been very patronising onstage and very rude offstage and he was altogether very full of himself and insincere. I suppose he was the obvious choice for a gig like this.

'Ladies and gentlemen!' he began, then waffled on in his oily voice about what a great job the Management was doing. 'Not only have they been solving the underworld's most challenging scientific problems, they have also been providing us with exciting new leisure activities.' What a load of nonsense! I couldn't stand this guy. At least he was too self-absorbed to notice me. Eventually he introduced the Management's glorious leader to the stage and there was a pathetic ripple of applause. As he stepped up to the platform, Big Moustache flashed a nervous glance at Quince, who grinned and gave a thumbs up.

'The underworld's first *upward* flume will be spouting any minute now,' Big Moustache declared, staring into the camera like the crazed dictator he was. 'The Management has been working tirelessly with technical specialists from every field to solve the tragic problem of our overcrowded population. We've even worked with plumbers. Allow me to introduce one such "expert" now. This is . . . I forget her name, but she can explain some of the technical jargon while we wait for the gloop to flow.'

Quince stepped up. 'Here's the thing,' she said, taking

the mic. 'This no-flow situation was never a "natural disaster".' The place went silent. Everyone stopped what they were doing and stared at the Dead Plumber with the microphone. She continued, 'The flow of purgatorial gloop was blocked. *Deliberately*. The Management stopped the flow because they don't *want* any more Restless Souls coming down here. Population overcrowding is a LIE, cooked up to justify their evil plan to evict so-called Undesirables.'

Mic drop! I mean, not literally – Quince kept hold of the mic, which was a relief because there didn't seem any point in damaging a perfectly good microphone. But her speech ended as if she'd dropped the mic. For several moments everyone was too stunned to react, frozen in disbelief at this revelation of the Management's Villainy.

Then Big Moustache calmly stepped forward and smiled into the camera.

'As every intelligent Soul is aware,' he said, 'there has been a prophecy.'

'Yes, the prophecy!' cried out a stripy-shirted Management official. 'The prophecy proves we were right! Doesn't it?'

'Ahem,' said a tall lady with eyebrows that got the audience's attention. 'If I may?'

'Indeed,' said Big Moustache, inviting her to join him onstage. 'Please welcome the chief spokesperson for the

Prophecy Department. I'm sure she can clarify matters for anyone who is still confused by the delirious rantings of a mad plumber.'

'Well, erm, actually –' The chief spokesperson for the Prophecy Department looked uncomfortable, despite the respect her eyebrows commanded. She took the microphone hesitantly, as a slimy Doubt and a bristly Regret twined their way round her neck like a damp scarf. 'In the last hour, we have run further tests on the recent prophecy and . . .' She paused again, as if she had unwelcome news to share. 'To be honest, this prophecy felt a little odd from the outset. I mean, prophecies are always odd – it's an odd line of business we work in. But this one felt particularly odd. This was the first prophecy we'd ever received as an anonymous email attachment. In our defence, it does *look* authentic.' She held her phone up to the camera so we could all see the photo of the prophecy on the TV crew's monitor.

**WHEN AN EXCESS OF FOULNESS DESCENDS,**
**ONLY AN ALMIGHTY SURGE**
**SHALL CLEANSE THIS PLACE.**

It was an ancient-looking script, carved into stone. Around the stone were clean blue tiles above what looked like a toilet cistern –

'Oy! Oy! Oy! I've *seen* that!' said Olly. 'That's in them Heroic Toilets on the Path of Heroes! I knew that prophecy sounded familiar –'

Quince was smiling mysteriously, and I remembered that she'd claimed to have seen it before too. Big Moustache was wringing his hands and edging slowly backwards, his moustache quivering like a cornered raccoon. Doubts and Regrets were circling him, greasily awaiting their moment to pounce.

'It seems that someone has been playing a little joke on us,' said Dr Radar, stepping forward. 'When one looks at the "prophecy" in situ, it is far easier to interpret. Evidently, **WHEN AN EXCESS OF FOULNESS DESCENDS, ONLY AN ALMIGHTY SURGE SHALL CLEANSE THIS PLACE** actually means, **PLEASE FLUSH THE LOO VIGOROUSLY AFTER YOU'VE DONE A SIZEABLE PLOP-PLOP**. I imagine some of those Beast Guardians on the Path of Heroes can do some very "foul deeds" after they've eaten a Legendary Hero . . . Cupcake, anyone?'

Quince raised the mic. 'So, there you have it! It's not a prophecy at all –' she said, before being tackled to the floor by one of Big Moustache's cronies. Stripy-shirted officials stumbled over each other trying to wrestle the microphone off Quince, though some held back, clearly unsure where their loyalty belonged after this revelation.

'Has all our hard work been based on a toilet sign?' one

of them cried out, as hordes of gristly, blubbery Doubts leapt on to the heads, shoulders and toes of his colleagues.

'Yes!' laughed Professor Yaxis. 'Isn't it funny? We were all fooled!'

Now the Dead Plumbers waded in to defend Quince and there was a big scuffle. Olly and I watched as the carnage unfolded – and the TV cameras watched too. Interestingly, I noticed that Bilbamýn the Bold and Vileeda the Valiant were also holding back, lurking in the shadows with their Deletion wands lowered.

As Mel shoved a clipboard-wielding Management official off Quince's back, the leader of the Dead Plumbers Society got her breath back and continued her denouncement into the mic: 'This isn't a fun water park!' she yelled. 'They wanted us to set these flumes up as waste pipes – to pump out unwanted Souls! *These* Souls – the scientists and activists and peacekeepers who'd have challenged their evil policies –' Quince rolled out of the way as a Management loyalist dived at her with a lever-arch file. 'They've been trapped in luxury to prevent them from seeing the truth. Fooled into thinking they were on a holiday reward treat, when really that upward flume would've ejected them into an eternity of restless misery!'

But wait. Who was this? Zooming out of the shadows in a mobile jacuzzi? It was Olly's dad, roused from his brainwashed stupor by Quince's compelling accusations of criminality and corruption! Leaping from the hot bubbles and dripping all over the stage, Sergeant Polliver whipped his whistle out of his trunks and –

*Phoop! Phoop!*

The authoritative squeal of his police whistle cut through the mayhem like scissors through cheese. Everyone stopped scuffling and looked up.

'Freeze!' said Olly's dad from his onstage puddle. 'Nobody move!' And nobody did move while Sergeant Polliver cordoned off the area. Then he got out his notebook and approached Big Moustache.

'So, what have you got to say for yourself?' he asked. 'You have the right to remain silent, but then I won't have anything to write in my notebook. So, it'd be much better if you could tell us about all these crimes you've been up to!'

Big Moustache glanced furtively at the corner where his Heroic Alliance lurked. 'Delete them!' he barked. 'Delete them all!'

Vileeda the Valiant pulled the plug on the TV cameras, then she and Bilbamýn the Bold swung their massive Deletion wands around, causing everyone to cower and duck, including Sergeant Polliver, who'd left his truncheon back at the castle.

'Who first?' asked Bilbamýn the Bold, his weapon crackling with demonic energy.

'Oliver Polliver and Harley Lenton,' hissed Big

Moustache without missing a beat. He hated us so much we were top of the list! It was almost touching. 'And *her*,' he added, pointing at Quince. 'Then this pesky police officer. Then *everyone else*, so there are no witnesses!'

# 27

## 8:19 a.m. TUESDAY

### 1 hour and 41 minutes until Eternal Damnation

Bilbamýn the Bold and Vileeda the Valiant tensed their enormous muscles, ready to strike.

'Go on,' said Big Moustache. 'Why are you hesitating?'

Well, I had a feeling I knew exactly why they were hesitating – and it gave me an idea.

'Not very good for your Legacy, this, is it?' I said, stepping towards the sizzling Deletion wands. A blubbery Doubt leapt on to Bilbamýn's shoulder, confirming my suspicions. 'If you get rid of everyone here, there'll be no one left who's witnessed any of your Heroism today. Just think of all those epic deeds you'll miss out on being remembered for: exposing the Management's evil conspiracy, getting the gloop flowing, fixing the Portals, saving all those future Restless Souls from an eternity of misery *up there*.'

'But they haven't done any of that!' said Big Moustache.

The Legendary Heroes swung their Deletion wands towards him.

'Shhh,' said Vileeda the Valiant. Then she turned to me. 'Say that again, Harley Lenton,' she said. 'Remind everyone once more of the epic deeds that have been undertaken by Bilbamýn the Bold and Vileeda the Valiant upon this day. Say it one more time, nice and loud.'

I repeated what I'd said about them exposing the Management's evil conspiracy and fixing the Portals of Doom and generally saving the day like the proper Heroes they were. As I spoke, they beamed proudly as if it were all true.

Then Vileeda the Valiant leered menacingly at Big Moustache. 'Do you remember now?' she said, her wand throbbing within millimetres of his vital organs. He nodded weakly. 'I thought you might.'

'Can we *all* remember the epic deeds accomplished by Bilbamýn the Bold and Vileeda the Valiant here today?' boomed Bilbamýn, waggling his wand as he stalked slowly round the room. 'Or does anyone need their memory jogged?'

Everyone shook their heads timidly.

'*I* certainly remember you doing all of those things,' said the silver-haired host, smiling his oily smile and sweating nervously. 'And you did them with style and panache and good old-fashioned courage. What a wondrous tale your epic deeds shall make! Such Legacies –'

'Film it,' said Vileeda the Valiant. 'Run the cameras. Let's broadcast this to the underworld.'

And they did. That slimy host interviewed those glossy Heroes about how great they were, and they all lied through their shiny teeth about everything that had happened. Big Moustache and his Management colleagues and the TV crews and everyone else kept their mouths shut, while the wands crackled menacingly out of shot – a constant reminder of the threat of Deletion for anyone who "forgot" the new version of how things went down today.

'Yes, the Portals of Doom must and shall reopen!' announced Vileeda the Valiant. 'That's why we've been working undercover to destroy the Management's wicked schemes from within! And now it only remains for us to heroically delegate the task of fixing the pipes to a crew of Souls who we've long admired and supported: the Legendary Dead Plumbers Society!'

As the TV crew applauded, Vileeda took Quince aside and said, 'Go and fix the pipes now. The caskets of gold are yours.'

The silver-haired host did a long piece to camera about how lucky we all were to have these Legendary

Heroes looking after us. For a moment, I forgot I was one of them, (officially). I wished I wasn't. Fortunately, I wasn't expected to share in any of Vileeda and Bilbamýn's glory this morning. As they continued the self-congratulatory interview, I could see the faces of their audience changing. The TV crew, the scientists in their swimming costumes, even the Dead Plumbers – their expressions were changing with each new line of smug nonsense these Legendary Heroes spoke. Ten minutes ago, we'd all known they were liars, in league with that sinister Big Moustache Villain. But now, for most of this audience, they were Heroes again, to be idolised and worshipped. They looked like Heroes, they spoke like Heroes, they *said* they were Heroes – I guess for most people, that was enough. After all, we had to believe someone was making things better.

'This is codswallop!' said Olly. 'These smarmy plonkers are taking the credit and the glory for all the Heroism *you* done, Harley-arley-arley!'

I shrugged. 'It wasn't just me,' I said.

'I s'pose,' said Olly. 'Hey, I'm sorry I went off earlier and got a job. That wasn't right. I promise I won't do it again.'

'What, you won't go off again, or you won't get another job?' I joked.

'I won't get another job,' said Olly gravely. 'I'm telling you, Harley-arley-arley – it's a mug's game, working. Look at the trouble it can get you in!'

It felt good, more like the old days. Me and Olly, having a laugh, vanquishing evil. But there was a sadness we couldn't escape. We'd both lost some of our most important people. Olly's friends, my grandparents, Bess. The thought of that Big Fish floated between us like a huge, sad elephant in the room.

'It really ain't fair,' said Olly, as the interview ended, and the Legendary Heroes marched away before any awkward questions were asked. 'We should get our revenge.'

'Against them?' I asked, as Vileeda and Bilbamýn disappeared into the shadows.

'No,' said Olly, staring angrily at his yo-yo. 'Not them. They ain't worth it.'

He was talking about the fish.

'It came for me again,' I said. 'In the reservoir.'

Olly looked up at me, concerned. 'Are you all right?'

I nodded. 'Went for Quince too,' I said. 'Goes for anyone I care about – I *know* it does.'

'We gotta hunt it down,' said Olly. 'You and me, uniting to do battle against a massive evil fish – that's just the sort of thing a Legendary Hero and her Loyal Sidekick *should* be doing, ain't it?'

'Maybe,' I said. 'Or would it be more Heroic to forgive it?'

Olly looked at his feet and thought about this one. 'I s'pose you'd better be getting Back to Life soon anyway,' he said. 'Can't be long now till the caravan's gonna get crushed and you'll be trapped forever with all the heart shrivelling and brain mushing and so on.'

'Yeah, thanks for that,' I said. He was right, of course. I'd better get a wiggle on if I was going to fend off Eternal Damnation. I hadn't forgotten, obviously – you don't forget a thing like that, even when your loved ones have been swallowed by a Big Fish. But in truth, I didn't want to go back without Bess. And not because everyone would think I'd exploded her in a caravan toilet. I just couldn't imagine it being any fun without her.

'Get in the van, kids!' Quince called, beckoning for us to join her and the Dead Plumbers. 'Gloop's gonna flow down that flume any minute now. We should get ahead of it, to check there's no blockages on its way round the system.'

'Come on,' I said to Olly. 'Let's go with them. This is what's important now.'

The other Dead Plumbers had gathered their stuff together and were hanging around Quince's van, even though they clearly weren't all going to fit.

'We ain't all gonna fit,' said Olly.

'You haven't seen what the boss's van can do,' said Rik proudly. 'It's a magic van. Try it. Get in and see what happens.' I got in and nothing happened. Then Olly got in and nothing happened. Then Rik got in and Mel got in and Nell got in and Jonah got in and all the other Dead Plumbers got in and still nothing happened. Nothing apart from the fact that we'd all somehow managed to fit in the front seats of a normal-sized van.

'Transcendental,' said Rik, grinning.

Peering through the grubby windscreen at the gaggle of scientists chatting to the TV crew, I noticed Big Moustache ducking under the police cordon and sneaking away while Sergeant Polliver was busily writing in his notebook.

'Oy! Oy! Oy! That hurts,' said Olly, as I nudged him in the ribs.

'Look!' I said, pointing. 'He's getting away from your dad!'

'That sneaky little –' Olly began. But he never finished. Because at that moment a torrent of cascading gloop came roaring down the flume – and riding it was the Big Fish, free-falling, skidding along the edge of the slide. Big Moustache looked up in disbelief, as the fish fell out of the sky and squashed him flat.

It fell with a crash and a clang and a thud. A scale fell off and rolled around like a hubcap. People screamed and ran for cover as the fish thrashed its tail, its great gills flickering, craving oxygen as it floundered on dry ground. I looked up into the mist of gloopy spray above us.

'A visitation!' declared the spokesperson for the Prophecy Department. 'Is this divine retribution?'

'Nah,' said Olly. 'It's basic plumbing.'

'Kid's right,' said Quince. 'That fish has been pumped up to the top of the flume and launched back down again. Don't know how it got *in* the system, though. Anyway, we've got a job to get to. Ain't no time for unexplained phenomena. Let's quit this joint.' She turned the key in the ignition and revved up the van's engine.

'Wait!' I said. 'I need to get out.'

Quince turned the engine off and leaned over the four Dead Plumbers sitting between us. 'You sure about this, kid?' But she knew I was. And those other Dead Plumbers must've seen how serious I was about confronting this fish too, because they shuffled out of my way to let me clamber across their laps and out the driver's door.

As I approached the Big Fish, its tail flapped slower and slower until it lay still. What *was* this creature that was so determined to get me, it was prepared to sacrifice itself on dry land?

'Be careful, kid.'

'Watch yourself, Harley-arley-arley!'

Neither Quince nor Olly offered to come with me, but I knew this was out of respect, not cowardice. They understood this was something I needed to do alone.

I walked slowly towards its monstrous head – and it winked at me. The Big Fish winked at me, and everyone saw it.

But this wink was different. This was a weary wink.

A final wink of surrender.

And now the mouth was opening, slowly and meaningfully, like an electric garage door. The upper jaw rose like a curtain in a theatre, revealing one, two, three, four . . . eight pairs of feet. Some of them in the same old shoes I'd been looking at since I only came up to those same old knees . . .

'Hello, Harley,' said Nana.

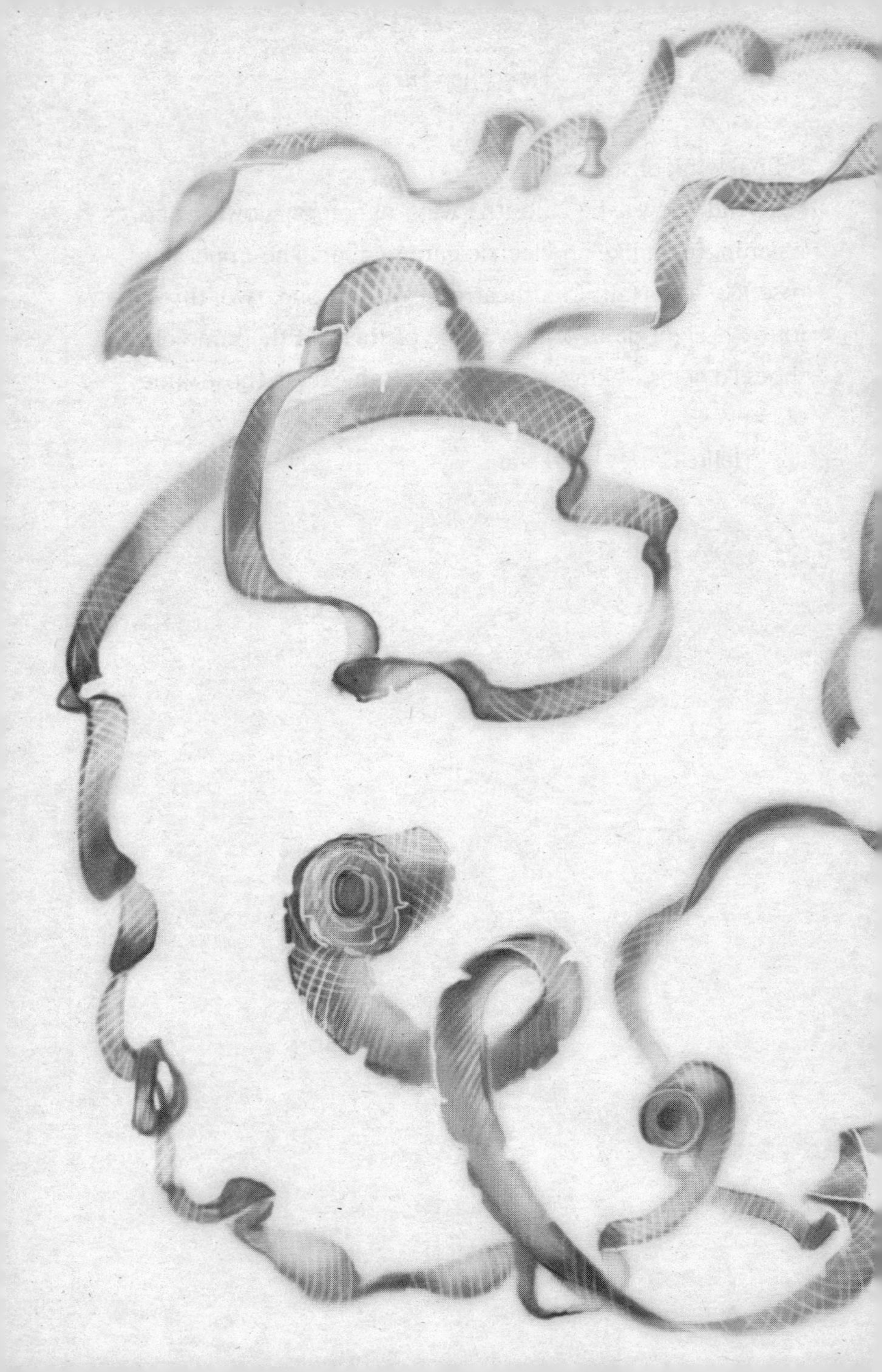

# PART FOUR

# REGULAR FOLK

# 28

## 9:02 a.m. TUESDAY

### 58 minutes
### until Eternal Damnation

Nana, Gran, Grandpa, Pops, Sparky, Frazzle, Elektra and Bess stood in the Big Fish's mouth. Then they stepped off its softly carpeted tongue and walked towards me.

'You're . . . not swallowed?' I gasped, as we gathered into a group hug. And that was all I could say, I was so overcome with joy and relief. Bess was alive! After all this. I just couldn't believe it.

Behind my grandparents, I was dimly aware of a hatch opening in the fish's head. J-Wolf climbed out and slid down its scaly cheek.

'Oy! Oy! Oy!' shouted Olly, leaping about gleefully

with his pylon mates. 'It ain't a real fish, Harley-arley-arley!'

'Yeah,' I said, noting that the hubcap-like scales were actual hubcaps.

'We've been trying to catch you all night!' said Grandpa.

'But you were so *quick*, Harley!' beamed Gran proudly. 'So good at dodging about and getting away!'

'You was sick on that jet ski,' said J-Wolf. 'Legendary skills.'

'Thanks,' I mumbled, bewildered by the revelation that *this* was what he and Grandpa had been working on at the docks. *This.* The enormous robot-submarine-fish-thing that had been terrorising me for hours.

Pops was on his knees, poking under the fish's belly where Big Moustache had been making his getaway a couple of minutes earlier.

'Squashed!' said Pops, chuckling to himself. 'Flat as a pancake!'

'Is he . . . *dead*?' asked Bess.

'We're all dead here, Bess-diddly-Bess-Bess,' said Olly. 'Apart from you and Harley-arley-arley! Vroom! Vroom! VROOM!'

'I know,' said Bess. 'But is he deader?'

'No, dear,' said Nana. 'Just flatter.'

'I *knew* this fish was chasing me!' I said. 'I knew it. But why? Why were you in it? Why did you build a Big Fish to swim around and swallow everyone in?'

'Reckon the kid's got a right to some answers,' said

Quince, stepping up to my grandparents.

'As soon as we saw where things were headed with the Management, we set to building this Big Fish,' said Grandpa. 'And as soon as it was ready, we launched it. The plan was we'd all hide in the fish, to keep us safe from the Management while we made preparations for the resistance. But it had to be top secret. We couldn't tell any of you what we were up to. What if someone overheard? So, we planned to swim up and catch everyone. That way, we'd all be safe, we'd all be together, and no one would suspect a thing.'

'But you were just too good at dodging its big mouth and saving the day without us,' said Bess.

It was so great to see her. She looked like she'd been having a whale of a time, swimming round the underworld in a big metal fish. They all did, and it was the best thing ever to discover they were safe.

Still, I couldn't help feeling that me and Olly would've avoided a lot of stress if they *hadn't* hidden in a Big Fish which went round swallowing people.

'Couldn't you have given me a clue?' I said. 'Some kind of warning about what you were up to – some hint that the fish was on my side?'

'Kept winking at you, innit,' said J-Wolf, clicking a remote control that made the lifeless fish machine flutter its big metal eyelid at me once more.

'It was the best we could think of,' said Gran

apologetically.

'I'll be honest, the winking was sinister,' I said.

'I warned you!' said Pops, shaking his stick at Grandpa and the others. 'Time and again I warned you all. Winking's never a good idea. A wink can so easily be misunderstood.'

'Couldn't you have texted me?' I asked.

'Management would've traced the signal,' said Grandpa. 'We had to keep all devices on airplane mode in the fish.'

'So, how *did* you get into the reservoir?' asked Boz.

'Come through the water-cooling system that runs from the river straight to the pump room, innit,' said J-Wolf. 'See, this fish was designed to cause an obstruction – as a last resort. If the Management *had* succeeded in reversing the flow, we was gonna, like, swim up the pipe and create a blockage. Then we worked out the plug was in, so we tried ramming it from underneath – that's why we come splurging up when you pulled it out.'

'So, let me get this straight,' said Olly, examining the fish-shaped submarine. 'This is a red herring, ain't it?'

'Reckon the kid's right about that,' said Quince. 'Said something along those lines myself, earlier tonight. This here fish is a red herring.'

'Well, here's the thing,' said Grandpa, his eyes twinkling like they always did when there was a chance to explain something complicated. 'Yes – it *is* a red herring. The design is inspired by a red herring; we even call it the Red Herring.

However – and here's the clever part – the Red Herring *wasn't* a "red herring". I mean, not in the figurative sense of a *distraction from the important clues.* The Shrinking Solution leafleting campaign was the real red herring in *that* sense. We came up with the Shrinking Solution as a deliberately absurd answer to a problem that we knew didn't really exist. We invented it to test whether the Management was genuinely looking for a solution to overcrowding, or whether they had an alternative agenda. And when they turned up all heavy-handed to shut it down, that proved our hypothesis – that the false claims about "overcrowding" were a cover story to hide their true motives. Meanwhile, we went undercover – in the Red Herring – to find out what those true motives were. But in the end, you did a better job of that yourself, Harley. By recruiting the Dead Plumbers Society like you'd planned all along, you were able to expose their wicked conspiracy and save an eternity of future Restless Souls.'

'I think I've got it,' I said. 'The Red Herring being a red herring was a red herring, but the Shrinking Solution was also a red herring.'

'Exactly,' said Grandpa. 'We made the Red Herring in the shape of a red herring as a red herring – so people would think it was a red herring when in fact it was just a red herring.'

'Okay,' I said.

'The Red Herring was a fake red herring, as well as being a fake red herring,' said Bess.

And I smiled and nodded, partly because Bess's explanation was the best one of all, but mainly because I'd had enough of this conversation now.

'I think we've all learned something here today,' said Gran.

'Yeah,' I said. And then I wondered what I actually *had* learned. I guess I'd learned that my friends and family were safe, and they'd been trying to protect me all along. I guess I'd learned that rumours and reputation didn't matter to the people who matter, because they know you too well. I guess I'd learned all that stuff about red herrings too, but I wasn't so sure about that.

'Hey, guess what?' said Bess, flapping her arms wildly in excitement.

'What?' I asked.

'The fish has got a pizza oven!'

'Let's CELEBRATE!' shouted Elektra.

'Pizza-za-za!' yelled Olly, launching his yo-yo into a Revolutionary Roundabout.

At the mention of the P-word, I nearly dribbled down my chin. I was *so* hungry! And this really did feel like the part of the story where we should have a feast in a giant mechanical fish and celebrate our victory.

But it was 9:20 on Tuesday morning. We had only forty

minutes to get Back to Life before the caravan would be crushed and we'd be trapped in an eternity of shrivelling. Only forty minutes to travel through *Beyond* and along the Path of Heroes to the Fire Exit. By this point, I wasn't even considering doing the Twelve Tasks – that would take *hours*. I guess I was hoping I'd done enough Heroic deeds to get away with skipping them this time. (Though I hadn't finished the Tasks last time either, so I knew it was a long shot . . .)

'Pizza sounds great,' I said. 'But we haven't got time.'

I really didn't want to have to remind Bess and everyone else about Eternal Damnation *again*. I was just too hungry. A soggy little Regret slipped on to my ankle.

'Oh, I wish you could stay for tea!' said Nana, a tear in the corner of her eye. 'It's been so lovely having you down here, and we really haven't spent enough time together.'

'If only we could have one more hour!' said Gran, as Regrets slid out of crevices all around us and began circling my grandparents.

'But you can,' said Boz. Behind us, the reunited Dead Plumbers Society were standing and kneeling in two rows like a team photo.

'Yeah,' said Rik. 'The boss has got a van, remember?'

I looked at Quince, who was kneeling at the front of the group holding some pipework. 'Hey, kid,' she said, standing and walking over to us. 'You've seen how my van defies the laws of space, fitting all those plumbers in when you didn't expect it? Well, it also defies the laws of time. That's right. My van doesn't care for the constraints of a conventional linear chronology. That's why I'm always late. But I could just as easily be early. I can take you along the Path of Heroes, check the gloop's okay, and be back here before we left.'

'Really?' I said.

'It's a magic van,' said Olly. 'It'll get us to the Archive *early* – with time to spare!'

'Us?' I said.

'Yeah, I'm coming with you,' said Olly.

Gradually, the Regrets slunk away as I saw how confident Quince and Olly were about the magic van plan. And having Olly with me at the Archive would be a massive help. The Archivist loved Olly. She'd let *him* sweet-talk her into getting the Fire Exit ignited – even if I hadn't done all the official Hero stuff like the Twelve Tasks.

'Okay,' I said. 'Let's stay for pizza!'

Everyone cheered and some people whooped, while others hugged and jumped up and down or did funny little dances. Then Pops and Gran went into the fish's mouth to fire up the pizza oven, while J-Wolf wowed the rest of us with the drink dispenser hidden under the dorsal fin. Then we all sat around on its softly carpeted tongue and joked and laughed as delicious cooking smells wafted out of its gills.

And after we'd stuffed ourselves silly, my grandparents regaled us with thrilling and wondrous tales of Legendary Heroes and Mythical Monsters. And even though I *knew* the actual Heroes weren't really so brave, and the real monsters weren't actually so fierce, the stories were as magical and inspirational as ever. So magical, in fact, that at one point Olly sat and listened without fiddling with his yo-yo.

But such jolly scenes can't last forever, and we weren't quite ready to live happily ever after yet.

'Time to go, kid,' said Quince, jingling her keys as she slid off the fish's tongue and walked over to her van.

I went up to each of my grandparents in turn to give them a hug goodbye. We'd meet again, but probably not for a lifetime.

'Bye, Grandpa,' I said, looking up at the tears on his cheeks and the garlic sauce in his beard. 'Bye, Pops. Bye, Nana. Bye, Gran – I wish I could stay!'

'You need to get Back to Life,' said Gran. 'That's the place for you now.'

'Don't worry about us,' sobbed Grandpa. 'We've got plenty of important things to be getting on with.'

'We really do,' said Nana. 'The Management has spread such a lot of nastiness around here lately. The Dead are going to need some wholesome truths after all this terrible nonsense about overcrowding and Undesirables.'

'We've got a plan!' said Elektra.

'A plan?' I said. 'Like the van?'

'Bigger than the van,' said Sparky.

'Dragons!' said Frazzle.

'We're gonna commandeer the airships!' said Olly, excitably catapulting his yo-yo into a Cosmic Croissant, which his pylon mates bounced in and out of in a frenzy of blimp-raiding celebration.

'Then we'll put cheery motivational slogans on the big screens instead of lies and propaganda,' said Gran.

'You know, nice things,' said Nana. 'Messages of peace and love and harmony.'

'Funny cat videos?' I asked.

'Innit, though,' said J-Wolf.

'You lot get started,' said Olly, 'and I'll join you as soon as I'm back from dropping off Harley-arley-arley and Bess-diddly-Bess-Bess! Oy! Oy! Oy!'

We squeezed out a few final hugs then piled into the van.

'I know a shortcut to the River Betwixt,' said Quince, as me, Bess, Olly and all the Dead Plumbers put the same seat belt on. 'A route that cuts out the Nothing and bypasses the Road to the Back of Beyond.'

Quince revved up the van into a frenzy, then released the handbrake. The van shot off like a rocket, lurching up the wall and back through the pipe to the empty reservoir, skidding along the rocky ground towards the sinkhole. 'This'll bring us out into the river!' she yelled above the screaming engine, as we gripped each other's hands in silent terror. 'Hold your breath!' she shouted – but it was too late because we were already hurtling over the edge and plunging into misty darkness. For a moment we fell, spinning, weightless – then Quince shifted through the gears and we torpedoed upward through murky water. It grew brighter as we neared the surface, until we exploded out of the river and soared into the eerie mists of the Badlands Beyond the Back of Beyond.

Landing with a thud, we banged our heads on the van's roof – and now we were teetering on the edge of the perilous Path of Heroes, only millimetres from plunging towards the eternal suffering of *Beneath,* where a gazillion Resentful Beasts lay in wait to tear us apart in slow motion for eternity . . . But before I knew it, Quince skidded to a stop in front of the three mysterious doors that marked the end of the Path of Heroes.

Either side of me, Dead Plumbers were frozen in wide-eyed terror.

'Sorry about the bumpy ride, kids,' said Quince. 'I should've explained – the quicker I drive, the more time we regain. Reckon that'll have clawed us back a few minutes.'

'Transcendental,' grinned Rik.

# 29

## 9:02 a.m. TUESDAY (again)

### Still 58 minutes until Eternal Damnation

Quince approached the three doors.

'Careful, boss,' Mel murmured over her shoulder. 'I heard that one of these doors leads to the Suffering of Ages and the other one leads to the Joys of Humanity.'

'Nah, mate,' said Olly. 'That one's a bathroom and that one's a library.'

'And that one's the staffroom where all the terrifying monsters who work as Beast Guardians of the Legendary Twelve Tasks sit around drinking coffee between shifts,' I said, pointing to the middle door.

'Been here before,' said Olly, totally showing off.

'So, this one's the bathroom?' asked Boz, pointing to the door on the left.

'Yeah,' I said. 'I'd suggest you knock first. Last time I was here, I saw a monster in the bath. Bit embarrassing.'

'Whoa!' said Bess. 'Is it a big bath?'

'No, it's a normal bath,' I said. 'It was a little monster.'

'Maybe the big ones don't wash?' pondered Nell.

Quince knocked on the door and waited a few seconds. Then she cautiously opened it and looked inside. She reached round to pull the light switch, and entered the empty bathroom. 'Only room for one more in here,' she called. 'Give us a hand will you, kid?'

Well, everyone assumed she meant me, so I joined her in the little bathroom. It was damp and had a mildewy smell, presumably because of the lack of ventilation.

'No window and the extractor fan's not working,' I mumbled to myself.

Quince grinned. 'Apparently the toilet's not either.'

A handwritten notice had been stuck on the wall behind the toilet.

OUT OF ORDER
DO NOT FLUSH

Quince knelt down and shone her torch behind the

sink. 'Nope, not there.' She glanced at the bath, then turned her attention to the fourth appliance in the room, which was like a small toilet but with taps and no seat.

'Aha!' she said. 'The *bidet*. This is something you don't see in every bathroom. Tell me, kid – do you know what this *bidet* is used for?'

I did know what a bidet was used for. 'You sit in it and wash your bum,' I said, proud of the knowledge I had gained over months of intense DIY experience, researching fittings and fixtures with my parents when I didn't have any friends.

'That's what a standard bidet is used for,' said Quince. 'But *this* bidet is a decoy. A red herring . . .'

Oh no! I couldn't be starting all that again.

'Look,' said Quince. 'It's a dummy bidet, a false bidet, placed here to conceal an important valve. Come and look.'

She shuffled up so that I could get down on my knees and squeeze in next to her, peering round the edge of the bidet. We had our noses disturbingly close to a bum-washing appliance in a bathroom for monsters. I screwed up my face and tried to act professionally. We had a job to do.

'See here, kid?' she said, pointing to a small lever on a narrow pipe. 'That's the stopcock. We just have to make sure it's turned to the left –'

It was turned to the left. Quince switched off her torch and stood up.

'Is that it?' I said in disbelief. 'We're just checking the

tap's turned on? You didn't even use the Legendary Pipe Wrench of Destiny!'

'Shh, not so loud,' said Quince. 'We don't need everyone to know. That's the way it is sometimes, kid. Sometimes a job's not quite as transcendental as people might imagine.' She leaned in and spoke conspiratorially. 'That's why I didn't want a big crowd in here. Trade secrets.' She tapped her nose and winked. I shuddered for a moment, reminded of the Big Fish. But that had turned out all right in the end, and I guess so had this. 'See, with this valve open,' Quince continued, 'when the gloop comes along the pipe that runs out here from the splash pools at the bottom of the flumes, it'll keep going, back round, under the river and into the reservoir. On it goes, round and round. It's the circle of life.'

Quince stood up and stepped over to the door.

'Shouldn't we try and fix the toilet?' I asked, looking at the DO NOT FLUSH sign.

'No,' said Quince. 'That toilet is in perfect working order.' Then she winked at me again and stepped out of the bathroom, turning off the light behind us.

'Job done,' said Quince.

'Cor, that was quick!' said Boz, beaming with admiration.

'Excuse me,' boomed someone behind the Dead Plumbers. They parted to reveal Bilbamýn the Bold and Vileeda the Valiant. 'Oh, it's you,' said Bilbamýn the Bold.

'Yeah, it's us,' Quince growled. 'We're here to make sure the gloop's flowing, remember? That epic deed you're planning to take all the glory for?'

'Yes, we remember,' said Vileeda the Valiant. 'That *well-paid* job you're doing for us. I don't see you've any reason to complain.'

'Well paid?' sneered Quince. 'A *billion* caskets of gold is my standard call-out fee. Seems to me you've had yourselves a bargain.'

'A deal's a deal,' said Vileeda the Valiant. 'Now please step aside.'

'What're *you* doing here anyway?' asked Olly, as he and Bess joined Quince to stand between the pushy Heroes and the three doors.

'We have come to speak with the Archivist,' boomed Bilbamýn the Bold grandly. 'We're just checking that the story of our Epic Heroism is recorded accurately. You know, how we were working undercover to expose the Management's evil conspiracy. How we saved the day. The trouble is, the Archivist *sees* everything, so we were a little worried that some of today's events might get misinterpreted. Like when we were following Harley on my yacht to protect her from dangerous river beasts, for example – one can easily imagine how that *could* have looked as if we were chasing her. So, we were just dropping by to check the Archivist has all the precise, correctly updated details for our story. It would be a shame if any of our epic deeds were misunderstood –'

'So, while we're here to fix up the pipes, you're here to fix up your Legacies?' said Mel in disgust.

'Indeed – that's very well put!' boomed Bilbamýn shamelessly. 'Now which of these is the door to the Archive?'

No one spoke. Obviously, none of us was going to help them out by showing them the right door. Or were we?

'If there's one thing I've learned today,' I said, 'it's that we Legendary Heroes must stick together. Now, as it happens, I am also on my way to the Archive. But since you are so much older and wiser and more Heroic than me, and your business is so much more important, I'm perfectly happy to wait. So, please, after you.' I stepped politely aside and gestured towards the middle door.

'Thank you, Harley the Legendary Hero,' boomed Bilbamýn the Bold, bowing gallantly. 'But I must insist – after *you*.'

'Yes,' said Vileeda the Valiant, eyeing me suspiciously. 'After you.' I could tell she suspected me of trying to trick them into opening the wrong door. And she was dead right – that's exactly what I was doing. But I wasn't going to be foiled by their fake politeness.

'Okay then,' I said, reaching towards the middle door.

'Stop!' snapped Vileeda the Valiant, pushing me aside. 'Our business *is* more important. Wait your turn, Harley.'

Barging Bess and Olly aside, she pulled the door open, convinced by my double bluff that this really was the entrance to the Archive. But of course, it wasn't. This was the door to the Beast Guardians' staffroom. And as luck would have it, the Many-Limbed Optimugoon and the Razor-Elbowed Glockenpard (who, according to legend, were SLAIN by these very same "HEROES") were at that precise moment doing a crossword together. But when the notoriously violent Many-Limbed Optimugoon and the famously short-tempered Razor-Elbowed Glockenpard saw that the annoying people who had opened the staffroom door without knocking were those same "Heroes" who had established their reputations by *lying* about hacking them to pieces, they were not best pleased.

'YOU!?' bellowed the Many-Limbed Optimugoon and the Razor-Elbowed Glockenpard. Then they let out a ferocious roar that shook the Path of Heroes like an earthquake – causing Olly's trousers to fall down – and Bilbamýn the Bold and Vileeda the Valiant to boldly, valiantly, scream and run away.

The Dead Plumbers laughed victoriously.

'Excuse me,' I said, turning to the enormous and terrifying Many-Limbed Optimugoon. 'Can I ask you something?'

The Many-Limbed Optimugoon roared.

'Are you going to ask us about the prophecy?' growled

the Razor-Elbowed Glockenpard.

'Yeah, I just wondered –'

'It was us,' the Many-Limbed Optimugoon admitted, hanging its head. 'We're sorry if it caused any bother in the Back of Beyond. It was just a little joke. Sometimes we get so *bored* up here . . . We didn't mean any harm.'

'You see, it wasn't really a prophecy at all,' the Razor-Elbowed Glockenpard chuckled. 'It sounded like one because it's a very ancient sign, but really it's just a fancy way of saying *Please flush after you've done a big one.*'

'It's hilarious!' laughed Bess.

'Oy! Oy! Oy!' giggled Olly, doubling over. 'Epic laughs!'

'I've got to admit, it was funny,' I agreed. 'Even if it nearly led to an eternity of misery for an infinite future of Restless Souls!'

And now we were all laughing our heads off. Monsters, Dead Plumbers, the Living, the Dead, chuckling happily together on the Path of Heroes.

Eventually, the Beast Guardians said goodbye and went back to their staffroom. And now it was time for yet another farewell. 'You done good, kid,' said Quince, putting a hand on my shoulder. 'Been good knowing you.' Then she stared at me thoughtfully for a minute, and I wondered if she was coming up with some wise words for our parting like a lot of people down here seemed to do. She stared and stared, still saying nothing, and I wondered if I might get away with just a bye bye. But then she said, 'Remember, kid. Ain't no job too big, so long as you got the right tools. Sometimes the right tool is in here.' She pointed to her tool bag. 'Sometimes, it's in here.' She pointed to her head. 'But mostly, it's in here.' She pointed to her heart.

'Thanks, Quince.'

'See you later, kid,' said Quince. Then she and the other Dead Plumbers crammed into her van – all, that is, apart from their newest apprentice.

'I'm gonna stay here,' said Olly. 'In case Harley-arley-arley and Bess need me. I mean, they won't, but –'

Olly stared at his trainers, scuffing them on the rocky ground. Then he looked up and called to his colleagues. 'To be honest, I don't think I'm cut out for this apprenticeship. No offence like, but the whole "work" thing – it just don't suit me. So, I'm just gonna see Harley-arley-arley and Bess-diddly-Bess-Bess off, then I'll make me own way back. I know it's a long walk, but I'm less likely to throw up than in the van.'

'You know where to find us,' said Quince. Then she opened the throttle and shot off down the path, leaving a dramatic dust cloud in her wake.

# 30

## 9:24 a.m. TUESDAY

### 36 minutes until Eternal Damnation

The Archive was full of books. Gazillions of ancient, dusty tomes filled with squidillions of tales of epic deeds and Heroic escapades. Last time I was here, I'd been confused about how true or accurate these myths and legends were. Today, I still was. If Bilbamýn the Bold and Vileeda the Valiant hadn't been scared off by the Many-Limbed Optimugoon and the Razor-Elbowed Glockenpard, would they have persuaded the Archivist to edit *their* story? Would it have been changed forever into a completely dishonest version of events, where they looked like true Heroes instead of the vain liars they were?

Anyway, I didn't have time to get bogged down in all that truth and reality stuff now. I got out my phone to text Miss Delaporte.

Hi Miss,
Me and Bess are at the Archive and will be going through the Fire Exit in the next few minutes.
Please could you arrange the Soul Swap?
Thanks, Harley Lenton

'Right,' I said, pressing SEND. 'Any moment now, my old teacher will swap Mr Purry Paws IN, to make sure the Portal opens when me and Bess go OUT. Just along here we'll find the Archivist, who'll waffle on a bit and tell me off for not completing the Twelve Tasks. Olly, you're going to sweet-talk her into giving us some clues about how we can light the Fire Exit in some other way.'

'You leave that to me, Harley-arley-arley! Vroom! Vroom! VROOM!'

'Thanks,' I said. 'Then me and Bess will sprint through the Fire Exit – which, I warn you, is HOT. But don't worry, it doesn't burn. Don't ask me how that works. Then, as soon as we get Back to Life, we need to work out some way of rescuing the caravan from being crushed and get to school before my parents find out I've snuck off to the Land of the

Dead without their permission.'

'Cool,' said Bess.

'Although, on second thoughts, maybe we should take you home first?' I said. 'To let your mums know you haven't been murdered?'

'Sure, whatever,' said Bess. 'I'm easy either way.'

'I'm gonna miss you guys so much!' said Olly, spinning his yo-yo in a slow, sad sort of swirl. I felt as sad as his yo-yo, so I did a sort of sad-shrug-smile instead of words.

'Gonna miss you too, Olly, you lunatic,' said Bess.

My phone buzzed. It was Miss Delaporte, and it wasn't good news.

> Sorry, Harley. Can't do the swap right now. Mr Purry Paws has wandered off and there's a real rush on at the cafe because Tam's called in sick again. I'll text when I get a moment to go and find your cat.

'Come on, Miss!' I called out to the eternally gloomy under-sky above us. 'If I get us trapped in the Land of the Dead, my parents will kill me!'

But as I stormed between looming bookshelves towards the Archivist's little desk, I realised it was already too late for that.

Because my parents were here.

'Hello, love,' said Dad, turning to face us.

Malcolm was sitting on his shoulders. 'Arwee!' he giggled, shaking Diddy Dino at me.

'Oy! Oy! Oy! Mr and Mrs Lenton!' said Olly.

'Hiya!' said Bess.

'Hello, everyone,' said Mum, sheepishly. 'I'm sorry we had to meet here like this, Harley. We were hoping to have been back home by now. We didn't want to worry you.'

'What are you doing here?' I finally managed to blurt out. 'And how did you get here?'

'We did a thing called a Soul Swap,' said Mum, looking embarrassed. 'My great aunts Mitsy, Bitsy and Pat are having a little day out in the Land of the Living. There's this place out the back of Pickerton Services . . .'

'You swapped with your aunties?' I said, shocked that my parents would do something as reckless as an illegal Soul Swap. 'What if they wander off?'

'Oh, I don't think they'd do that,' said Mum. 'Not with Mitsy's knee and Bitsy's hip and Pat's fondness for sitting.'

'We've been on a mission,' said Dad, waving some papers at me.

'We managed to get that old document re-signed by Sue the Landowner,' Mum explained. 'But unfortunately, the Archivist says we're not allowed through the Fire Exit – which is rather disappointing, since none of us really fancies Eternal Damnation.'

'*And* we did it all properly!' Dad moaned. 'Spent *hours* completing the Twelve Tasks along the Path of Heroes.'

'You don't need to bother with them,' said Olly, which wasn't quite accurate – but I didn't say anything, because I was still dealing with my parents' poor behaviour.

'What do you mean you're not allowed through?' I asked, exasperated.

'Apparently, getting an ancient decree re-signed to prove the legal status of an old caravan isn't Heroic enough to ignite the Fire Exit,' said Dad sulkily.

'The Archivist has just stepped out to discuss the matter with colleagues,' Mum said. 'Maybe they'll persuade her to change her mind . . .'

'I can't believe how irresponsible you are!' I said. 'Bringing Malcolm down here and risking Eternal Damnation! And now look what's happened. You're trapped! For eternity! I'm very disappointed.'

Mum and Dad hung their heads in shame. I wasn't *enjoying* telling them off, but it sure made a change.

'So that *was* you I saw out on the river earlier,' I said. 'Dodging the Big Fish in your little boat?'

Mum nodded.

'Oh, yeah, I forgot to tell you about that, Harley!' said Bess. 'We tried to swallow your family to keep them safe from the Management. Sorry, I should've mentioned it before, but it slipped my mind when I discovered that pizza oven. Tell you what, though – your mum's got epic fish-dodging skills. Just like you!'

'Thanks,' I said, wondering how chuffed I ought to be about the Lentons' fish-dodging skills. As a talent, it had been very unhelpful so far.

'Don't be cross with us, Harley love,' said Dad miserably. 'We only came *Beyond* so you wouldn't have to. We knew how concerned you were about saving the caravan, so we decided to pop down and get that old decree re-signed.'

'By the way,' said Mum, 'we called in at the Ragged Goose and told Bess's mums she was staying at ours. You know, so they wouldn't worry –'

'You lied to my mums!?' gasped Bess. 'That is so cool!'

Mum and Dad looked ashamed and a little bewildered. I don't think anyone had ever accused them of being "cool" before. I felt oddly pleased for them, and grateful to Bess. She was so generous.

'I'm sorry we messed up,' said Dad. 'We're just not Heroic types, Harley. Not like you. We're just regular folk.'

Well, now wasn't the time to get into a discussion about Heroes and Villains and Regular Folk and what any of that really meant, because we urgently needed to do something drastic about this Eternal Damnation situation. And just at that moment, the clip-clopping of a pair of very sensible and self-assured shoes reverberated into our ears as the Archivist came marching down an aisle towards us.

'Good morning, Harley the Legendary Hero,' she declared as she slid into place behind her desk. 'Oliver the Loyal Sidekick. Bess.' She nodded at the others in turn, then peered over her spectacles at my parents. 'Now, I have spoken with my colleagues and our view is unanimous. Minor administrative errands such as getting documents re-signed do not constitute epic deeds.' Mum and Dad looked crestfallen. 'I'm sorry, Mr and Mrs Lenton. But just think what would happen if we were to bend the rules for you. Imagine if every time someone filled in a form or updated a spreadsheet, they were declared an official Legendary Hero! The idea is absurd. Before long, there'd be no ordinary people like you left.'

'But the Legendary Heroes are fake!' I interrupted.

'Ah!' said the Archivist, lowering her spectacles even further down her nose. 'I suspect you are referring to the pitiful attempt by Bilbamýn the Bold and Vileeda the Valiant to amend their Legacies just now? Fear not, Harley. I am the Archivist. I see everything. I cannot be fooled! Bilbamýn and Vileeda shall be recast as Villains, so that future generations may learn from their wickedness! None shall bring the Archive into disrepute by muddling Heroism with Villainy and muddying the truth with false reports!'

*Apart from you*, I thought. Last time we were here, the Archivist had made it very clear that inventing and exaggerating the facts was her standard approach to recording the "true" stories of epic deeds in her Archive. "All stories can benefit from a little embellishment" – that's what she'd said, or something like that. I bet Bilbamýn the Bold and Vileeda the Valiant would be made to seem a lot more villainous and scary than they really were now. I didn't care about them – they deserved it. But how could any of us learn to be better if we just set them down as evil? They'd been greedy and vain and selfish and jealous and dishonest – all the exact same things Quince had been. And I'd been guilty of most of that too. And we'd *all* lied – even my parents. Even the Archivist who recorded the "truth".

It made my head hurt coming here. This place was even more intense than a normal library. I should probably just keep quiet and let Olly do the talking.

'How delightfully lovely it is to see you again, Mrs Book Lady!' he said, bowing and curtseying and doing a little twirl.

A flicker of a smile appeared at the corners of the Archivist's mouth. It was working! She loved Olly.

'It's a pleasure to see you again too, Oliver the Loyal Sidekick,' said the Archivist.

'So, here's the thing,' said Olly. 'Far as I can tell, you're an *expert* on the TRUTH. Am I right?'

'Truth is sacred!' declared the Archivist, enjoying her captive audience. 'Indeed, I have just been conversing with fellow members of the Guild of Dead Librarians. There is concern about a dangerous faction who have spoken of *consolidating* all the stories . . . Anyway, such matters are for another day. Who would like a grape? Or an orange? I also have apples, kiwis, bananas and a perfectly ripe cantaloupe melon.' The Archivist pushed her large bowl of fruit towards us and everyone took some.

As Mum passed grapes to Malcolm and Olly peeled a satsuma's skin into the shape of a little man, the Archivist continued.

'These dusty tomes have made me very wise,' she said, gesturing towards the looming bookshelves. 'Harley, this

quest has taught you that stories cannot be fixed. Their flow cannot be stemmed. Nor can an individual narrative be fished out from the swirling sea of tales in which all our stories flow together, mingling and blending into one great mass –'

We all nodded in agreement. I had to admit the Archivist *was* good at saying wise stuff, even if she was annoying and ate too much fruit.

'Diddy, Diddy!' said Malcolm, waggling his dinosaur.

I checked my phone. Still no message from Miss Delaporte. Come on, Mr Purry Paws!

'Thing is, Mrs Wise Old Book Lady,' said Olly. 'Harley is a proper Legendary Hero, ain't she? I mean, you've *seen* it all – how she teamed up with Quince and done her brave and clever plan to get those pipes fixed. She's saved an eternity of future Restless Souls! That's proper Heroism, eh?'

The Archivist pushed her fruit bowl aside and looked at Olly suspiciously.

'So, like, since she's such a Hero, would you mind opening the Fire Exit?' he asked, in a much smaller voice. I could see his confidence shrivelling under her gaze. Even Olly was no match for *this* librarian!

The Archivist sighed wearily.

'You know the rules,' she said. 'I cannot ignite the Fire Exit; it is an automated system. Firstly, a Noble Quest must be ratified by the Hero Welcoming Committee – Harley's has not been. Secondly, a Legendary Hero must complete the Twelve Tasks upon the Path of Heroes – Harley has made no attempt whatsoever.'

My phone buzzed with a message from Miss Delaporte.

Good news, Harley. Mr Purry Paws has returned! Hooray! Now there's nothing to stop you from passing Back to Life.

btw, if you happen to see your parents down there, can you tell them Mitsy and Bitsy have woken from their nap, so the aunts are ready to swap back too? I tried the number your dad gave me, but it won't send for some reason.

Okay. So Miss Delaporte's 'good news' wasn't looking all that relevant any more. Sure, we could pass safely through the Portal of Doom now, but what use was that when we had no way of getting *to* the Portal? It was a catastrophe!

'Put your phone away, Harley love,' said Dad. 'We're in a bit of a pickle here. You can text your friends later.'

I rolled my eyes. 'Dad, I am *literally* trying to save us from Eternal Damnation.' I turned back to my phone, ignoring the tutting and sighing from the Archivist and my mum, as another message came through.

> It just occurred to me that maybe you didn't know your parents had gone down after you. Perhaps they came to surprise you? Sorry about that. Pretend I didn't say anything.
>
> Btw, you and Bess should pop in for an ice cream when you're back, tell me all about your adventures. Good luck! :)

'Arwee?' said Malcolm. I looked up from my phone and saw that everyone was watching me. My brother's worried little face made me want to cry. Even Bess looked nervous. I didn't know what to say. Any minute now, the caravan would be crushed, and we'd be trapped.

Mum turned to the Archivist. 'Look, I do understand the difficult situation we've put you in,' she said. 'But we really do need to get back. The children are meant to be at school –'

Bess gasped. 'Seriously?' she said. 'What time is it?'

'It's 9:45,' I said hopelessly.

'I can't *believe* it . . .' Bess was wide-eyed and grinning. 'We're missing History!'

'No, Bess,' said the Archivist solemnly. 'We're making history.'

'Sorry to interrupt,' said Dad, jiggling from one foot to the other, 'but does anyone know if there's a loo around here? We brought the big flask, see, and I haven't been since the Back of Beyond.'

'There's a bathroom just out there,' said Bess helpfully.

'NO!' gasped the Archivist. 'You can't use that! It's staff only. And the toilet's broken.'

The Archivist seemed oddly flustered by Bess's suggestion – and for some reason I couldn't immediately pin down, that gave me hope.

'What's wrong with it?' I asked, recalling the DO NOT FLUSH sign and Quince's mysterious insistence that the toilet was "in perfect working order".

'Oh, a blockage or something,' the Archivist replied evasively. 'But you really *mustn't* flush it, that's very important. On no account should you flush it! Anyway, it's staff only, so you're not allowed in. You can use any of the other toilets along the Path of Heroes, *just not that one*.'

Why was she so keen for us not to use it? And especially not to flush it? From what I knew of the Archivist, this might well be a HINT –

And suddenly, it hit me. There *was* another way out. It might not be safe, it might not be clean, but it'd be fast.

'Follow me,' I said.

# 31

## 9:50 a.m. TUESDAY

### 10 minutes
### until Eternal Damnation

I led everyone out of the Archive to the room next door: the little bathroom at the end of the Path of Heroes. Bess joined me inside, while Mum and Dad and Olly peered round the doorway.

'Look,' I said, pointing at the handwritten notice above the toilet cistern.

OUT OF ORDER
DO NOT FLUSH

'Oy! Oy! Oy!' said Olly, shuffling up between my parents. 'I would offer to fix it, but I'm recently retired.'

I tore off the notice to reveal the ancient "prophecy" behind it.

**WHEN AN EXCESS OF FOULNESS DESCENDS,**
**ONLY AN ALMIGHTY SURGE**
**SHALL CLEANSE THIS PLACE.**

Everyone gasped like I'd pulled a rabbit out of a top hat.

'The prophecy!' chorused Mum and Dad.

'I thought it *wasn't* a prophecy?' said Bess. 'Those monsters pretended it was a prophecy as a joke, but really it's just a sign telling you to flush the toilet?'

Olly doubled up giggling again.

'It does mean that,' I said. 'But it doesn't *only* mean that. It's like Miss Delaporte taught us in Year 5: *There are always at least two ways of looking at everything. Sometimes, many more.* Before she worked at a transport cafe for drivers of the Dead, Miss Delaporte was the best teacher.'

'Oy! Oy! Oy!' said Olly for some reason.

'THIS is the Legendary Reverse Flow,' I said, pointing at the flush on the cistern. 'Earlier, while she was dangling over the Lake of Lost Souls, Quince hinted that anyone looking for the Legendary Reverse Flow should *follow the prophecy to its source.* And that's here. You see, every toilet along the

Path of Heroes has a sign like this. But this one has been deliberately hidden because it's not like the others –'

'It clearly said DO NOT FLUSH,' said Mum.

'Yes,' I said. 'And that's why we need to flush it.'

'I'm really not sure I should use this toilet,' said Dad.

'No,' I agreed. 'Please don't use this toilet, Dad. We're going down it.'

'We're what?' gasped Bess.

'Usually, this toilet must *never* be flushed because this flush is the Legendary Reverse Flow. And that's how we're going to get home. Olly, you need to make sure you're holding on tight, otherwise it'll drag you along with us.'

I stuck the DO NOT FLUSH notice back over the **FOULNESS DESCENDS** sign.

'Olly, as soon as I've flushed, hold on tight. Everyone else be ready to jump in. We can't hang around because we'll only have one **ALMIGHTY SURGE** to get us all the way along to the Front of Beyond, up the Flume of Infinite Terror and out through the Portal of Doom.'

'But the Legendary Reverse Flow was the Management's evil scheme!' gasped Bess.

'Yes, but we're using it for Good rather than Evil,' I said. 'Well, for convenience. Olly, it's really important that you close the toilet lid as soon as we're all through.'

'Oy! Oy! Oy! This'll be epic!' He spun his yo-yo in a figure of eight, a move that he called the Dynamic Hawk.

'This is important, Olly,' I said. 'You've got to take this seriously. We don't want any curious Souls jumping on for the ride or getting accidentally swept up in the current. We can't risk another catastrophe like what happened to Bess in reverse.'

'I think we can trust the lad,' said Dad.

'I've got total faith in you, Olly,' said Mum. 'Despite your limited training and your reluctance to take up transcendental plumbing as a profession.'

'It is an honourable profession,' said Olly, 'but it's a profession, nonetheless. And today I have made a sacred vow never to work again. Oy! Oy! Oy!'

'Just try not to think about the eternity of future Restless Souls who are relying on you to not mess this up,'

said Dad unhelpfully.

Olly held on tight to the edge of the bath, and I pressed the flush. Immediately, the toilet bowl expanded into a swirling vortex of gushing wind with a hint of lemon-scented bleach. A violent gust swept through the little bathroom, pulling us towards it like a giant vacuum cleaner.

'Hold on!' I yelled above the howl of the gale and the distant roar of gushing gloop echoing out of the tunnel. Dad gripped the door and held on to Mum; Bess grabbed the bath and Olly clung to the sink. Malcolm squeezed

Diddy Dino like that squidgy dinosaur was the last bit of toothpaste in the tube.

'Olly, remember,' I yelled. 'As soon as we're through, close the lid!' Olly gave a thumbs up. 'We all need to jump in immediately after the person before us, so that we join up into the most aerodynamic shape we can be – like a string of sausages. Dad – you and Malcolm go first. Then Mum, then Bess, then me. On the count of three. One, two, three!'

'Oy! Oy! Oy!'

We leapt into the windy tunnel.

# 32

## 9:59 a.m. TUESDAY

**1 minute until Caravan Crushing**

**581 hours and 16 minutes until the Summer Holidays**

Hurtling through that pipe was like being back in Quince's van, but gustier and gloopier, and without a seat belt. We whooshed through it on a tidal wave of gravity-defying purgatorial gloop, landing with a reverse splash in the swiftly refilling reservoir, only to be sucked up into the side tunnel and swept out through the hatch and up the Flume of Infinite Terror. It felt like we were being rewound, played backwards, unburied alive and reconstituted. Eventually, we burst through the Portal of

Doom feet first, and landed in a bruised and sticky heap in my grandparents' caravan.

'Crikey,' said Dad.

Daylight glimmered round the edges of the caravan's closed curtains. Outside, we could hear voices approaching.

'Okay,' I said. 'What shall we do?'

'I'd say we face the music, love,' said Dad. 'We've nothing to hide.'

I looked from my gloop-soaked companions to the Portal of Doom disguised as a chemical toilet in the corner.

'I reckon we do have *something* to hide,' I said. 'They're gonna wonder how we magically transported through the locked gate, past the guard dogs and into a caravan.'

'And why we're so sticky,' said Bess.

'Fair point,' Dad replied. 'But it'll be fun to freak them out a bit, eh?'

No one could argue with that. I opened the door and stepped on to the tarmac while the others remained hidden in the caravan.

'You?!' said Councillor Meadows, halting her march towards my late grandparents' home. 'But . . . What . . . How . . .?' She spun round, trying to work out how I'd got in there. Watching her befuddlement *was* fun, like Dad had suggested. But Ambary's mum was a professional meanie, so she soon recovered her nastiness and sneered at me. Then she got out her phone.

'Police,' she said. She smiled spitefully while they connected her. 'Good morning, I'd like to report a break-in. And a murder.' She gave the address of the wrecker's yard as its owner strolled up beside her. Then, as she described to the operator how I'd broken in, her bratty kids appeared at her other side. Ambary looked kind of sad. Rocky-Nathaniel had jam round his mouth. 'We can't explain *how* the murder was committed,' her mum snapped, in that snooty voice, which was probably making the emergency operator dislike her. 'That's *your* job,' she said. 'But we have CCTV footage of Harley Lenton and Bess Macadamia breaking in together, and only Harley Lenton leaving. Furthermore, my son, who is a most reliable and trustworthy boy, witnessed the whole thing. He saw Bess explode. I don't know if it was a bomb or some nasty chemical reaction – but anyway, the suspect is here now, so hurry along. We shall detain her until you arrive.' She ended the call.

'I can't believe someone in my class is a murderer,' wept Ambary.

'Have you seen the last Ofsted report?' I asked. 'By the way, there's someone in here you might like to say hi to.'

And then, with perfect timing, Bess stuck her head round the door. 'Hiya!' she said, grinning her big grin.

'Mummy!' whimpered Rocky-Nathaniel. 'Is that a ghost?'

Rocky-Nathaniel's mummy was speechless. It was a wonderful sound.

'Is that you, Bess?' asked Ambary with a look of disgust.

'Yeah, it's me,' said Bess.

'Why are you both covered in slime?'

'Is it ghostly ectoplasm?' asked Rocky-Nathaniel, shuddering.

'No, it's just where I sneezed on her,' I said. 'I've had a nasty cold.'

'Then I caught her cold and sneezed back at her,' said Bess. 'It's okay, though, because we're friends. We'll try not to sneeze on you, Ambary.'

'Ha ha ha!' the scrap dealer laughed at Ambary's mum. 'They're winding you up! She hasn't been murdered at all – and you called the police! What a nincompoop.'

'We've just been having a sleepover in my grandparents' caravan,' I explained.

'And what do you think your parents will have to say about this?' blustered the councillor, finally recovering her voice and fumbling for her phone.

'Oh, we're here too,' said Mum, stepping out of the caravan beside Bess. She put Malcolm down and he shuffled around on his bum.

'Incapoop!' he giggled, and the wrecker laughed along with him.

Dad stepped out too, and the councillor stared at my

parents in horror as they dripped globules of purgatorial gloop over the tarmac. 'Mucky, mucky people,' she muttered to herself, then tapped her phone. 'Police,' she said. Then she explained to the operator that her call about the murder was a mistake, but she was sure that some kind of crime had occurred here this morning and she'd call back as soon as she worked out what it was. Then she stuck her nose in the air and inhaled her humiliation until it puffed back out as a vindictive smile.

'It is ten o'clock,' she said. 'Fire up the car crusher, Mr Binks.'

Mr Binks frowned at Councillor Meadows. 'But there's people in the caravan,' he said. 'And they're saying it's theirs.'

'But it's not theirs,' said the councillor, smiling evilly.

Looking at Ambary and Rocky-Nathaniel standing beside their mum, I suddenly felt sorry for them. They were trying to be snooty and mean like her, but their faces looked exhausted from being screwed up into cruelty. Their expressions reminded me of angry emoji balloons whose sneers had deflated and shrivelled into almost-niceness. Councillor Meadows was still bloated with years of nastiness, but her children were running out of evil steam. I made a mental note to be nice to Ambary when I saw her at school later. (Would any of us ever go to school again? Why weren't these two there now? Had their mum bunked them off just to watch our caravan getting crushed!?) Yeah, next time I saw Ambary, I'd be nice. Not too nice, but a bit nice.

'This caravan is ours,' said Dad, holding out the ancient decree with its fresh signature. Ambary's mum recoiled from his slimy hand, but Mr Binks took it and skimmed through.

'Yep,' he said. 'It's theirs all right.'

'Which means,' said Mum, 'that the Tidy Village People entered private land unlawfully, took possession of the caravan unlawfully, and towed it away unlawfully –'

'Oh, so *that's* the heinous crime that took place here this morning!' said Bess, grinning.

'Fine,' said the councillor through gritted teeth. 'I'll just take my deposit back and we'll be leaving.'

'Deposit's non-refundable,' said the scrap dealer. 'You signed a contract. Right, I've got work to do. I'll be in the office if you need me.' He wandered off to the Portakabin whistling to himself. As he approached, the ferocious guard dogs chained up beside it wagged their tails and jumped up to lick him.

'Councillor, before you go,' said Mum, 'I wanted to let you know that we won't be reporting your crimes to the police. On one condition.' Councillor Meadows glowered nervously, like a rat in a trap. 'We won't call the police if you arrange a Preservation Order for our caravan, like the ones they put on special trees or listed buildings.'

Councillor Meadows thought about Mum's proposal for a moment. Then she made another one of her sneery faces and said, 'The police would never believe people like you over someone like me! You're all sticky and gooey and you own a rusty caravan in a field; I'm an upstanding citizen, an elected member of Risborough Council!'

'Let me put it another way,' said Dad. 'Do as we say, or I'll set my ghost cat on you.'

'Your what?' Councillor Meadows looked at my dad like he was crazy. 'Are you talking in slang? Well, let me tell you, Mr Lenton, I'm not afraid of any of your "ghost cat" – aaarrgghhh!'

And now Councillor Meadows was screaming and running around the wrecker's yard, flapping her arms like *she* was crazy. Because what she and her kids *couldn't* see was that Mr Purry Paws had leapt on to her head and was clinging to her hair like a rancher at a rodeo. I had no idea why he was still in the Land of the Living, but it was hilarious! Ambary and Rocky-Nathaniel were terrified, and I felt a bit sorry for them again – but I couldn't help laughing at their mum as she flapped and squealed.

There were several others the ordinary Living couldn't see in the yard now too. Miss Delaporte, who'd brought the cat with her, had arrived in the coach with BK and a long trail of Restless Souls. The non-Visionaries had no clue of their presence, until the car parts some of the Souls were fiddling with started floating about by themselves – at which point Ambary and Rocky-Nathaniel got even more freaked out. Eventually, Mr Purry Paws jumped to the ground and sidled up to me for a stroke.

'Fine!' snapped Councillor Meadows, looking furious and terrified and dishevelled. 'I shall set up a Preservation Order for your smelly caravan. Good day to you!' She stormed off, Ambary and Rocky-Nathaniel scuttling after her.

'I've just come from the cafe,' said Miss Delaporte, handing out cans of Coke. 'And I'm pleased to report that the Restless Souls have finally upped and left! Drivers from all over have been reporting that every Portal of Doom in Biddumshire is working fine again. Well done, Harley the Legendary Hero and Bess!'

'How come Mr Purry Paws is still here?' I asked. 'Why did the Portal let me through if you hadn't swapped him back? I thought it was the rules . . .'

'Rules,' said Miss Delaporte, 'can be flexible. Your cat looked like he was enjoying himself up here. So, I painted some whiskers on one of those eager Restless Souls in the cafe and let her swap through instead. She'd already made friends with Bitsy and Mitsy and Pat. Now everyone's a winner! Just keep it hush-hush.'

Outside the gates, Ambary was getting into her mum's flashy car. She and Rocky-Nathaniel cowered as Councillor Meadows angrily slammed the door. Imagine having her as a mum! It was weird. I'd spent so long believing Ambary's life was better than mine, but I realised now that this was just another made-up story – made up in my own head.

Maybe Orlando and that lot's lives weren't so enviable either. And now I came to think about it, who even *were* "that lot"? All this time I'd spent being jealous and afraid of Ambary and Orlando and *that lot* – and now I couldn't even think who "that lot" were. Who had I meant? Had my mind invented them too?

Maybe I'd need a little sleep when we got home.

BK reversed the coach into the wrecker's yard and hooked the caravan up to the tow bar. As we bumped along the backstreets of Risborough to our patch of moor at the edge of Kesmitherly, my parents and I repaired the tea machine. And as soon as we arrived, we began sending Restless Souls through. After queuing for a mug of *Special Tea*, the Dead sat about on the grass and heather, sipping and savouring their final moments in the Land of the Living. Gradually, one by one, they popped into the caravan's toilet and exploded through the Portal of Doom to *Beyond*.

'Piddle piddle, bang bang, job done!' said BK.

Finally, there was only one Restless Soul remaining. Mr Purry Paws sniffed at a saucer of very milky *Special Tea*, then turned his nose up and wandered over to Malcolm to have his tail pulled.

'What do you reckon to keeping him?' said Dad, all misty-eyed.

'Oh, could we?' said Mum, clapping her hands. 'Look how well Maccy and Mr Purry Paws get on! It'd be so lovely to have a dead pet.'

BK shook his head warily. 'Dodgy business keeping a ghost cat,' he said disapprovingly. 'It's against the rules, you know.'

'We'll be careful,' said Dad, staring lovingly at his resurrected moggy.

BK, Bess and I looked on. 'I don't know what's got into them, all this daredevil rule-breaking and risk-taking,' I said. 'They used to leave the room when Nana watched the wrestling.'

'Must be your influence,' said Bess.

BK dropped us off at the Ragged Goose. We took Bess in to be reunited with her mums and my parents immediately confessed everything because they couldn't bear any more fibbing. Bess's mums were totally fine about it. This was a massive relief to my mum and dad because not only had they lied about Bess being safe and well (which was outrageous when I thought about it), but also, Bess's mums were the first non-Visionaries my parents had *ever* shared the truth about our family with. Really, it was amazing. They seemed totally unfazed by the Land of the Dead stuff, just like Bess had been. I mean, they were interested – they just didn't make a big deal out of it.

We sat in for lunch. Afterwards, while our parents chatted about the roadworks, Bess and I went out to the beer garden. The beer garden was a bench by some bins, which was great because it never got busy.

'Weird that Ambary and Rocky-Nathaniel weren't at school, isn't it?' said Bess, staring thoughtfully at her feet. 'By the way, thanks for coming down to save me.'

'That's okay,' I said. 'I didn't do a very good job of it, though. Anyway, you didn't even need saving. I'm just sorry you got sucked into the Land of the Dead in the first place. And swallowed by a fish – even though it turned out to be kind of a party fish.'

'Yeah,' said Bess, placing one of her trainers on the bench beside her. 'The fish was cool. Would've been better if you were in it, though.'

I smiled.

'To be honest, Harley, I'm really glad *all* that stuff happened.'

'What, even though you came so close to Eternal Damnation?' I asked.

'Yeah,' said Bess. 'It was fun.'

'I wish you could see dead people too,' I said, watching a crisp packet blowing in the breeze. 'Up here, I mean.'

Bess shrugged. 'At least I can do this.' She stood up and walked around with her shoes on the wrong feet. I laughed like a drain – it was hilarious!

'That's the weirdest thing I've seen all day!' I said. And even though we both knew it *really* wasn't, this was our story, and we were sticking to it.

*

Meanwhile, a life and a death away, the Archivist was nibbling a plum and putting the finishing touches to the story of Harley the Legendary Hero's latest adventure. This volume was provisionally titled *Foul Prophecy*, but she wondered if that might be a bit over the top, considering how boringly ordinary the girl Harley seemed. The Archivist had enjoyed the Big Fish moments, but she did wish Oliver Polliver had featured more in this adventure – he was *so* her favourite character! She flicked back through the pages, wondering how she could build Olly's part . . .

Then the Archivist paused, as a shadow swept across the page. Slowly, she looked up – and gasped. Before her stood three terrible figures. They wore hooded cloaks that concealed their faces, and they smelled of nightmares.

'Good morning,' said the Archivist nervously. 'Would you like a tangerine?' The ominous beings said nothing. As they loomed over her, she felt their warm breath on her knuckles. 'Do you prefer satsumas? G-g-grapes –?' Quaking in terror, the Archivist squeezed her pencil until it snapped. 'Who *are* you?' she whispered, as tears ran down her cheeks.

'We,' replied the central figure, in a voice that stung her heart, 'are the new librarians.'

# Health and Safety Incident Report Form



| NAME | JOB TITLE |
| --- | --- |
| Bilbamýn the Bold | Legendary Hero, Slayer of Monsters, Saviour of Innocents and All-Round Good Guy |

| LOCATION OF INCIDENT | TIME OF INCIDENT | WITNESSES |
| --- | --- | --- |
| The Path of Heroes | Before breakfast | My colleague, Vileeda the Valiant |

**INCIDENT DESCRIPTION**

While DOING BATTLE with a horde of terrifying MONSTERS, I sustained multiple injuries. Although I fought bravely, there were literally hundreds of Beasts, including the Many-Limbed Optimugoon, the Razor-Elbowed Glockenpard, the Swift-Footed Gazellopuss, Gobbo Mawjaw, the Sporgal, the Spifflemucus and the Spikanik. I COULD have slain them ALL (easily), but I'd been up all night saving Innocent Souls from a terrible VILLAIN, so I was very sleepy and I hadn't had any breakfast either. Also, they took us by surprise, which in my opinion is CHEATING. We basically WON the fight (if they hadn't cheated) and we definitely weren't scared. And if anyone says I tripped up while running away they are LIARS and their pants should be set on fire immediately.

# Health and Safety Incident Report Form



**INJURIES SUSTAINED**

Stubbed my toe, grazed my knee, banged my funny bone and it really hurt and will take AGES to get better.

**WHAT COULD HAVE BEEN DONE TO PREVENT THESE INJURIES**

I could have been less BRAVE and stayed away from the battlefield – but that would have been in denial of my True Heroic Self, so really there was no way of avoiding it. We Legendary Heroes must place ourselves in harm's way for the good of Innocent Souls; it is our DESTINY!

Actually, I could've worn knee and elbow pads, like when I go on my scooter.

**FIRST AID AND RECOMMENDATIONS FOR TREATMENT**

Craemog the Intrepid put a plaster on my knee and Vileeda the Valiant made me a hot chocolate with pink marshmallows in it, but I will still have to have at least a YEAR'S holiday and a new sun lounger.

| SIGNED | Bilbamýn the Bold |
| --- | --- |

YOUR SMILE LIGHTS UP MY HEART
LIKE THE NEW STREET LIGHTING
ON THE RISBOROUGH BYPASS.
YOU FILL MY SOUL WITH JOY
EVEN MORE THAN THE £15.99
BUMPER BEAKY BARGAIN BUCKET
FILLS MY TUMMY WITH CHICKEN.

BEFORE, I WAS LONELIER
THAN THE LAST MINT
IN A DEAD MAN'S POCKET,
BUT WHEN WE'RE TOGETHER
I WISH TIME COULD STAND STILL
LIKE A TRAFFIC JAM
AT THE KESMITHERLY ROADWORKS.

SHALL I COMPARE YOU
TO MY LIVER AND ONIONS?
NO. YOU'RE EVEN LOVELIER
AND LESS GREASY.
I WOULD TRAVEL TO BEYOND
AND BACK FOR YOU,
MORGANA DELAPORTE

LOVE BK :)

LOOK OUT FOR
BOOK ONE!
INFO
for NEW ARRIVALS

KEEP READING FOR
A SNEAK PEEK . . .

Come for a holiday. Stay for eternity. . .

The Caravan at the Edge of Doom

JIM BECKETT

Illustrated by Olia Muza

# 1

## 3:57 a.m. THURSDAY

### 30 hours and 3 minutes until Eternal Damnation

I knew my grandparents had been ill, but I hadn't expected them to explode. Not all on the same night anyway.

Pops went off first, with a bone-rattling blast that rocked the caravan and echoed across the moonlit moor. He was in the loo at the time – *Boom!* – right in the middle of a wee.

Gran blew up next, before I had a chance to rub the sleep out of my eyes. She went into the tiny toilet and did such a big *BOOM* that I fell out of my bunk bed.

Green smoke seeped round the edges of the bathroom door. When I saw Grandpa shuffling towards it, I leapt into action, determined to prevent any more grandparents from exploding.

'Noooooo!!! Grandpa! Don't GOOOO!!!'

Except I couldn't actually *leap* because the zip on my sleeping bag was stuck, so I had to squirm to the loo like a desperate caterpillar – and as soon as Grandpa tinkled, I was thrown back by the biggest *BOOM* yet.

For a moment, the world was strangely silent. Apart from the smoke and the lack of grandparents, everything in the caravan looked normal. Neatly folded bedding, half-finished crossword, tea-stained mugs stacked by the sink . . .

'Peepo!'

Malcolm's grinning face popped out the top of Nana's wheelie bag like a cheeky bargain from Meg's Mini Mart. The first time he did this, we all thought it was hilarious – but he'd hidden in "Nana wee-wee gag" about a thousand times since Monday, and the joke had lost its edge. Still, it was a relief to see my little brother hadn't exploded too. Mum and Dad would've been furious.

('Don't get into trouble – *and keep an eye on Malcolm*!' That was Mum when they dropped us off on Sunday night. 'Be good for your grandparents, do your homework – *and look after your little brother*!' That was Dad. No *'Have fun!'* or *'Enjoy your holiday!'* Not that there was much danger of that.)

'Pop BAM! Gam BAM! Gampa BAM!' said Malcolm, summarising the main events of the last twenty minutes as he hugged his Diddy Dino.

'Yeah,' I said. 'They did.'

He'd had an eventful week for a sixteen-month-old. On Monday, a dog stole our picnic. On Tuesday, an ant crawled on to his knee. On Wednesday, he lost a sock. So far, Malcolm seemed to be coping pretty well with tonight's exploding grandparents catastrophe. It had taken him much longer to get over the 'woof-woof num-num nic-nic' incident.

When I finally managed to escape from my sleeping bag, I tiptoed towards the toilet.

'Grandpa?' I whispered. 'Gran? Pops? Nana?'

I gently pulled the door (the lock hadn't worked for years) and peered in, afraid of the mess I might find. But the loo was empty. No splattered flesh, no smouldering slippers, no charred pyjamas. Nothing but hot smoke and a disturbing pong.

My grandparents had vanished.

Suddenly, I heard a rattling behind me. Someone –

or some*thing* – was trying to break into the caravan! But what kind of maniac would be lurking on a lonely moor at midnight? What kind of *monster* would attack a child whose grandparents had just exploded?

I scrabbled about for a weapon, grabbing the first thing I could find. Whatever was jiggling that rusty door was about to get whacked with a rolled-up *Risborough Gazette.* Pops and Grandpa always complained the local newspaper was covered in adverts – it would soon be covered in blood and guts!

My heart was thumping. The longer I waited, the less confident I felt about the *covered in blood and guts* idea. Maybe a few nasty bruises would be enough to get the message across. Some stern words might even do the trick. After all, it was half-term. I was meant to be relaxing, not slaying Hell Beasts.

Also, I couldn't help worrying that an epic battle would be quite noisy. Bloodcurdling screams risked drawing attention to the fact that I spent my holidays in the creepy abandoned caravan on the edge of the village – and *then* someone might find out that the creepy abandoned caravan wasn't really abandoned at all. My grandparents lived here, all four of them squashed in together.

Well, they used to.

The door rattled violently. This Hell Beast wasn't going away, so I'd have to wreak havoc whether I felt like it or not.

I raised the rolled-up *Risborough Gazette*, ready to strike . . .

The door burst open, and moonlight flooded the caravan.

'Aaaaaggghhhh!!!!' I yelled, lunging at the vicious fiend in its dressing gown and slippers . . . 'Nana?'

'Hello, Harley,' said Nana. 'Did I wake you? Sorry. This door keeps sticking – needs a drop of oil.'

I caught my breath and lowered my weapon. *THREE* explosions, *FOUR* grandparents: I still had one left! What a relief! And what terrible counting! Must've been the adrenaline.

'I popped out to get a closer look at the moon,' said Nana, stepping into the caravan. 'One last look at the beautiful night sky before . . . Oh!'

Her voice cracked as she noticed the empty beds.

'They went without me!'